THICK GIRLS FALL IN LOVE

PEACHES & POLE BOOK FOUR

TINA GALLAGHER

Thick Girls Fall in Love

By: Tina Gallagher

Published by Galsalla Press

Copyright © 2025

Cover Design: Qamber Designs & Emporium

Editor: Jeannine Luby

THICK GIRLS FALL IN LOVE

TINA GALLAGHER

CHAPTER 1

Shannon

I PLACED THE LAST STACK OF T-SHIRTS INTO THE DRAWER AND closed it with a sigh of relief. It's taken nearly a week, but most of my stuff is finally put away. Once I get rid of the packing supplies, there won't be any more clutter, just a neatly arranged apartment that looks like it belongs to someone who has her life together.

Grabbing the empty box, I broke it down as I walked into the living room. After stashing it by the door, I paused to glance around my new place, reminding myself this is home for now.

Home. In Scranton. Once I left, I never thought I'd move back.

But when Manhattan lost its luster, I needed somewhere to regroup, reset, and resolve my next steps. And here, surrounded by family and friends, seems like the best place to do that.

A knock at the door interrupted my thoughts.

I crossed the living room and opened the door to find Anjannette, Keera, and Sophie on the other side.

"Surprise housewarming!" Keera announced, her grin as big as the brown bag she hoisted. "Since you didn't want to join us for taco night, we decided to bring it to you."

"And margaritas, of course," Anjannette added with a wink, holding up a pitcher that glistened with condensation.

"Plus chocolate." Sophie expertly balanced a plate of brownies as she pulled me into a quick one-armed hug.

She released me and we followed Keera and Anjannette into the kitchen.

"You guys are the best," I said, my voice thick with gratitude.

"We know." Keera dropped the bag on the table. "It's part of our charm."

I grabbed four plates from the cupboard and placed them on the counter. Moving to the next cabinet, I scanned the shelves.

"I don't have margarita glasses," I said, holding up a juice glass apologetically.

Keera waved it off with a dramatic flair.

"As long as it holds the nectar of the gods, the shape is irrelevant."

"Practicality over aesthetics, ladies. Let's get these filled." Anjannette nudged me aside and took over, rimming the glasses with salt and pouring with precision.

I placed the dishes on the table next to the takeout containers.

"What is all this?"

"Shrimp, beef, and chicken tacos." Keera pointed to each container in turn. "And of course, chips and guac."

We filled our plates and carried them and our drinks into the living room. Keera and I settled on opposite ends of the couch while Anjannette and Sophie sat in the chairs across from us.

After setting my drink on the coffee table, I picked up my shrimp taco and took one big bite, then another. I hadn't eaten since breakfast and I was starving.

I finished that taco in record time and took a sip of my margarita before moving onto the second.

"You ladies know how to make a girl feel at home."

"That's what friends are for," Sophie said. "Besides, we wanted to see your new place now that it's all set up." She looked around. "It looks great."

Along with my family, they'd offered to help me unpack, but I decided to do it myself. I needed time alone in this space to really settle in and make it my own.

"It's getting there." I said. "I still need to figure out where to hang some pictures and maybe buy a few extra pieces of furniture. I had a decent one-bedroom in Manhattan, but even so, it was tiny compared to this apartment."

"I bet this is way cheaper too," Anjannette said.

"That's for sure. Plus, I have a second bedroom and in-unit laundry."

"The lease is for a year, right?" Sophie asked.

I nodded as I chewed and swallowed the guac-loaded chip I'd just shoved into my mouth.

"That should give me enough time to figure my shit out."

Keera, Sophie, and Anjannette exchanged glances, but didn't say anything. Instead, they quietly continued eating, the silence hanging heavy with unasked questions.

Over the past year, I visited home more frequently and talked about moving back but never told anyone why. I know they're curious, anyone would be. While they didn't question me, their silence spoke volumes.

After what seemed like forever, Keera said, "Simon still can't believe you're back."

"I know. My parents are in shock, too." I let out a small sigh, feeling the weight of the past year settle on my shoulders. "I never thought I'd leave Manhattan, especially to come back here, but..." I held up my hands, "...here I am."

Sophie leaned forward and set her empty plate on the coffee table, then settled back in her chair.

"So, what's next?" she asked.

"That's something I need to figure out," I said.

Thankfully my career as a makeup artist was lucrative and my dad helped me invest well, so I have a decent nest egg. So financially, I'll be okay for a little while.

"I totally get that," Keera said. "As freaked out as I was when I got laid off from my job, I just wanted to take time to breathe before jumping back into the corporate grind." She smiled. "But thankfully, the lovely Anjannette saved me from having to do that."

"It was my pleasure." Anjannette blew her a kiss then turned her attention to me. "So are we going to address the elephant in the room?" I raised my brow. "Why did you leave Manhattan?"

I opened my mouth, but no sound came out. I'm rarely speechless, but I hadn't been expecting that.

"I mean, if you're not comfortable telling us, that's okay, but it might help to talk about It."

After saying that, Anjannette stood and walked to the kitchen. I heard the refrigerator door open and close, and a second later she was back, refilling our glasses. She set the nearly-empty pitcher on the coffee table and settled back into her chair.

I shifted my gaze between them, wondering if she's right. I've been dealing with this alone for the past year, replaying it endlessly in my own mind. Maybe talking it out with someone besides me, myself, and I will be helpful.

It's just so embarrassing. I'm usually a pretty smart person, so how could I have been so foolish? I've been pondering that question for a year and still don't have an answer.

"Basically my love life, friendships, and career all blew up at the same time. It was like a trifecta of shit showered down on me." I picked up my margarita and drained the glass. "But I'll fill you in on all the gory details another night if that's okay. Tonight, I just want to enjoy hanging out with you in my new apartment."

"We're here whenever you want to talk," Anjannette said.

The air felt lighter as we shifted the conversation to Sophie's newish boyfriend Jamie and Anjannette's upcoming wedding. Before long, the last of the tacos were eaten and empty plates littered the coffee table.

Anjannette gestured toward me with her glass.

"You know, Keera, Sophie, and I each had major changes in our lives before we met our guys. So did Eve."

"That's really great for all of you, but the last thing I want is another man in my life. I plan to live a dick-free lifestyle going forward."

The three of them burst out laughing.

When they finally settled down, Sophie said, "Famous last words."

"Yeah, we were all on dick-free diets too," Keera said.

"And remember, living well is the best revenge," Anjannette added.

"I don't need a dick to live well."

Keera smirked.

"But when you find the right dick, life is so much more fun."

"Ewww, that's my twin brother's *thing* you're talking about," I said. "Stop it."

Her smile widened just before she finished her margarita in one, long gulp.

"Dicks aside, just be sure to keep yourself open to whatever, or whoever, may come along," Anjannette said.

"I promise I'll be as open as I can be while I'm figuring out my life."

"That sounds like a good compromise," Sophie said, raising her glass. "To new beginnings and figuring things out."

"Wait, wait, wait," Anjannette jumped out of her chair. "It's bad luck to toast with empty glasses."

She grabbed the pitcher and divided the last of the margarita among our glasses, then nodded. We clinked them together, and I tossed back a mouthful of the tepid drink to seal a toast I had no intention of honoring.

ANDREW

I SLID INTO THE DRIVER'S SEAT AND STARTED THE CAR.

"Well, that was something," I muttered, snapping my seat belt into place.

It wasn't the worst blind date I'd ever been on. She was nice. Smart. Even understood my *Star Wars* references. But it was glaringly clear by the salad course that we weren't heading for a grand love story.

All in all, the evening was perfectly fine. But that's the

problem. It was just *fine*. There was no spark, no pull, no reason to consider a second date. And our awkward goodnight handshake made it obvious she felt the same way.

I shot Simon a text to make sure he and Archer were still hanging out. His response was immediate—a thumbs-up emoji that somehow managed to look smug. I could already imagine his expression when I recounted details of my night. Simon had suffered through plenty of cringe-worthy blind dates before getting together with Keera. Every time I told him I had another lined up, he'd laugh and say, "Good luck," in an I-feel-sorry-for-you kind of way.

And now that Archer has found love, I'm sure he'll have words of wisdom to offer as well.

Ten minutes later, I pulled into his driveway, ready for the inevitable teasing. The back door was unlocked, and I let myself in.

"I have returned, defeated in battle," I announced.

"In here!" Simon yelled.

I followed the sound of his voice to the living room and found my two friends hunched over their controllers, eyes fixed on the TV. Instead of the fantasy or sci-fi mayhem I'd expected, the screen showed a baseball game.

"What are you playing?"

"*Ultimate Baseball Unleashed*," Archer said.

"That's...different."

"Leo is in this game and gave me a copy," Simon said, then added, "There's pizza on the table if you're hungry."

"I'm good, thanks."

I settled into the recliner and watched them play, amazed at the image on the screen. The graphics are pretty sweet, detailing the texture of the grass and even the stitching on the baseball.

Even though I've only met Anjannette's fiancé Leo

Marakis a few times, it's still cool seeing someone I know in the game.

"So, how'd it go?" Simon asked, without taking his eyes off the screen.

"About as well as the others." At their stifled laughter, I added, "Yeah, I'm done being set up."

"Right," Archer said. "Until some well-meaning co-worker says they have the perfect match for you."

"Seriously, no more. I'm too busy to waste my time on dates that go nowhere. I'd rather spend my days off doing things I actually enjoy."

Simon turned to look at me.

"You say that every time."

"This time I mean it," I said, shaking my head. "I'm done. No more setups."

I ignored their shared smirks and settled into my seat, watching as Simon's batter crushed a walk-off homerun to seal the win. Archer tossed his controller onto the coffee table and leaned back with a satisfied sigh.

"Now that you've sworn off blind dates, what's the plan?" he asked, his tone light but teasing.

"Honestly, I'm looking forward to some downtime. Maybe I'll finally tackle my to-be-read pile or start a new TV series."

"Edge-of-your-seat stuff," Simon added.

"Hey, after med school and residency, a quiet night off is pretty thrilling."

I thought about pointing out that not so long ago, they weren't authorities on relationships themselves but I let it go. Among the three of us, I was always the one perfectly fine being single. Which, let's be honest, worked out, given my serious lack of options.

Let's just say none of us were lady magnets back in high

school or college. We were the quintessential nerds who hung out together, eating fast food or pizza, and playing video games. But for me, that dry spell ended after med school. Once I started my residency, it seemed like everywhere I turned, someone was eager to set me up with their daughter, niece, or best friend. I figured it was simply because my social circle had expanded. My sister, however, has another theory.

"Nerds are hot now," she said, then added, "And it doesn't hurt that you're a doctor."

I'll admit that at first, I was excited at the possibility of every blind date. There'd be this little thrill, a shot of adrenaline when I walked into the bar or coffee shop, scanning the room for the woman whose picture I'd studied on my phone like I was cramming for an exam.

But none of them ever led to a connection. Only a handful turned into a second date, and a fraction of those made it to a third. I dated one girl for a few weeks, but that fizzled out too, for whatever reason.

I'd like to think it's not me, but maybe it is. I'm a simple guy. I've got my routine, my hobbies, and my quirks. Sure I'm willing to branch out and try new things, but at the end of the day, I'm just me. And maybe I'm not enough.

But here's the thing, I'm done apologizing for who I am. That realization hit me one night after yet another date that ended with, "You're really nice, but..." Nice, but. Like being nice is some kind of consolation prize.

I went home that night, stared at my reflection in the bathroom mirror, and decided I wasn't going to change just to fit someone else's mold. I'm not a chameleon, shifting colors to blend into someone else's world. I'm me. Take it or leave it.

That's when I got the tattoo.

"No Apologies."

It's inked in Elvish, a nod to my lifelong obsession with Tolkien. People who see it usually ask if it's Hebrew or a tribal design, but I'm fine with that. I know what it means. It's a reminder, etched into my skin, that I'm not here to apologize for who I am or what I want.

Some days it's harder to live up to than others. It's easy to fall back into old habits, to overthink the way I talk, the way I dress, the way I exist. But I try. Because I'd rather wait for someone who gets me, who sees me and doesn't want me to be anything else, than keep settling for the dates who wish I were just a little more this or a little less that.

"Mirabelle has a new colleague you might like," Archer said.

I shook my head.

"She's an adjunct professor of biology, so you'd have science in common."

"I'm good, thanks."

Before he could add more, we heard the back door open, then close, and a second later,

Keera walked into the room.

"Hey, guys. What are you up to?"

"Andrew was telling us about his latest disaster date and Archer was trying to set him up on another one," Simon said.

She gave him a quick kiss, then offered me a conciliatory look as she settled next to him on the couch.

"The right person will come along when you least expect it."

I wanted to tell her that finding the right person isn't really a top priority, but figured protesting would make me sound pathetic. So, I just nodded. And thankfully Simon shifted the conversation.

"How's Shannon's place? Is she all settled in?"

"It's nice," she said. "And mostly."

"Did she enjoy the housewarming?"

Keera smiled.

"How could she not? We showed up armed with tacos, margaritas, and chocolate."

"Any word on her plans?" he asked.

I half-listened to their conversation as my mind drifted back to the last time I saw Shannon at Simon and Keera's engagement party last year. Wearing a burgundy dress that hugged curves that were softer and fuller than I remembered, she moved with an effortless confidence that made it impossible to look away.

She caught me in mid-stare and smiled. Then, with an easy grace, she walked toward me, the dress shifting with every step, giving me fleeting glimpses of her shapely thigh. We were only able to exchange a few words before she got swept away by other guests. And since I had to leave early to head to work, I never caught up with her again.

Not that it would have made a difference if I had. It's not like I would have asked her out or anything. Aside from the fact she's my best friend's sister, she's way out of my league.

Instead of falling down that rabbit hole, I focused on what Keera was saying.

"It's a big change from Manhattan, but she seems excited to start a new chapter of her
Life."

"I just wish she'd talk about what made her move back." Simon held up his hands. "Don't get me wrong, I'm happy she's here. So are Mom and Dad. But Shannon has wanted to move out of Scranton as long as I can remember."

"She'll talk when she's ready."

"So there *is* something?"

"I don't imagine she'd uproot her life if there wasn't," she said.

"That's what I've been saying."

"Well, like *I've* been saying, she'll talk about whatever it is when she's ready."

"Alrighty then, I guess we're done discussing Shannon." Simon looked at me and smiled. "I guess we're back to talking about your dating life."

"How about we find another topic?"

"Before you got here, Andrew was telling us that he's done with blind dates," Simon told Keera.

"That's totally understandable," she said. "They get old."

"Maybe Simon can set you up with Shannon," Archer said.

At his words, my heart skidded to a stop, then started pounding. I've never told anyone about my lifelong crush on Shannon, but both Simon and Archer have caught me staring at her enough through the years to have a clue.

"Very funny," I said, trying to play it off, but my casual tone sounded a little too forced, even to my own ears.

"If anyone could make you change your mind about setups, it'd be Shannon," Simon said.

"And technically, it's not a blind date since you already know her," Archer added.

I just rolled my eyes and stood.

"I'm going to the bathroom and when I come back, we're going to find a subject that has nothing to do with Shannon or me."

But as I walked out of the room, I couldn't help but wonder *what if.*

CHAPTER 2

Shannon

I tucked the pole into my inside bicep and wrapped my hands around it in a tight grip.

Moving my hips slightly forward, I took a deep breath in, letting the smooth strains of "Don't Look Back in Anger" by Oasis wash over me as I blew it out.

"You can do this," I muttered.

Pulling my elbows in, I engaged my core and tucked my knees up toward my chest. As I tipped back into the invert, it all fell apart just like it had all the other times I've attempted this.

I fought to hold on, determined to tip back, but my aching muscles and raw skin begged me to stop. As my hands began to slip, I finally gave in and slid down to the floor, defeated. Sweat dripped down my back, and my face burned, though I wasn't sure if it was from exertion or embarrassment.

Resting against the pole, I picked up my tumbler and

took a long drink of water. As I cooled off, I focused on the others through the mirrors, watching as they performed tricks with varying levels of ease.

Sophie effortlessly moved from a deadlift to a butterfly split. Tasha's shoulder mount took some effort, but she seamlessly transitioned into a brass monkey. Elsie, Vanessa, and Chelsea worked on their reverse grabs, with varying degrees of success.

Meanwhile I can't execute a simple invert.

I shifted my gaze to focus on my body, but before I could start to mentally criticize it, Anjannette approached.

"You okay?" I looked up at her and nodded. "You sure?"

She gracefully lowered herself to the floor, crossing her legs as she settled next to me.

"It's nothing."

Her perfectly arched brow lifted.

"You sure? You're giving off some serious I-need-a-margarita vibes."

I couldn't help but smile at her words, even as my shoulders sagged. After giving myself one last glance in the mirror, I shrugged.

"I'm just having a day."

"Want to talk about it?"

"It's just the usual," I said. "I have no idea what I'm doing with my life. Some days, I feel excited about all the possibilities, but sometimes doubt floods my thoughts, making me question if coming home was the right call. Today is the latter."

"Not to sound cliche, but it will all work out." She reached over and gave my hand a quick squeeze. "You're smart, resourceful, and amazing at what you do. You'll figure out your next moves soon enough."

"Theoretically I know that, but..." I had no clue how to

finish that sentence, so I just let it trail off. "Anyway, I decided to come to open pole to cheer myself up but ended up getting humbled by my invert."

"Inverts have kicked many a pole dancer's ass," she said in a haughty British accent.

"Well, if this pole dancer's ass wasn't so big, I'm guessing it would be much easier."

"Shannon, none of this is easy. You've only been coming to class regularly for a few weeks and you're killing it," she said, her voice warm and encouraging. "And for the record, I would do anything short of surgery to have an ass like yours."

I glanced at my reflection in the mirror. For someone who never had to worry about her weight until a couple years ago, the extra pounds my body insists on holding onto have been a shock.

"Thanks."

"It's amazing how one word can convey such doubt," she said. "Do you seriously not think you look amazing?"

Looking back at Anjannette, I shrugged.

"My thyroid basically stopped working a couple years ago and I'm still not used to the weight I put on," I said. "But my doctor thinks we've finally got the meds right, so hopefully it'll even out soon."

Behind me, Sophie finished a spin, grabbed her drink, and walked toward us.

"Don't mind me inserting myself into your conversation." She sat next to me. "I hope it doesn't straighten itself out. Those curves are in all the right places, and you look fabulous."

Their faces blurred as I swallowed the lump forming in my throat.

"I don't know what I'd do without you ladies," I said.

Without another word, they pulled me into a group hug, their arms wrapping around me like a warm, impenetrable shield. I blinked rapidly, trying to hold back my tears, but a few escaped anyway. When we finally pulled apart, I wiped my eyes, my heart lighter than before.

"Come on." Anjannette stood and held her hand out to me.

I took it and she pulled me up. Sophie followed

"Where are we going?"

"Right here." She pointed to the pole I'd just been sitting against. "Sophie and I are going to help you invert."

"You don't have to do that."

"That's a great idea," Sophie said to Anjannette, then turned to me. "It took me two months to climb the pole. Then one day, Anjannette stood in front of me and literally squeezed my knees together and demanded I push up. And once I felt the motion, I was able to climb, no problem."

I scrunched my nose and eyed the pole.

"That pole has defeated me too many times today."

"One last time," Sophie said. "We'll help you get there."

Anjannette bounced on her heels.

"Let's do this!"

I took in a deep breath and squared my shoulders.

"Okay."

Stepping up to the pole, I wrapped my hands around it, my determination renewed.

"That looks good," Anjannette said. "Move your butt over in front of the pole just a little bit more."

"Okay, now tuck your knees up and tilt back."

As had happened before, I got stuck and started to slip. But before that happened, Sophie and Anjannette supported my hips on each side and held me in place.

"Keep going," Anjannette said. "Keep your back engaged and let your head and shoulders drop back."

I did as I was told and this time, it worked. Well, it worked with Anjannette and Sophie pushing my hips.

"Put your legs out straight in a straddle."

They stepped away as I settled into my invert.

"Great job, Shannon!" Anjannette yelled. "You've got this!"

"Hold it, I'm gonna grab my phone."

My fingers threatened to cramp as I held onto the pole with a death grip and watched Sophie run across the room and come back.

"Fix your face," she said.

I did my best to smile, but I'm sure I looked like a demented gargoyle.

Once Sophie was done snapping pictures, I dropped my feet to the floor and released my hold on the pole.

"You did it!" they screeched in unison.

"With help from you guys."

I grabbed my water.

"*That's what friends are for...*" Anjannette sang.

"And you did it mostly yourself. We just gave you a little boost." Sophie cupped her hand and lifted it, mimicking the movement. Lifting the other hand, she held out her phone. "Check it out."

I took the phone and swiped through the pictures. My face looked awful and my legs weren't perfectly straight, but for the most part, the invert looked okay. It wasn't perfect, but it was progress. And for now, that's enough.

ANDREW

. . .

I FINISHED DICTATING NOTES ON MY LAST PATIENT AND PAUSED for a moment to make sure I hadn't missed anything. I'm happy with the progress Jan Evans has made after meniscus surgery, and so is she. Her range of motion is excellent, and she's been hitting all her physical therapy milestones. It was a great way to end the day and a good reminder of why I decided to go into orthopedics. It's nice helping someone return to her normal life, one careful step at a time.

I stopped by Sarah's desk on my way out. She's been managing this office nearly as long as I've been alive and somehow keeps the chaos organized.

"I'll be at the hospital tomorrow morning, so I won't be here until noon, but call if you need me."

"You know I will." She finished typing and looked up at me. "Have any fun plans tonight?"

"No, just heading home." I chuckled at her raised brow. "What?"

"I'm just surprised you don't have a date. You had quite a streak going for a while there."

"Just heading home for some much-needed sleep," I said, then added, "And I wouldn't call it a streak. Just a few dates."

"Mmmm Hmmm."

"On that note, I'm heading out."

"Get some rest. I'll see you tomorrow."

"See you."

I headed out the side door to the parking lot. My stomach let out a loud growl as I slid behind the wheel, reminding me I didn't eat lunch. Between the rotator cuff surgery this morning, post-op visits at the hospital, and back-to-back patient consultations at the office, food wasn't even on my radar.

Anything in my refrigerator is probably growing new life forms by now, so I definitely need to stop for food. I'll pass at least five fast food places on my way home, but I've been eating way too much of that lately. So instead of grabbing another drive-through burger, I decided to stop at Shoprite.

I can't even remember the last time I actually stepped foot in a supermarket. Between Instacart, takeout, and raiding my mom's pantry, I've managed to avoid it for a long time.

The automatic doors whooshed open, and I grabbed a basket near the entrance, adjusting my grip as I walked past the fresh produce toward the deli. Two guys were cleaning up behind the counter and one stopped what he was doing to wait on me. I asked for a pound of ham and perused the case of prepared foods as he sliced it.

Since it's so late in the day, there's not much of a selection, but everything looks good. Probably because I'm really hungry.

After deciding on roast chicken, I added a container of mashed potatoes and steamed broccoli to the basket.

"Can I get anything else for you?" the counter guy asked.

"No thanks."

"Have a great night."

"You too," I said as I grabbed the pack of ham he'd set on the counter.

As much as I'm dying to get home, I figured I should pick up some basics while I'm here. I headed to the other end of the store and after adding milk, eggs, bread, bagels, and cream cheese to the basket, it was overflowing. I thought about grabbing orange juice, but decided to just get oranges instead and walked back toward the produce.

I'd just finished bagging oranges when I spotted her.

Shannon.

She stood directly across from me, methodically selecting apples, examining each one before placing them in her bag. Even in simple black leggings, an oversized T-shirt, and her hair pulled into a messy bun, she's stunning.

My feet moved toward her before my brain could overthink.

"Hi."

She looked up, and her brows knitted together for a moment as she took me in.

"Hi Andrew." Her mouth curled into a smile. "Sorry, I'm still not used to seeing you without your glasses. And with the new 'do."

As she gestured toward my freshly-cut hair, her sleeve slid back, revealing a nasty bruise on the inside of her forearm.

Instead of addressing what she'd said about me, my doctor instincts kicked in and I gestured toward her arm.

"What'd you do to yourself?"

She glanced down, and shrugged.

"It's from pole class," she said.

"It looks painful."

"Honestly, it looks worse than it feels."

"You should get some arnica cream. It'll help with the healing."

A ghost of a smile touched her lips.

"The pole ladies swear by it. I've got some at home." Her eyes shifted toward my chest. "So, scrubs, huh? Just getting off work?"

I glanced down at myself like I forgot what I'm wearing, then nodded.

"Yeah. It was a long day."

"You always said you wanted to be a doctor. Do you like it?"

"I do," I said without pause. "It's demanding and exhausting, but I love it."

"That's great."

As she said those two words, something shifted in her expression and the light in her eyes dimmed, like a cloud passing over the sun. I'm not sure what prompted her move back to Scranton, but I'm guessing whatever it is caused that flicker.

Even if I felt comfortable asking her if she wanted to talk about whatever's wrong, it's not a conversation to have in the produce aisle of Shoprite. Before I could think of something else to say, my stomach let out a loud growl. We both laughed, breaking the moment.

"I better let you go so you can eat." She gestured toward the apples. "And I need to finish shopping so I can do the same."

If I had the guts, I'd ask her to join me for dinner, but I'm not that smooth. And even if I was, I probably wouldn't ask. After all, she's Shannon, not some random woman.

"It was great seeing you," I said.

"You too."

I paid for the groceries and headed to the car, my mind replaying every second of our exchange during the drive home.

Something is different with her. Shannon always had this energy about her, a sparkle, like she was lit from within. The woman I just talked to is beautiful, yes, but that inner light seems dimmer.

I know people change. Hell, I'm living proof of that. But this feels different. This feels like something broke her, and I can't help wondering what—or who—is responsible.

CHAPTER 3

Shannon

After unleashing a cloud of hairspray, I stepped back to evaluate my work. I didn't expect to spend part of my afternoon doing hair and makeup at my friend Phoebe's boudoir studio, but she was in a bind, and I had nothing else going on, so why not?

Satisfied that Ella was camera ready, I looked at her and smiled.

"Ready to see yourself?"

At her nod, I turned the chair so she faced the mirror.

"Oh wow. I don't even recognize myself." She touched her cheek, then her hair. "I've *never* looked this good in my entire life. You're a miracle worker."

"That's all you. I just highlighted your natural beauty."

She'd given me carte blanche for her makeup and only requested that her hair remain down. I styled the latter in loose curls that tumbled in a sexy cascade over her shoulders. For the former, I decided on a soft smokey eye that made her green eyes pop. Instead of a standard red lip, I went with a perfect shade of berry that compliments her skin tone and works well with a variety of outfits.

"Thank you so much."

"You're very welcome."

"I can't stop looking at myself." Ella beamed at her reflection.

"You look amazing," I said, giving her shoulder a light squeeze. "Phoebe's going to get some gorgeous shots."

Phoebe poked her head into the dressing room.

"How's it going in here?" Her eyes widened. "Oh Ella, you look gorgeous. You did an amazing job, Shannon."

"Thanks, but it was easy working with such a beautiful canvas."

I gathered my brushes while Phoebe looked through the items Ella brought to wear. As I finished packing my makeup kit, they decided on a fuchsia lingerie set beneath a delicate black lace robe. After I said goodbye to Ella, Phoebe and I left the room so she could change.

"Thank you so much, Shannon, you're a lifesaver," she said as I followed her into the studio.

Phoebe had called me in a panic yesterday when her regular makeup artist, Amy, had some sort of medical emergency and had to cancel.

"I'm happy to help out," I said. "I hope everything is okay with Amy."

"Actually, it's not. She's been having issues with high blood pressure and the doctor wants her to reduce activity for the rest of her pregnancy."

"I'm sorry to hear that."

"Me too," she said. "I thought I had a couple more

months before I'd need to find a fill-in for her." Holding her hands up in prayer position, she added, "Would you be interested in covering until I find someone?"

"Oh. Wow."

"I know what I pay isn't anywhere near your normal rate, but I'd be eternally grateful if you'd say yes."

I'm not sure why I hesitated. Aside from pole classes and taco night, there's nothing on my calendar. And even though I'm relatively stable financially speaking, extra cash is never a bad thing.

"Sure, why not?"

"You're the best!" She gave me a quick hug. "I'll text you my schedule. If there are any days you're not available, just let me know."

"Sounds good."

We walked toward the door.

"Thank you so much. You're a lifesaver."

I waved off her thanks.

"I'm glad I could help."

She opened the door.

"I'll see you at pole next week."

"See you then."

I left the converted warehouse that housed Phoebe's studio and walked toward my car. I stood in the parking lot for a moment enjoying the feel of the late afternoon sun on my face. I breathed the brisk winter air into my lungs before sliding behind the wheel.

Instead of heading back to my apartment, I decided to stop by my parents' house. It's been a long time since I could just pop in for a visit, so I'm determined to make it a regular occurrence now that I can.

Fifteen minutes later, I pulled into the familiar driveway

and took in the sight of my childhood home, settled deep in winter. The front porch was empty, aside from a thin layer of salt dust and the outline of where the holiday decorations had been. No wreath, no lights, just the quiet stillness that settled in after the new year.

I made my way around the side, the frozen ground crunching under my boots, and headed for the back door like always.

My mom sat at the kitchen island and looked up from her iPad as I entered.

"I thought I heard a car," she said. "What a nice surprise."

"Mmm, it smells yummy in here."

"There are brownies cooling on the counter and the chocolate chip cookies should be done in a minute."

"Looks like I stopped by at the perfect time." I settled onto a stool at the island.

"Were you at pole class?"

"No, I was actually at Phoebe's boudoir studio." At my mom's raised eyebrows, I explained. "Her makeup artist is pregnant and she's having some issues, so Phoebe asked me to fill in."

"It's good you were available to help out."

"Yeah."

Her phone alarm chimed and she got up to take the cookies out of the oven. After setting them on the counter next to the brownies, she sat across from me again.

"Is she okay? The makeup artist?"

"Actually, no. She has high blood pressure and the doctor told her to restrict her activity."

"Oh no. I hope everything will be alright."

"Yeah, hopefully it will be."

I stood and grabbed a glass from the cupboard and filled it with water. The fresh-from-the-oven cookies called to me and I grabbed one before sitting back down. I took a bite of the still-warm cookie and moaned as the chocolate melted on my tongue.

"You're going to get a stomachache eating hot cookies."

"It will be totally worth it." I popped the last bite into my mouth and chewed. "So Phoebe asked if I'd fill in while Jenna's out."

"What did you say?"

"I told her I would." I shrugged. "I'm not doing anything else, so there's no reason I can't help her out."

"That's great. I'm sure she's happy to have you, you're so talented." She shook her head and smiled. "As someone who can barely apply mascara without poking myself in the eye, I've always been amazed at how good you are."

"Thanks Mom."

She reached across the table and squeezed my hand.

"I'm so proud of everything you've accomplished. From the time you were little, you knew what you wanted to do and exactly where you were headed. You never strayed from that path."

"Until now."

"Why do I have a feeling that outside forces are more to blame for that than anything?"

I blinked to prevent the tears that threatened to fill my eyes. Instead of answering her question, I changed the subject.

"Oh, I almost forgot," I said. "I saw Andrew at the grocery store yesterday. It took me a second to recognize him."

"Really? Why?"

"He looks different." I held my hands out next to my shoulders. "Broader. And he wasn't wearing his glasses."

My brother's gangly best friend is looking good, but I kept that to myself.

"He's really growing into himself," she said.

"Yeah." I traced the rim of the glass with my index finger. "And he seems more confident...or something."

"That confidence has probably evolved from making it through medical school and his residency. Those aren't easy feats."

"True."

"Plus, Simon mentioned that Andrew's co-workers have been setting him up on a bunch of blind dates. He's probably getting more comfortable in social situations." She flashed a self-deprecating smile. "You know casual conversation doesn't come naturally to nerds like Andrew, Simon, and me."

I laughed at her last sentence instead of focusing on the way my stomach twisted unexpectedly at the thought of Andrew dating. Because that doesn't make any sense at all.

"Well, he said he loves what he does, so I'm happy for him."

"Like you, he always had a clear vision of his future."

Hopefully his future stays in focus, unlike mine.

I didn't realize I'd said those words out loud until my mother responded to them.

"Honey, there's nothing wrong with changing your path. Sometimes the detour leads you exactly where you're meant to be."

My mom stood, giving my shoulder a gentle squeeze as she moved to the cupboard. She pulled out a plate and busied herself arranging cookies on it, probably giving me some quiet time to absorb her words. And it worked.

I found myself reflecting on how genuine my new friends are—they laugh, care, and live authentically. A far cry from the superficiality I left behind in New York. It's also nice being so close to my family. With a short drive, I can see them in person anytime.

Amid those thoughts, an image of Andrew flashed across my mind, a fleeting glimpse that made my heart skip a beat. Maybe my mom is right, the unexpected detour might just be guiding me exactly where I'm meant to be.

ANDREW

I'M LATE. AGAIN.

But at this point, I'm pretty sure my family is used to it.

I raked a hand through my hair as I hurried up the walkway to my parents' house, a gift bag swinging from my hand.

The light from the kitchen spilled onto the lawn, and as I jogged up the front porch steps, I heard my family's voices inside. I pushed open the door and all eyes turned to me.

"Andrew!" My mom stood and pulled me into a hug that smelled like home—a mixture of vanilla body lotion, fabric softener, and hair spray. "I was about to send out a search party."

"Sorry I'm late," I said as I pulled back.

"There he is," my brother Bobby announced like he was emceeing a roast. "Our very own McDreamy, gracing us with his presence."

My sister Claire smirked and said, "Do you think if we all fake an injury, we can get him to show up on time?"

My siblings are just busting my ass like usual, but I offered an explanation anyway.

"We were behind all day at the office, and I had to stop at the hospital to check on a post-op patient on the way here."

"Can't even argue with that excuse." Claire wrinkled her nose. "That's just cheating."

Bobby looked at her, brows raised.

"He walks in with a halo and a stethoscope, and we're supposed to just forgive him?"

"Yes, that's exactly what you're supposed to do," Mom said.

"See?" I said. "Mom gets it."

I kissed each of my three nieces on the top of their heads as I made my way to my usual seat at the table.

Claire raised her glass.

"To our little brother, saving the world one late dinner at a time."

"And remember that it doesn't matter how many degrees you have, you'll always be the one who had a meltdown when Mom wouldn't let you wear your Flash costume to my high school graduation," Bobby said.

My nieces always enjoy watching us banter, and tonight is no exception. Harper hid a smile behind her napkin, Maddy glanced among the three of us with open amusement, and Karli's brow lifted as the corner of her mouth twitched.

I gestured toward them and my sister-in-law Maria.

"Did you have to bring that up in front of witnesses?"

At my half-groaned words, laughter erupted around the table. And I couldn't help but join in. My siblings are eight and ten years older, so they have an endless supply of embarrassing stories about me. Or as our mom likes to call them, "treasured family secrets."

And embarrassing or not, they're also the stories that make us who we are. The inside jokes, the relentless teasing, the way we fall right back into rhythm whenever we're together.

Our family can be loud and a little chaotic, but when I was in Arizona, knee-deep in residency, this is what I missed. It's partially what convinced me to turn down better-paying jobs in more-exciting cities to come back home when I was done.

Before I could keep moving down that sentimental road and dissect the other part of why I came back to Scranton, I smiled at Maddy and held out the gift bag. "Happy Birthday, Maddy Moo."

"Thanks Uncle A."

She pushed her plate forward, set the bag down, and dug through the tissue paper.

"What'd you get?" Harper asked.

Maddy pulled out the Sheetz gift card and smiled.

"This will come in handy for my new wheels."

"I heard you bought a car. Congratulations! I can't wait to see it."

"Thanks. I saved for two years but still needed help from the Bank of Mom and Dad."

"There's nothing wrong with that if they're willing to help," I said. "I would have starved through medical school and residency if it wasn't for the Bank of Mom and Dad."

After stashing the gift card in the holder attached to her phone, she reached into the bag and removed the small box. A smile spread across her face as she opened it.

"Uncle Andrew! This is gorgeous!"

"What is it?" her mom, Maria, asked.

"It's a sterling silver friendship bracelet." She picked it out of the box. "It has eighteen beads." She turned it to show the other side of the bracelet. "And look, there's an M on the little slide fastener."

"That's so pretty." Maria smiled at me. "And thoughtful."

"It seemed like the perfect gift for a girl who came out of the womb singing Taylor Swift songs."

Maddy fastened it around her wrist, turning it to catch the light.

"I love it! Thank you!"

"You're very welcome," I said as I grabbed a plate and filled it with fried chicken, a generous scoop of macaroni and cheese, and a few stalks of broccoli that I knew would make Mom happy to see.

Mom stood and held her hand out.

"I can pop that in the microwave."

I shook my head.

"It's perfect just like this."

I took a bite of the cold chicken to prove my point. And I wasn't lying. Mom's fried chicken is delicious at any temperature. The mac and cheese wasn't bad either, but I forced myself to chew and swallow the cold broccoli. I took another bite of chicken to wipe the taste out of my mouth.

"So, Maddy," I said, "all set for your party tomorrow night?"

"Yeah. We're going for a hibachi dinner, then having a movie marathon in our basement."

"I don't know why we can't come," Karli said, her thirteen-year-old face scrunching into a pout.

"Yeah, we like movies too," Harper said.

"It's friends only," Maddy said.

"Let your sister have her night," Maria said to her daughters. "When you turn eighteen, you can have whatever kind of party you want."

"That's forever away," Karli groaned dramatically.

"It'll be here faster than you think," I said.

"What did you do for your eighteenth birthday, Uncle A?" Maddy asked.

I paused with a drumstick halfway to my mouth, thinking back.

"Actually," I chuckled, "nothing too different from your plans. Simon, Archer, and I went to see whatever superhero movie was out that weekend, then played video games until sunrise." I shook my head. "We did that pretty much every weekend and birthday. I wasn't as cool as you are."

Maddy smiled.

"I think you're cool. Not everyone has an uncle who's a surgeon."

"Thanks Maddy McFluff."

"Since you mentioned Simon," Mom chimed in. "I ran into Lily at the grocery store yesterday. Did you know Shannon moved back to town?"

I nodded, suddenly very interested in my plate.

"Yeah, Simon mentioned that."

"Do you know if she's planning to stay permanently?"

"I don't really know her plans," I said, shoving a forkful of mac and cheese into my mouth.

Claire and Bobby exchanged a look that I pretended not to notice.

"Well," Mom said, clearly disappointed by my lack of information, "I always thought she was lovely."

Dad, bless him, changed the subject.

"Are you working this weekend, Andrew?"

I shook my head.

"I'm not scheduled. The only way I'd get called in is if there's a surgery I haven't assisted with or done yet, and the chances of that happening are slim to none." I took a sip of water. "I'm actually heading to The Ritz Theater for a *Star Wars* marathon with Simon and Archer."

"Just like old times," Bobby said with a grin. "Some things never change, huh?"

"Nope," I agreed, grateful for the shift in conversation.

Because while some people might suspect I had a crush on Shannon, Bobby and Claire know it for a fact. And that's one treasured family secret I'd rather they not share.

CHAPTER 4

Shannon

The studio lights cast a warm glow across the hardwood floors as I focused on mimicking Anjannette's movements. She'd put together a light, slow-burn routine tonight with hair flips, heel clacks, and confidence in every move.

I'm so grateful the goal of this class isn't nailing hard tricks, it's about moving with intention and perfecting the moves. The other ladies in class—Sophie, Keera, and Amber—are way ahead of me skill-wise. It's nice being able to keep up with them.

"Looking good in those heels, Shannon!" she said as I extended my leg straight out in front of me, then executed a sexy hip bump against the pole.

"Thanks to Keera for giving me her hand-me-downs."

"Anything for my sister from another mister," Keera said.

Keera had moved on to eight-inch Pleasers and since we take the same size shoe, gifted me her seven-inch. I have to admit I look pretty badass in the black patent leather boots. It's my third class wearing them and they're finally starting to feel like extensions of my feet rather than death-defying stilts.

I'm no stranger to heels, so I was shocked the first time I put them on and wobbled around like a newborn giraffe. But my Jimmy Choos are totally different and were made for power walking down the streets of Manhattan, not strutting around a pole.

"Okay, let's do a full run through to music," Anjannette said. "I'll call out the moves this time."

I eased into position, my fingertips brushing the pole before curling around the cool chrome. Anjannette tapped her iPad screen and the dark, moody notes of "Make It Rain" by Ed Sheeran filled the room.

Anjannette's voice cut through the music, "Body waves."

And we were off.

I moved through the routine, my heels clicking and scraping in time with the others, creating a rhythm that danced beneath the music. We weren't perfectly in sync, but the difference in timing had more to do with each woman letting the beat move through her body in a slightly different way.

"Okay, let's finish strong," Anjannette yelled. "Fan leg pirouette, thread the needle to the floor, slide up to your knees, and sexy hair flip." As soon as we executed the last move, the sound of her clapping filled the room. "You ladies are amazing! Take a short break and grab a drink, then we'll do it one last time."

I shifted onto my butt and reached for my tumbler.

"Anyone want to grab dinner after class?" Keera asked, brushing sweat off her brow.

"I can't," Sophie said with a sly wink. "Jamie and I have the house to ourselves tonight."

"Oooh, sexy time," Keera teased. "Have fun!"

"I'm out too," Amber added. "Matt got called into work, so my mom's watching the baby. She's got plans tonight, so I promised I'd be home right after class."

Keera turned to me.

"I'm in," I said with a shrug and a grin.

"Yesss!" She beamed, then turned toward Anjannette, who was scrolling on the iPad, probably picking out a song. "Are you heading to Leo's parents'?"

"Yeah, we're leaving as soon as I get home."

"Looks like it's just the two of us," Keera said.

Before I could respond, Anjannette stood and clapped her hands.

"Set up your phone if you want to record and we'll take it from the top," she said.

After grabbing my phone, I set it against the wall and checked to make sure my pole was in frame. Keera had talked me into recording myself to track my progress, but honestly, I almost never watch them. Seeing myself on video makes me hyper-aware of every curve I haven't made peace with.

When I'm dancing, I feel strong, powerful, like I belong in my body. But studying myself too closely, on screen or in the mirror, pulls my focus to the parts I wish were smaller, tighter, different. I'd rather hold on to the strength than get lost in the flaws.

"Last time through, ladies!" Anjannette called out.

We all scurried to our phones to hit record. Once we were back in position, she started the music. I faced the pole and flowed into body waves, starting with a tilt of my head, then rolling my chest forward, stomach following, hips last.

My body knew the next move and without having to think about it, I executed a perfect step-around, adding an extra dip in the middle.

When it came time for the hip bump, I hit the pole with confidence, a grin tugging at my lips.

This time through, we moved in perfect harmony, the sound of our heels marking each flawless step. As I circled the pole, I caught fleeting glimpses of my friends, their faces lighting up with the same joy and energy flowing I felt through me. It was almost bittersweet as we moved into the final steps of the routine.

I swept through the final step-around and tightened my grip as I pushed into the fan leg pirouette. A rush of satisfaction bloomed in my chest as I prepared to finish strong.

And then something went wrong. Very wrong.

When I shifted my weight to step down from the fan leg pirouette to thread the needle, the solid platform of my Pleasers suddenly vanished beneath me. My ankle rolled hard, twisting in a way it was never meant to. I heard a pop a split second before the pain hit, radiating like shockwaves.

I hit the floor hard, the impact registering as I fought to catch my breath. My stomach lurched as I looked down, unable to comprehend the sight of my foot bent at an impossible angle. I blinked, hoping my eyes were playing tricks on me. They weren't.

Over the sound of the music, I heard Anjannette yell, "Holy shit! Call an ambulance."

A second later, I was surrounded by concerned faces.

I held still, leaning on my right side, propped against my elbow, too afraid to move. Keera dropped to her knees beside me, eyes wide.

"I'm going to move behind you, so you can rest against me," she said.

Her eyes locked onto mine, searching, waiting for a response. I managed the smallest nod, careful not to move more than necessary.

She shifted toward my back and eased me into her arms, cradling me against her. I let myself sink into the embrace as the pain in my ankle throbbed in time with my heartbeat.

The music had stopped, leaving the studio eerily silent, no clacking heels, no beat to move to, just the sharpness of my breath. Anjannette, Sophie, and Amber gathered in front of me, their expressions mirroring the panic clawing at my chest.

Sophie's voice cut through the haze, soft but urgent, telling me an ambulance was on the way. Amber and Anjannette murmured reassurances, but their words felt distant, like they were coming from somewhere far away.

"She looks really pale," Anjannette said.

Keera's warm hand brushed away damp strands of hair off my forehead.

"Let's take some yoga breaths, Shan," she said. "In for four, hold for four, and out for four. Ready?"

If I wasn't in agonizing pain, I would have chuckled. How could something as simple as breathing possibly make a difference? But I didn't have the energy to argue. And if it didn't help, at least it's something to focus on.

Together we breathed in beats of four until the studio door burst open and the paramedics approached..

"Hi there." A woman with a long brown ponytail and kind blue eyes crouched next to me. "I'm Dani and this is Mike. Can you tell me your name?"

"Shannon," I said, my voice barely above a whisper.

"Nice to meet you, Shannon. We're going to take care of you." She secured a blood pressure cuff around my right bicep. "Can you tell me what happened?"

"I landed wrong," I managed, breath catching. "My ankle popped."

I followed her gaze to Mike, who knelt next to my foot.

"Okay," she said. "We're going to take care of you, but first I need to ask…on a scale from one to ten, how bad is the pain right now?"

"Eleven," I breathed, trying not to move.

She nodded, calm and focused.

"Alright. We're going to give you something to help with that. Then we'll stabilize your ankle for transport. We're not going to remove the boot, it's important we keep everything in place until we get imaging at the hospital. Sound good?"

"Mmm Hmm."

My whole world had narrowed to the throbbing in my ankle, pulsing tighter with every second, like my boot was shrinking around it. I couldn't tell if sweat or tears were running down my face, but I didn't have the energy to care.

"Quick check," Dani said. "Do you have any allergies I need to know about?"

"No."

"I'm going to start an IV and give you some morphine to help manage the pain. It should take the edge off pretty quickly." She reached into her bag several times, pulling out supplies. "Okay, small pick coming."

I barely felt the needle when Dani slipped it into my arm. Maybe the blinding pain in my ankle was stealing all my focus, but the sting I expected never came.

"There you go." She taped the line down with practiced ease. "We'll give the meds a few minutes to kick in. Hang tight for me."

She stood and walked over to Mike. They kept looking over at me. Based on their gestures, I'm guessing they're discussing a plan of attack.

"You hanging in there?"

I startled at the sound of Keera's voice coming from behind me. I'd forgotten she was there which is ridiculous considering I'm lying against her.

"I am," I said. "I just feel so stupid. This is so embarrassing."

She gave my shoulder a reassuring squeeze.

"There's no reason to be embarrassed. Especially with us. Accidents happen."

"Yeah, but this one is a doozy."

"It definitely doesn't look great," she said. "But they'll get you to the hospital and you'll be in good hands."

"Can you call Simon and my parents and let them know?"

"I will. And Simon is with—"

Dani interrupted before she could finish.

"You feeling a little better?"

As I looked up at her, I realized that while the pain wasn't totally gone, it was definitely more tolerable.

"I am, thanks."

"Good. We'll go ahead and get your leg splinted," she said, turning to Keera. "I'll support her shoulders so you can carefully slide out from behind her, nice and slow. We'll keep her leg as still as possible."

Once Keera moved, Dani slowly lowered me until I was lying flat on the floor.

I've always been the type to deal with pain privately. I prefer to curl up alone and wait for it to pass. But as Mike and Dani moved in to take off the boot, I was thankful not to be alone. Anjannette and Keera knelt beside me, each gripping one of my hands, their presence steadying me more than I could say. Sophie and Amber stood behind, offering quiet support.

"Alright, Shannon," Dani said gently. "We're going to keep the boot on and immobilize everything as it is. The hospital will handle removal once they've got imaging and better pain control. Our goal is to keep things stable right now."

Mike knelt beside me and pulled out what looked like a thick, padded wrap with straps hanging off the sides.

"This is called a vacuum splint," he explained. "We're going to slide it under your leg, wrap it around, and then suck the air out so it firms up around you. It'll feel snug, but it shouldn't make things worse."

I nodded, bracing myself. Even with the meds, the idea of being moved made my stomach twist.

"Okay, Shannon," Dani said calmly, shifting to one side. "We're going to lift your leg a little. Stay as relaxed as you can. We've got you."

I focused on breathing as they worked together, Dani supporting above the injury while Mike gently slid the splint beneath my leg.

"You're doing great," Dani said.

Once the splint was in place, Mike wrapped it around my leg, adjusting the edges so they didn't press on any one spot. Then I heard a soft hiss as he used the pump to draw the air out. The wrap slowly tightened, firming up around my leg and boot like a custom mold.

It was a strange sensation, like a firm hug wrapping around something fragile. I could feel it molding to every curve, locking me in place without digging in or forcing anything to move. The pressure was even, supportive, not sharp or suffocating, just contained. For the first time since I hit the floor, my leg didn't feel like it was dangling off a cliff.

"There we go," Mike said once it was fully set. "That'll keep everything stable on the ride."

I let out a long, shaky breath. The worst of it was over, for now, at least. I still couldn't look at my leg, but it was wrapped, supported, and no longer felt like it was about to detach from my body. And somehow, in the middle of all this, that tiny bit of stability made me feel a little more okay.

Mike walked across the studio and retrieved the gurney he'd brought in and wheeled it to my side. Anjannette and Keera let go of my hands and backed away from me.

"We're going to roll you onto your side and move you to the gurney now, nice and easy," he said.

Dani slid one hand behind my back while Mike supported my leg, their movements practiced and smooth. With one gentle pull and a slow, controlled shift, they rolled me onto the stretcher. Every motion still lit up my ankle, but the pain had softened so it was less like a knife, more a throbbing ache. The meds had to be working better now, because a few minutes ago, that would've sent me through the roof.

Once I was settled onto the gurney, Dani adjusted a blanket around me and strapped me in. They raised it to full height and unlocked the wheels. The ladies followed us out the door.

"I talked to your parents," Keera said. "They're on the way to the hospital."

I nodded, my hands holding the sides of the gurney in a death grip as Mike and Dani wheeled me toward the waiting ambulance and pushed me inside.

ANDREW

. . .

THE FINAL CREDITS OF *THE EMPIRE STRIKES BACK* FINISHED and the lights flickered on. I blinked, half-dazed from the emotional gut punch of Darth Vader's confession. I've lost count of how many times I've seen this movie, but it still gets me.

I stood to stretch and my spine popped in protest, a reminder I should've moved between movies instead of remaining stuck to the seat inhaling popcorn.

"Shit!"

Simon's sharp tone made me stop mid-stretch to look at him.

"What's wrong?" Archer asked before I could.

"I've got..." He studied his phone for a second. "...nine missed calls and six texts from Keera. Something happened to Shannon," he said, already dialing.

My heart skidded to a halt then started pounding at that last sentence. I exchanged a look with Archer as Simon paced the aisle, phone pressed to his ear.

"Keera? What happened?" Simon's voice tightened. "She what? Which hospital? I'm coming right now."

He shoved his phone into his back pocket and raked a hand through his hair, leaving it sticking up in frustrated spikes.

"Well?"

I held my hands out, brows raised.

"Shannon fell during pole class and Keera said her ankle is in pretty bad shape," he said. "They took her to the hospital by ambulance."

"Which hospital?"

"Yours," he said.

Meaning Lehigh Valley Hospital in Dickson City. It makes sense they took her there because it's in the same building as the orthopedic institute, which just so happens to be where I work.

"Okay, let's go."

As we rushed out of the theater and headed to our cars, Archer looked at us with panicked eyes. He hates hospitals. Like, *viscerally* hates them. I didn't get it at first, not until he told me about all the time he spent in one as a kid. His grandma had kidney disease and was in and out for treatments all the time. His mom dragged him along like it was a family field trip. He talks about the smell, like it still lingers in his nose if he thinks about it too hard.

"Simon, I want to be supportive, but..."

"I know," Simon said. "You don't have to come."

"Are you sure?"

"Go home. I'll text when I know something."

Archer nodded and got into his car.

"Come on, I'll drive. We can pick up your car later."

Simon must be shaken because he didn't argue and got into the passenger seat.

The ride to the hospital was quiet and tense. Simon checked his phone repeatedly while I tried to reassure him that ankle injuries, while painful, usually heal well. Still, I couldn't stop thinking about Shannon. The thought of her being hurt made my chest ache.

"Did Keera mention if it was a lateral or medial injury? Did she see any deformity?" I asked Simon, needing more clinical details.

He looked at me like I had three heads.

"No, she just said Shannon fell and it looked really bad."

I nodded, reminding myself most people don't think in medical terminology during emergencies.

When we got to the emergency room, we found Shannon's friends and family in the waiting room. Lily and John sat stiffly in uncomfortable chairs, Keera stood, her eyes glued to a *Friends* rerun on the TV, and Anjannette and Sophie huddled together in the corner, speaking in hushed tones.

Keera's eyes widened when she spotted Simon. She ran over and flung her arms around him in a desperate hug, her voice thick as she said, "I'm so glad you're here."

Simon squeezed her tight and kissed the top of her head. I gave them a moment then touched Keera's arm to get her attention.

"Keera, what happened?"

Before she could answer, Lily and John came over. Lily gave Simon and then me a hug.

"Andrew, can you find out what's happening with Shannon?" she asked. "We haven't heard anything since they told us she was taken to X-ray."

"I will," I said, slipping into my calm, doctor voice. "But first I want Keera to tell me what happened."

Keera rubbed her forehead and dragged her fingers through her hair.

"We were almost finished with our routine and she was moving from a fan leg pirouette to thread the needle." She held out her arms and shook her head. "I heard her scream and when I looked over, she was on the ground and her ankle was sideways. Like seriously, *sideways*." She shuddered. "It looked so bad."

"Okay, let me see what I can find out," I said. "Sit tight."

I headed toward the department's secure entrance and swiped my badge. Thankfully I keep it in my car so I didn't have to run home to get it.

As I stepped through the door, I approached the unit secretary.

"Hi Larissa."

"Dr. Bowen," she said. "I thought you were off today."

"I am, but my friend's sister was brought in with an ankle injury. Shannon Parker? Is she back from X-ray?"

"She is, and Dr. Reade called Dr. Chen for an orthopedic consult. He's reviewing the X-rays now."

"Any idea where he is?"

"In the workroom."

"Thanks."

I found him exactly where Larissa said he'd be. He looked over when I entered the room.

"Andrew, aren't you supposed to be off this weekend?"

"I am, but the ankle on the X-ray belongs to my best friend's sister. I was with him when he got the call she was brought here, so I came with him."

"Well, since you're here, would you want to stay and assist in her surgery?"

"She needs surgery?"

He nodded and pointed to the monitor.

"She's got a bimalleolar fracture," he said. "Clean breaks on both the medial and lateral malleolus."

"How bad?"

He shifted so I could see the X-rays on the monitor. I studied them as he answered my question.

"Not the worst I've seen," he said. "Displacement's moderate. No open wound, no neurovascular compromise. Could've been a hell of a lot worse."

I nodded, hands tightening at my sides.

"I'll definitely stay and assist," I said, then chuckled. "The person I had plans with tonight is the patient's sister, so I'm suddenly free."

Dr. Chen looked over his glasses, studying me.

"Do you feel comfortable assisting with this case, given your personal relationship to the patient?"

"Yeah, it's fine. Shannon and I aren't really close, I'm friends with her brother."

It's not a total lie. Shannon and I have been around each other most of our lives, but we've never hung out without Simon there.

"Let's go talk her through the plan," he said, getting to his feet. "I had Larissa call her parents back right before you showed up, so they should be with her already."

I followed Dr. Chen down the hallway to Shannon's room, my mind running through surgical protocols and post-op care plans. Even though he'd be leading the surgery, I wanted to be as prepared as if it were my own.

We entered the room to find John and Lily standing on either side of the bed. Shannon's face looked pale and the harsh lights accentuated the pain etched into her features. Her eyes caught mine and for a split second, everything went still.

"Andrew?"

Her voice sounded thick from the medication.

"Yeah, it's me." I stepped forward, giving her a small, comforting smile. "I was with Simon when Keera called, so I came along to see if I could help."

Before she could comment, Dr. Chen stepped in, his presence calm and professional.

"Shannon, I'm Dr. Chen, the orthopedic surgeon. I'll be taking care of you today."

"Surgeon?" Lily asked.

He nodded and even though Lily asked the question, he directed the answer to Shannon.

"Dr. Reade called me in after looking at your X-rays. I reviewed them before coming in here. It looks like you've got a bimalleolar fracture, which means you've broken both sides of your ankle, what we call the medial and lateral malleolus. The good news is it's a clean break, and we can fix it with surgery. The goal is to realign the bones and secure them with plates and screws so they heal properly. That'll help you regain full range of motion once everything's healed."

"How long is the recovery?" John asked.

"Barring any complications, Shannon should be able to go home within a day or two after the surgery. She'll need to stay off the ankle for several weeks, and we'll keep a close eye on her recovery to watch for any signs of infection or other issues."

"But I'll be okay? I'll be able to walk?"

"You will." He smiled. "It will take some time, patience, and physical therapy, but you'll be back to dancing in no time."

Shannon looked up at me then, her eyes a little glassy but locked on mine, like I was the only thing keeping her steady.

"Are you gonna be there for the surgery, too?"

Years of training helped me maintain my professional demeanor, but inside, something protective and personal stirred.

"Yes, I'll be assisting Dr. Chen."

The way Shannon and her parents seemed to relax after I answered meant more than I expected. It felt good, knowing they had so much faith in me.

"When will you be doing the surgery?" John asked.

"We're just waiting for the anesthesiologist to arrive. Once he's here, an orderly will take Shannon upstairs and we'll get her prepped and into the OR. Larissa will direct you to the waiting area."

"How long will it take?"

That question came from Lily.

"About two hours," he said, then turned to Shannon with a reassuring smile. "Once it's done, you'll be on the road to feeling like yourself again."

Lily walked over and pulled me into a hug.

"Take care of her, Andrew."

She said it like she's trying to hold on to the little bit of control left in a situation she can't change.

"I will," I said.

She pulled back and nodded.

After making sure no one had any more questions, Dr. Chen and I headed upstairs to get ready. The locker room smelled of antiseptic and felt unusually quiet, a sharp contrast to the typical pre-surgery buzz during the week.

I'd just changed into fresh scrubs when Dr. Chen glanced over.

"Dr. Lu's here," he said. "We're good to go."

As I followed him into the scrub room, the weight of it all settled over me. This wasn't just another surgery. This was Shannon.

CHAPTER 5

Shannon

I woke to a soft beeping and the scent of antiseptic in the air. The room was dark, with a greenish glow coming from a monitor next to me. It took me a moment to figure out where I was, and why.

Then it hit me.

My ankle.

I tilted my head and spotted thick white gauze poking out from beneath the covers. My foot lay on a pillow, wrapped snug in bandages climbing up to my mid-calf. From the knee down, my leg felt heavy and oddly distant, like it wasn't really part of me.

My butt was completely numb. and I tried to shift, but my limbs felt sluggish and didn't want to cooperate. I wiggled the best I could, awkward and slow, until I settled into a slightly different position.

As I settled back against the pillow, a prickle of aware-ness stirred at the base of my neck, an unshakable sense I wasn't alone. The room was quiet, but not completely empty.

I blinked, trying to clear the fog, as I glanced around the room. Shapes slowly came into focus, and I spotted Andrew sitting a few feet away across from my bed. He sat straight, his head resting against the back of the chair, eyes closed, breathing steady.

"Andrew?"

My voice cracked, more air than sound. But he heard me.

His eyes snapped open and he straightened immediately.

"Hey," he said, rubbing a hand over his face. "You're awake."

"I think so." I gave a faint, wry smile. "Unless this is a weird painkiller dream."

He smiled back, and it made something twist in my chest. Something that had nothing to do with the painkillers.

"No dream. You're really here. Hospital room and all."

I glanced at my ankle then back at him.

"How did it go?"

"It went well," Andrew said softly. "No complications."

"So I have screws in my ankle now?"

"You do. Screws and plates." He smirked. "Think of them as your personal hardware upgrade."

I let out a half-laugh, half-groan.

"You're funny. I thought you were a doctor, not a comedian."

"I'm multi-talented." Leaning forward, he rested his elbows on his knees. "How are you feeling?"

"A little fuzzy."

"That's from the anesthesia and pain meds and it's

totally normal." He glanced at me with concern. "Are you feeling any pain right now?"

"Not sharp pain, no. It's more like pressure or tightness around my ankle, kind of heavy and dull." I cringed. "But I'm guessing I will be in pain once the pain meds wear off."

"Yeah, unfortunately," he said with a small nod. "But don't worry, you'll have a pain management plan to keep it under control."

"Sounds like fun." He nodded, stifling a yawn. "You look exhausted. How long have you been here?"

"Since after they brought you back from recovery."

"I'm surprised my mom isn't here."

"She was here for a while after you got out of surgery, along with your dad, Simon, and Keera," I frowned, trying to sort the fragments in my head. "You don't remember talking to them?"

I shook my head carefully.

"Not at all."

"That's totally normal," he said. "Dr. Chen went over everything with all of you after the surgery. Once you fell asleep, I told them you'd probably sleep through the night and convinced them to go home."

"I can't believe they listened to you."

"Well, I promised them I'd keep an eye on you."

"So you're still here because you promised them?"

He hesitated.

It was quick—just a beat—but there was weight in it. More than he probably meant to show. And even in my semi-groggy state, I didn't miss it.

Maybe it was the too-easy tone in his voice, or the way his eyes didn't quite meet mine. Either way, something about his answer felt off, like there was more he wasn't saying.

"Is that the only reason?"

Instead of answering, he stood and moved to the monitor beside my bed. He stared at it like it held the secrets of the universe.

"Your vitals look good," he said quietly, avoiding my eyes.

I watched him, a strange ache rising beneath the haze. He's my brother's best friend, someone I'd grown up with, trusted without thinking. So why did my heart feel tight all of a sudden, like it was trying to tell me something I didn't quite understand?

"You didn't answer my question."

Maybe if he did, it would help me make sense of this tangled mess inside.

He didn't look at me, instead focused on adjusting the corner of the blanket near my arm.

"You're on a lot of medication," he said gently, like I might not even remember this later.

Maybe I wouldn't.

But I felt it now, and that probably wouldn't go away. The way the air shifted between us. The way his silence said everything.

He ran a hand through his hair, still not quite meeting my gaze.

I sighed and let my eyes drift closed for a moment. When I opened them again, he was still standing there, his expression unreadable.

"You didn't have to stay, but I'm glad you did."

Finally, his eyes found mine. And there it was—something unspoken flickering beneath the surface. Something too big, too complicated for this dim hospital room in the middle of the night.

"I wasn't going to leave you," he said, his voice thick with something I couldn't quite place. After a pause, he added, "I should let you rest."

My chest tightened as I watched him settle back into the chair.

"Will you be here when I wake up?" I asked.

He looked at me for a long moment. Then nodded.

"Yeah. I'll be here."

His words settled over me offering quiet comfort, though I couldn't quite grasp why they mattered so much. I'd figure it out once the haze lifted and my mind was clear again.

For now, I just believed him.

ANDREW

THE MORNING LIGHT FILTERED THROUGH THE BLINDS AS I watched Shannon sleep. Her hair was a little messy, her lashes resting against her cheeks like they'd been painted on, and her lips parted slightly as she breathed deeply.

There was something vulnerable about her like this, something I wasn't used to seeing. Shannon was usually sharp-eyed and quick-witted, always the most competent person in the room. Seeing her like this—small and hurting and asleep—did something weird to my chest.

I kept thinking about what she'd said earlier, her words half-slurred but laced with something more personal than gratitude.

"You didn't have to stay, but I'm glad you did."

Maybe it was the drugs talking, maybe it wasn't. Or maybe it was wishful thinking on my part.

I didn't have a great track record when it came to reading

signals. But I couldn't shake the feeling there'd been more there, something unspoken pressing against the edges of her words like fog against glass.

Her breathing slowly changed and became lighter, more aware.

She blinked her eyes open and winced.

"Hey," she croaked.

"You okay?"

She groaned.

"Define okay."

Before I could ask about her pain level, the nurse stepped into the room.

"Good morning, Shannon. I'm Maria, your nurse this morning," she said warmly, glancing briefly at me. "How are you feeling?"

"A little sore," she murmured.

"That's normal after surgery," Maria replied. "Any sharp pain or numbness?"

"There's no numbness and it's more of an ache than a sharp pain."

"What's your pain level from one to ten?"

"About a seven, maybe eight," Shannon said, cringing as she shifted.

Maria checked the IV in her arm.

"I'm going to give you some pain meds through your IV now to give you some relief."

"Thank you."

"You're very welcome," Maria said. "If you need me, just hit the call button. I'll be right in." She smiled and looked at me. "Although with Dr. Bowen here watching over you, I doubt you'll need my help."

"Thanks for the confidence, Maria." I said.

She gave a playful smirk and slipped out of the room,

the door whispering shut behind her.

Shannon looked over at me.

"So I guess you're my bodyguard now."

"Guess so. Though I left my suit and earpiece at home."

She laughed, then winced.

"Okay, that hurts. No more jokes."

"Noted," I said. "The meds Maria gave you should kick in any minute and take the edge off."

She sank back into the pillows with a sigh, just as a soft knock sounded at the door. A second later, her parents eased the door open and stepped inside.

"Hey, sweetie," Lily said softly, eyes full of worry. "How are you feeling?"

"Tired and sore," Shannon said, her voice scratchy. "But the meds must be kicking in, because the pain isn't as bad as it was when I woke up and I'm starting to feel a little fuzzy again."

John stepped closer and kissed her forehead.

"You'll be up and kicking in no time."

She groaned.

"That was such a bad dad joke."

John grinned and looked around the room, his eyes landing on me.

"I thought it was a pretty good dad joke."

I chuckled and nodded.

"Classic delivery. Solid eight out of ten."

Lily rolled her eyes.

"Don't encourage him."

I smiled, but the weight of the past twenty-four hours was catching up with me. I scrubbed a hand over my face and stood.

"You're in good hands, so I'm going to head home for a bit," I glanced between Shannon and her parents. "I need to shower and put on some clean clothes." Looking at Shannon, I added, "I'll stop back in later, okay?"

"Sounds good," she murmured. "Thanks for staying."

There was something quiet and tentative in her voice. But before I could overthink that, John stepped forward and rested his hand on my shoulder.

"Thanks for staying with her, Andrew. It's really above and beyond. We appreciate it."

"I'm happy to help," I said.

With that, I stepped out and headed for the parking garage.

When I got home, I kicked off my shoes, got undressed, and headed straight for the shower. I stayed in there a long time letting the hot water wash away the stiffness from my night spent in the hospital chair.

Once I dried off, I tugged on a clean T-shirt and some old sweatpants, then dropped into bed with a groan. After spending the night in a chair, being horizontal felt like heaven. I didn't even bother pulling the blanket up, just closed my eyes and let sleep take over.

I woke up groggy, blinking against the afternoon light slanting through the blinds. The clock told me I should get moving and head back to the hospital, but instead I rolled over and stared at the ceiling.

Sleep had helped with my exhaustion, but not the mess in my head. Being near Shannon, feeling like she might want me around for more than moral support, made me nervous. Not bad nervous, but the kind that curled low in my stomach and made me second-guess every casual touch, every word.

I've known Shannon since preschool, and yeah, somewhere along the way, I developed a crush. A quiet one. The kind I kept tucked away like a secret, because she never gave me a reason to think she saw me as anything other than her brother's best friend.

But something felt different now.

Maybe it's the way she looked at me in the hospital room, a softness in her eyes that hadn't been there before. Or how she relaxed when I said I wasn't going anywhere. It could've started even earlier, back in the produce section of the supermarket, when something between us shifted, like the air had rearranged itself.

Whatever it was, it felt new. And it made it a hell of a lot harder to pretend I wasn't still half in love with her.

I didn't have answers yet, but lying around wasn't going to give me any. With a sigh, I dragged myself out of bed, threw on clean clothes, and grabbed my keys. It was time to head back to the hospital.

The drive over passed in a blur, my mind looping through every look, word, and small shift in the way she'd been with me. By the time I pushed open the door to her room, my heart was already racing. She greeted me with a smile.

"Hey, you're back."

"I told you I would be." I grinned and eased into the chair. "So, did anything exciting happen while I was gone?"

"I don't know how exciting it was, but the physical therapist was here."

"How'd it go?"

She let out a long breath and leaned her head back against the pillow.

"I survived. Barely. Pretty sure my ankle is trying to kill me. But the pain meds are finally kicking in again, so I'm not planning to die dramatically in the next hour."

"Glad to hear it. I draw the line at dramatic death scenes."

She chuckled.

"My parents took off for a late lunch or early dinner, whichever you want to call it. They said they'd bring me something that doesn't taste like sadness."

"Good. You deserve at least slightly cheerful food."

She glanced at me with a raised eyebrow, a teasing smile tugging at her lips.

"Have you always been this funny, or is it a new thing?"

I shrugged, trying to sound casual.

"Of course I've always been like this."

Her answering nod led to a quiet beat between us, the kind that felt loaded with unasked questions and maybe a few unsaid admissions.

"I'm actually going home tomorrow," she said. "Well, to my parents' house."

"Yeah?"

"Just until I can put weight on my foot," she said. "Mom suggested it and I agreed because I knew it would make her feel better. And because she'll be able to take care of me without sprinting across town every time I drop my phone or want coffee."

"She'll love that," I said. "Though I'm sure she wishes it wasn't under these circumstances."

"She will. And honestly, having her around will make things a lot easier while I'm stuck on crutches." She scrunched her nose. "But, it'll be an adjustment. I haven't lived with anyone—especially my parents—in a long time."

I nodded.

"I stayed with my parents for a month after residency. It wasn't easy, but we made it work. You'll be fine."

"Maybe you'll have to come over and coach me through it."

"No problem," I replied.

"Would you actually come over just to play referee or something?"

"I'd come over for you."

The words left my mouth before I could stop them.

She blinked slowly, like she wasn't sure she'd heard me right.

I cleared my throat and tried to play it off with a shrug.

"I mean yeah, I'd come to coach you through it."

"You're terrible at casual," she said, but there was a smile in her voice.

"I'm aware."

She looked down at her blanket and picked at the edge.

"I meant it, you know. When I said I was glad you stayed."

My heart thudded in my chest, loud enough I was half-convinced she could hear it.

"I wanted to," I said quietly. "I wanted to be here."

She looked up at me then, and her expression was so open it made my breath catch.

"So...what now?"

The question hung there between us, innocent and enormous.

I leaned back in the chair, feeling suddenly calm, like everything was shifting into place.

"Now, I make good on my promise to teach you how to survive living with your parents again. And maybe I can help you escape in a week or so when you're going stir-crazy."

"Are you planning a rescue mission?"

"Operation Shannon Liberation," I said, deadpan. "Highly classified. Code name: Sneaky Crutch Escape."

She laughed again, then the sound softened into a quiet smile.

"Thank you," she said. "For being here. For everything."

I nodded, my chest tight in that good, terrifying way.

"Anytime."

And I meant it. Because this wasn't only a favor to her parents. It never had been.

Maybe this was the start of something that had been quietly building between us all along.

CHAPTER 6

Shannon

BEING WHEELED OUT OF THE HOSPITAL FELT MORE AWKWARD than freeing, like I was part of a slow parade I hadn't signed up for. But now, tucked into my childhood bed with my leg propped on a stack of pillows, the real discomfort wasn't physical. It was the strange sense of being thrust back into a life I left behind years ago.

It's a bit surreal. My room hasn't changed one bit.

Same fuchsia walls with the metallic polka dot decals my mom helped me stick up freshman year. The same white furniture set I'd begged for from IKEA after watching a bedroom makeover on HGTV.

The corkboard above my desk was cluttered with a collage of photo booth strips, graduation announcements, and crumpled notes from friends. Bottles of nail polish in every shimmer and shade, a lineup of Victoria's Secret body sprays, and a sparkly tumbler with its straw bent to spell out my name littered the surface of my makeup table.

I have no idea why I never threw any of it away. I stayed in this room every time I visited over the years, so there were plenty of chances to clear it out.

Mom sat on the edge of the bed, looking around.

"I always told myself I'd redo this room into a guest space. Simon's too. But I couldn't bring myself to change them."

It was like she read my mind.

I smiled.

"It's kind of like stepping into a museum exhibit. 'Life of a Teenage Girl Circa 2006.'"

She laughed.

"Well, I liked keeping the memories close." She brushed my hair back gently, like she used to when I had the flu or a heartbreak. "I've got a Zoom call starting in five minutes, so I'll be in the office for about an hour. Simon and Keera said they're coming over, but if you need anything in the meantime, text me."

"Thanks Mom. For everything."

"You're welcome, honey."

She stood and gave me a kiss on the top of my head before heading out the door. As it clicked shut behind her, I sank deeper into the pillows and let my eyes fall closed.

I don't know how long I was sleeping before I heard a soft knock on the door.

"Permission to enter," Simon said, in a mock-serious tone.

"Come on in. Be careful you don't trip on the time warp."

He stepped inside, followed closely by Keera, who immediately paused and took in the room with a slow, nostalgic smile.

"This room is awesome," she said, eyes sweeping from

the twinkle lights above the bed to the bookshelf packed with worn paperbacks and ceramic trinkets.

"Shannon begged for this setup for a year before our parents finally caved," Simon said.

"It's true. I recorded the show I saw it on and made Mom watch it over and over."

"You were relentless," he said, shaking his head.

Keera wandered the room as we chatted. Occasionally, she pointed to an item and asked about it. Then Simon's phone buzzed. He checked the screen and groaned.

"Mom needs help with her computer. Something is wrong with her second monitor."

He ducked out, and Keera dragged the papasan chair closer to the bed and settled into it cross-legged.

"How are you doing?"

"My ankle hurts, but it's only really bad when the pain meds wear off."

"I'm glad you're mostly not in pain, but how are *you* doing? Your vibe seems off."

What a loaded question. I'd had surgery less than forty-eight hours ago, moved back into my childhood bedroom like I'd hit rewind on my entire adult life, and I was still trying to make sense of what happened in New York. My vibe was off because I was off balance, off center, off everything. But how was I supposed to explain it all without sounding like a total mess?

I could lie and say I was tired or adjusting. Blame the meds or the pain or the weirdness of the situation. But Keera would know I wasn't telling the truth. And honestly it might actually be nice to talk about it, maybe get someone else's perspective of what happened.

"It's weird." I looked around the room. "Obviously I've slept here over the years, but now it seems different. It's like

I fell through a crack in time and landed back in high school. I keep half-expecting a text about senior skip day or to hear Mom yell at me to get up for school." I fiddled with the edge of my blanket for a few seconds before adding, "Maybe the difference is before, I always knew I was heading back to the life I built in New York. Now, even though I have my own place here, it feels like I've hit pause on everything. Like I pressed rewind without meaning to. I'm staying here because of the surgery, but it's more than that. After everything that happened last year, I don't know what I'm doing anymore. I don't have a job or a real direction. It feels like I'm standing in the middle of my own life and somehow got lost. Like I'm having an early midlife crisis or something."

Keera didn't say anything right away. Instead, she tilted her head slightly, her expression softening as she studied me. Then she finally spoke, her voice low and steady.

"You know I'm here to listen, right?" she said. "When you're ready to talk about what happened in New York."

Her words hung in the air between us, and for a moment I considered deflecting, making some joke about how I was being dramatic. But looking at Keera's face, at the genuine concern there, something inside me cracked open.

I let out a breath, steeling myself, and blurted it all out.

"I was dating this guy, John, for close to two years. Things were pretty serious, and we were talking about moving in together." My throat tightened. "Then I found out he'd been sleeping with someone I considered a good friend for at least six months."

Keera's eyes widened.

"Are you serious?"

"Yep. And the worst part? When I confronted him, he

didn't even apologize. He just kind of shrugged, like I should've seen it coming."

She crossed her arms and said, "Please tell me you at least threw something at him. Or dramatically stormed out. Bonus points if there was background music."

"Unfortunately, no," I said with a chuckle. "I collected my things and left his apartment." I let the smile fade as I added, "Afterwards, I called my brunch crew—the ladies I considered my best friends—to commiserate. They said all the right things. Told me I was better off without him, that I deserved more."

Keera's expression softened.

"Of course they did. It's what best friends do when your boyfriend turns out to be a garbage human." She paused, then raised an eyebrow. "Let me guess, there's a 'but' coming?"

I shrugged and nodded.

"But a couple days later, I was the last to arrive at brunch and as I approached the table, I heard them talking about me." I swallowed hard. "Maya said she couldn't really blame John, not with how fat I'd gotten. Laura laughed about how I used to be the pretty one. I stood there frozen for a full thirty seconds listening to them confirm every insecurity I'd tried to ignore for months."

I stared at the blanket covering my legs, tracing the pattern with my finger.

"When I finally stepped up to the table, they froze. I didn't say anything, just shook my head, turned around, and left." I blinked hard, willing the sting in my eyes to go away. "It was like something cracked open inside me. Not only because of what they said, but because I knew I'd never go back. Not to that table, not to our friendship, or that version of my life. It was like a switch flipped, like I finally saw everything for what it was, and I knew I couldn't unsee it."

Keera's jaw tightened so hard I thought she might crack a tooth.

"Those bitches. I hope you know you're better off without them."

"In my head I do, but sometimes my heart has a different opinion—one tangled up with memories of what I thought was real friendship." I blew out a long breath. "Maya, Laura, and Jess were my first real friends in the city. We even lived together for a few years before we each made enough money to afford our own apartments."

"Have you talked to them since?"

"No, Jess called and left a message apologizing for the three of them." I shrugged, the memory still faintly bitter. "At first, hearing her voice brought everything rushing back. But the more I listened to it, the more her words sounded stupid and shallow. Like she was saying what she thought she was supposed to, not because she meant any of it. So, I removed myself from the group chat and deleted their numbers from my phone." I smiled. "And shortly after I met you and Anjannette and all the pole ladies. You all reminded me what real friendship looks like. No judgment. Just showing up, cheering each other on, and laughing until we cry."

"I know coming back here wasn't part of your plan, but I'm so glad you did. Walking away from your job, your apartment, and everything you built had to be brutal. But staying in that mess would've wrecked your mental health. I'm proud of you for choosing peace over pretending everything was fine."

"About my job..."

"Are you kidding me?"

"I wish I was," I said. "That's the third part of my shit trifecta."

"What happened?"

"The agency I worked for was owned by Lila, who I loved. When she retired, her son Nick took over, and he's a total creep. Through the years, he hit on me constantly, and I always shut him down. Once he was in charge, he started sidelining me...cutting my bookings, passing me over. When my contract was up, he didn't renew it and I was out."

Keera blinked, like she was trying to absorb it all.

"So you literally lost your relationship, your friends, and your job all at once."

"Yeah." Silence stretched between us for a moment. "And sometimes I wonder if I overreacted. Like maybe I should've stayed. Maybe it wasn't as bad as I made it out to be."

Those last two sentences came out more like questions.

Keera sat up straighter, her eyes fierce.

"Shannon, *no*. You absolutely didn't overreact. Any one of those things would've knocked most people off balance. But all three at once?" She shook her head. "You were dealing with betrayal, emotional abuse, body shaming, and a toxic work environment. Of course you were looking for a way out. Anyone would have."

Tears stung my eyes, but I blinked them back. Her words hit me right in the center of my chest.

"Thank you," I whispered.

Keera reached over and took my hand, squeezing it. "You don't have to justify protecting yourself. You were drowning, and you swam for shore. That takes strength."

I swallowed hard, emotion knotting in my throat.

"I guess I've been trying to make sense of it all. It still feels messy."

"Of course it does," she said gently. "But you're not alone anymore."

The sound of voices floated up from downstairs, Simon's and someone else.

"Is Andrew here?" she asked.

I felt the heat rise to my cheeks before I could stop it. I looked away, but not fast enough.

Keera's eyes lit up.

"Is there anything you'd like to share with the class, Ms. Parker?"

I bit back a smile, tucking my hair behind my ear.

"Not yet."

Her eyes shifted toward the doorway as Andrew's footsteps sounded on the stairs.

"That's not what it looks like from where I'm sitting."

Andrew appeared in the doorway a second later, his expression softening when he saw me.

"Hi Andrew," Keera said as she stood. She leaned over, giving my hand one last squeeze. "We'll finish this later."

She winked as she passed Andrew on her way out, and I caught the amused expression he gave her before turning his full attention back to me.

And even though I was still in my teenage bedroom with a messed-up ankle and more emotional baggage than I knew what to do with, somehow seeing him made everything feel a little bit lighter.

ANDREW

. . .

Keera gave me a knowing little wink as she slipped out of the room, which was my first hint I was walking into something. The second? Shannon's eyes were a little too shiny, like she'd either just cried or was about to. And the third? The room felt heavy, like whatever she'd been feeling hadn't quite settled yet.

Shannon shifted, slow and careful, and for a second her face tightened like it hurt more than she wanted me to see. Her ankle was bandaged up and propped on a pile of pillows, peeking out from the blanket like something that might break if you looked at it wrong.

"Hey," I said, settling into the papasan chair next to the bed. "How are you doing?"

She offered a forced smile.

"Not too bad as long as I don't move certain ways and the meds don't wear off." Her voice had that half-drained rasp I recognized from post-op patients—part exhaustion, part irritation because her body wasn't cooperating. "I've been doing the toe curls and the isometric exercises, like they told me."

"Good. They'll help maintain muscle tone while you're immobilized."

She gave a one-shouldered shrug.

"If nothing else, they keep my butt from falling asleep."

"Critical post-op strategy," I said around a chuckle.

I let my gaze wander around the room, really taking in the details for the first time. I'd spent countless hours in this house, but Simon, Archer, and I usually stuck to the basement controllers in hand, arguing over who got the next turn.

It's interesting being in what had been Shannon's inner sanctum and taking it all in. I remember when John and Lily finally gave in to her begging and redid the whole room. Now it looked like a time capsule of her high school life.

The walls were lined with framed photos and trophies—cheerleading medals, school awards, snapshots of smiling girls in matching dresses with perfect hair. A tiara from prom. A bulletin board with fading notes and an ancient corsage.

It was quintessentially Shannon—the Shannon I remembered from high school, anyway. Head cheerleader, prom queen, the girl every guy wanted to date and every girl wanted to be. She'd inhabited a stratosphere I could only observe from a distance.

"What are you thinking about?" she asked, following my gaze around the room.

I turned back to her, debating how honest I should be, then decided to just go for it.

"I was remembering how you were the 'it girl' back in high school," I said. "Head cheerleader, prom queen, the whole package."

She let out a soft laugh, but there was something wistful in it.

"Yeah, I guess I was. It's funny how at seventeen I thought I had the whole world figured out."

"Didn't we all?" I let that sit between us for a moment, then added, "You seemed to do pretty well for yourself, though."

She hesitated, then nodded.

"I did. For a while."

The words hung between us, heavy with implication. I could have let it go, changed the subject, kept things surface-level like we always had. But something about the vulnerability in her voice, the way she was looking at me like she wanted to say more, made me push.

"What happened, Shannon? Why'd you move back?"

I expected her to dodge the question. Maybe crack a joke or change the subject. But instead, she took a shaky breath and told me everything.

It was tough to listen to. The kind of slow-burn mess that makes you question everything—who you are, who you can trust, if you're even worth the effort anymore.

"So, there you have it," she said, her voice barely above a whisper. "The complete implosion of my life in Manhattan."

She looked down at the edge of the blanket, jaw clenched, like maybe she wished she'd kept it all to herself.

"That explains a lot." She glanced up at me, her right brow raised. "For as long as I remember, you had an air of confidence about you, like you knew exactly who you were. It doesn't feel like it's there anymore."

Her smile was faint and a little sad.

"I guess that's what happens when your life implodes."

"Shannon—" I shook my head. "That's all bullshit. Painful bullshit, but still bullshit."

"What do you mean?"

"Shannon, you're amazing," I said, my voice low but firm. "And you're gorgeous. Anyone with eyes can see that. And those curves? Damn." I shook my head, a small smile breaking through. "But it's not only physical. You're smart, funny, and you've got this way of making people feel like they matter. Plus, you're actually there for people when they need you."

I paused, watching her eyes flicker like maybe she didn't believe me.

"Any guy who'd cheat on you is a straight-up asshole. And those women you called friends? They weren't friends. They were jealous. Plain and simple. You shine, Shan. They couldn't stand being in the shadow of someone real."

Her eyes widened, and I felt heat creep up my neck.

"Did I say too much?" I asked.

But instead of retreating or looking uncomfortable, she smiled. A real smile this time, the first genuine one I'd seen since walking into her room.

"No," she said softly. "It wasn't too much."

Something shifted between us in that moment. The air felt charged, different. I found myself leaning forward slightly.

"Good."

Her expression turned curious, almost amused.

"You know, I don't remember high school Andrew being this...bold. Talk about confidence."

"High school Andrew was too busy sweating through his undershirt anytime a girl made eye contact." I laughed. "Although not that many did."

She sighed, shaking her head.

"Then they were all idiots, Andrew."

I ran a hand through my hair, then looked back at her with a soft smile.

"You can't let what happened with those jerks in New York define you or drag you down. You're Shannon Parker—strong, smart, and amazing. Don't forget who you are," I smirked. "Don't be a hard rock when you really are a gem."

"Did you just quote Lauryn Hill?"

"I did."

"I'm surprised you even know that song. It's not exactly your kind of music."

"You used to blast "Doo Wop" nonstop so it's burned into my brain."

She actually laughed—not the fake, polite kind, but the real deal that made her eyes squint and her whole body shift with it.

"God, I haven't listened to that song in years."

"It's a classic."

She settled back against the pillows.

"I can't believe you quoted Lauryn Hill to make me feel better."

"Well, it's true. You are a gem, Shannon. Don't let anyone make you think otherwise."

Pink tinged her cheeks, and she looked down at her hands fidgeting with the edge of the blanket.

"You know, in all the years we've known each other, I don't think the two of us have ever really talked like this."

"No," I agreed. "We haven't."

"Why do you think that is?"

I considered the question, thinking about the invisible barriers that had kept us in separate orbits for so long.

"Because you were Shannon Parker, and I was just Simon's nerdy best friend. We existed in completely different worlds."

"And now?"

The question hung between us, loaded with possibility. I looked at her—really looked at her. Not the untouchable cheerleader from high school or my best friend's sister, but Shannon. The woman who'd trusted me enough to share her deepest hurts, who was strong enough to rebuild her life from scratch, who made my heart race every time she smiled.

"Now I think maybe our worlds aren't so far apart."

She held my gaze for a long moment, and I swear I could feel something building between us. Something that had maybe always been there, waiting for the right moment to surface.

A door slammed downstairs, followed by the sound of John's voice calling out letting us know he was back. The spell between us broke, but not entirely. Shannon's cheeks were still pink, and she was looking at me like she was seeing me for the first time.

"I should probably go," I said. "Let you get some rest."

"Probably," she agreed, but she didn't sound like she wanted me to leave any more than I wanted to go.

I stood, then paused at the foot of her bed.

"Shannon?"

"Yeah?"

"For what it's worth, I think seventeen-year-old you would be pretty impressed with who you turned out to be. Curves and all."

Her mouth curled into a sweet smile.

"Thanks, Andrew. For listening. And for everything."

"Anytime."

I headed for the door, but her voice stopped me.

"Andrew?"

I turned back.

"Next time you want to quote '90s R&B to cheer me up, I'm partial to TLC too."

"I'll keep that in mind."

As I walked downstairs to find Simon, I couldn't stop grinning. Something had definitely shifted between Shannon and me. Something that felt like the beginning of everything I'd never dared to hope for.

And if she wanted TLC quotes, I'd better brush up on my "Waterfalls" lyrics.

CHAPTER 7

Shannon

AFTER FOUR DAYS TRAPPED IN MY ROOM, I SERIOUSLY couldn't take the isolation anymore. Dad and Simon helped haul me down to the couch. At least now, when people come to visit, it's in the living room and not my bedroom, so it doesn't feel like they're holding some kind of vigil over me.

The couch is a step up from my room, but sitting around all day still sucks. I'm used to being on the move. But, I'm not dumb enough to push it. The doctor said no weight on my ankle for about six weeks, and I'm not about to screw up. I want this thing to heal right.

While I hunted for a series to binge to kill time, I did some toe curls and isometric exercises. I'm used to working out or at least stretching every day, so my body's been feeling ridiculously tight. Even those tiny movements help a bit.

I stopped taking my prescription pain meds and my ankle's been throbbing a bit. Ibuprofen doesn't cut the pain completely, but as long as it's manageable, I'd rather skip anything stronger.

I finally settled on *Gilmore Girls* and sank back into the pillows, ready to get lost in Rory and Lorelai's world. I was about halfway through the first episode when Mom appeared at the edge of the couch.

"Shannon honey, do you need anything?"

I shook my head, forcing a small smile.

"No, I'm good, Mom. Thanks."

"Are the girls still planning on coming over tonight?"

"Yeah, they'll be here in a couple hours."

"Is it okay if your dad and I go out to dinner tonight?" she asked, her voice a little hesitant.

Honestly, I wasn't the only one struggling with all this downtime. My parents are always on the go—weekend projects, dinners with friends, volunteer stuff—but they've been home with me every day since the surgery. I know it's because they want to be here for me, but none of us are used to this much sitting still.

"Yeah, of course it's okay," I said.

"Joe and Mary are going to The Loading Dock for dinner, so as long as you won't be alone, we'll join them."

"Even if the girls weren't coming over, I'd be fine."

"I'm not comfortable leaving you by yourself yet," she said. "Once you can put weight on your ankle, I'll probably feel better about it."

"You're such a mom," I said with a sassy smirk.

"Guilty." She walked over and gave me a kiss on the forehead. "I still have some work to do so I'll be in my office. Text if you need anything."

She disappeared down the hallway as I turned my attention back to *Gilmore Girls*. Lorelai was mid-rant about wanting coffee, and I felt that in my soul. But I've been keeping my liquid intake to a minimum because every bathroom trip feels like planning a mission to Mars. I adjusted the pillows under my ankle, grabbed the remote, and let the familiar rhythm of Stars Hollow take over.

I must have fallen asleep because the next thing I knew, I was waking to voices in the foyer. My parents let my ladies in as they were leaving to meet their friends for dinner.

"Oh good, you're awake," Keera said, grinning as she stepped around the couch, arms loaded with takeout bags from Italo's. "We brought sustenance."

Anjannette was right behind her.

"And I've got everything we need for margaritas. No store-bought mix crap, either. Tonight we're making them from scratch," she said, then headed straight for the kitchen.

"We have chorizo, steak, and shrimp tacos." Keera set the bag on the coffee table and started unloading it. "There's also guac and chips," she said, plopping a container down. "Because obviously."

Sophie added a foil-covered tray to the growing spread on the coffee table, like she was completing some kind of sacred offering to the gods of comfort food.

"And I brought homemade Tandycakes," she said as she settled into the chair across from me, like it was no big deal, even though bringing baked goods basically made her a hero.

"You guys are actual angels."

"We try," Keera said, as she piled a taco, a generous scoop of guac, and a handful of chips onto a plate. She handed it to me with a flourish along with a napkin, because she knows me.

Anjannette reappeared from the kitchen balancing a tray loaded with the blender jar and four glasses, each with a perfectly salted rim. "Margaritas are served," she declared, beaming like a proud bartender as she set the tray down and began pouring and handing out drinks.

"Don't forget about Eve," Sophie said as she accepted a glass.

Keera grabbed her laptop from her bag and cleared a space on the coffee table for it. A few taps later, the Zoom screen blinked to life.

Sophie and Anjannette adjusted the chairs to fit within the camera frame, while I scooted back and sat up straighter, trying to get comfortable enough to eat. Keera adjusted the tower of pillows under my ankle before settling in near my feet with her own taco-laden plate.

We had just finished getting settled when Eve's smiling face popped onto the screen.

"Sorry, I was having issues logging on," she said, then her eyes widened as she took us in, or more specifically, the food in front of us. "Oh my God, I can practically *smell* that. I'm so jealous."

"That's what you get for moving across the country," Sophie said, lifting her margarita with a wink. "And even though I love Max and I'm thrilled you're happy, I'll never stop reminding you of how you abandoned us."

"I know, I know," Eve said. "I love both Max and Seaside, but the two drawbacks are you're all not here and I can't find a pole studio to compare to Peaches & Pole."

"Well of course not," Anjannette said with a smirk, dunking a chip into the guac. "My studio is the best."

"But I'm happy to say Max surprised me and installed a pole in the garage yesterday. I'm so excited I could cry. I can dance regularly again."

"That's amazing!" Sophie said.

While Keera and Anjannette chimed in, chatting about the possibility of Eve attending class virtually, I found myself drifting. I stared at my plate, the corner of a tortilla folded perfectly, and all I could think about was how long it would be before I could dance again. The ache in my ankle was nothing compared to that.

"What's wrong?" Keera asked.

I looked around and found all eyes on me.

"Sorry, I was thinking about how it's going to be a long time before I can get on the pole again," I said. "And I hate to think about how long it'll take me to get back to where I was skill-wise."

"Shannon, it won't take long," Keera said gently. "It's like riding a bike. Your body remembers."

"I hope so." I sighed. "I was finally making progress on my invert and pretty much nailed my jasmine to Superman."

"And you will again," Eve said firmly from the screen. "But how are you doing otherwise?"

I took a sip of my margarita, the salt stinging a little at the corner of my mouth as I considered the question.

"I'm bored to tears. I still have weeks left of not putting weight on my ankle, and I honestly don't know how I'll keep from going completely insane."

"We'll visit and keep you occupied," Keera said, then added with a mischievous smile, "As will other people."

All eyes shifted to look at me and the silence stretched long enough to be uncomfortable.

"What?" I asked, though I have a sinking feeling I know.

"You know what and *who* I'm talking about," Keera said with a grin.

My gaze slipped to the tiny echeveria perched on the edge of the coffee table, its pink ceramic pot dusted with specks of glitter that caught the light and sparkled softly. Andrew brought me the succulent two days ago, claiming my recovery space needed "something alive that won't judge you for lying around watching TV all day."

Of course, they noticed, and four sets of eyes followed mine almost instantly.

Anjannette touched the tip of one of the plump leaves. "What do we have here?"

"It's a plant," I said, trying to sound casual, but the blush creeping up my face completely ruined the effect.

"It's a gesture," Eve chimed in. "That's not just any succulent, it's an echeveria in a handmade pot. Someone went to a real plant shop, not the supermarket."

"How can you even tell what it is from Oregon?" I asked.

"Because I have eyes," she laughed.

"It's definitely a thing," Anjannette agreed, scooting closer with her drink.

"Andrew's been 'checking on Shannon' a lot," Keera said, actually using air quotes.

"Can we not analyze my visitors? I'm injured, people visit injured people. It's basic human decency."

"Basic human decency doesn't usually involve artisanal plant pots," Sophie pointed out. "That's thoughtful human decency. Maybe even romantic human decency."

"Okay, fine," I said, throwing my hands up in defeat. "Maybe there's...something. I don't know what it is, but things between us feel different than they used to."

"Different how?" Keera whispered, leaning in like we're sharing state secrets.

I looked at the echeveria again, remembering the way Andrew's fingers brushed mine when he handed it to me, the electricity that shot through me at the contact.

"Like there's something in the air between us. Like he's not only here to 'check on me.'"

If Keera can pull out the air quotes, so can I.

"And how do you feel about it?" Eve asked gently.

"Terrified," I admitted. "He's Simon's best friend. If this goes wrong, it could be...awkward."

"And if it goes right?" Anjannette asked with a knowing smile

"Then maybe breaking my ankle turned out to be the best thing ever."

"Now that's what I like to hear," Eve grinned from the screen. "Sometimes the universe has to force us to slow down so we can finally see what's right in front of us."

I looked around at these women and felt a flicker of something I hadn't felt in a long time...gratitude. Maybe being stuck in one place wasn't the worst thing. Maybe it was exactly where I needed to be to slow down, take a breath, and finally figure out what I really want.

ANDREW

I HADN'T PLANNED ON STOPPING BY SHANNON'S TONIGHT.

She'd texted earlier letting me know her friends were coming by for tacos and margaritas. It didn't read like an invite exactly, more like a gentle way of telling me not to show up and find myself the only guy in the middle of girls' night.

I'd texted back—

Enjoy!

—figuring that was it for the night.

Then came her reply.

Oh. Okay.

The three dots appeared and disappeared three times before she added,

I'll miss you.

Nothing dramatic. No pressure. Just honest. Somehow, it hit harder because of it.

Which is how I ended up heading to see her after leaving the hospital.

Yesterday's conversation was still sitting with me—how she opened up about everything in New York. The fact that she trusted me with what happened, meant more than I could say.

Yeah, something had shifted between us. No question.

I wasn't in my best form tonight. I'd gotten something unidentifiable on my shirt during rounds at the hospital, and when I checked the spare clothes in my gym bag, they were already in questionable condition. So I ended up driving across town in a clean pair of blue scrubs that made me look like I'd either come straight from surgery or was headed to a bachelorette party as someone's fantasy.

The porch lights were on, and through the front window I could see the soft flicker of the TV and several figures shifting around the living room.

I knocked once on the front door, then let myself in, like I've done since I was a kid.

The living room looked like what I imagined a cozy sleepover would, the kind of relaxed chaos that made the whole place feel warm and lived-in. Shannon was on the couch, her leg propped on a pillow, a soft blanket thrown across her lap. Keera sat near her feet, elbow on the armrest, laughing at something on the laptop. Anjannette and Sophie had pulled the chairs from across the room so they were right up against the ends of the couch. And a laptop sat in the middle of the coffee table among empty plates and glasses, with the smiling face of a woman I didn't know on the screen.

All eyes were on me as I walked toward them.

"Do doctors still made house calls," Keera said.

"I got something on my clothes and had to change," I said with a sheepish smile.

"Oh, we're not complaining," Anjannette said as she stood and gestured toward the chair she'd vacated. "Have a seat."

When I opened my mouth to decline her offer, she raised her brows and pointed at the chair. I wasn't going to argue.

I sat and Shannon looked at me with a smile.

"I didn't think you were coming over tonight."

"I wasn't, but then decided I didn't want to ruin my streak."

"So, he's cute and funny," the woman on the laptop said.

"Andrew, this is Eve." Keera said, nodding toward the laptop. "She used to be part of our taco crew but moved to Oregon."

"Hi Eve."

"It's very nice to meet you, Andrew."

Anjannette sat on the floor with her legs tucked under her. She peeked into the paper bag on the coffee table.

"There's a couple tacos left," she said. "I'm not sure what kind they are though."

"Sold." I reached out as she handed me the bag. "Thank you."

"Do you want me to pop them in the microwave?" Keera asked.

"No, this is good."

"Well, I'm going to grab water for everyone. After the salty chips and margaritas, we could probably use it."

I glanced at the empty glasses littering the table then at Shannon.

"Did you have a margarita?"

She nodded.

"I had one."

"When's the last time you took your pain meds?"

"Yesterday afternoon," she said. "They make me feel weird so I'm trying to manage the pain with ibuprofen and it's going well for the most part."

"For the most part?"

"It's throbbing a little, but nothing I can't handle."

Keera returned holding five bottles of water and she passed them out before sitting on the end of the couch again. Shannon opened her bottle and took a long drink. I decided to let the pain meds thing go. I'm sure she'll switch back to her prescription if her ankle hurts too much.

I bit into a shrimp taco. It's cold, but had a little kick of heat and a bright, citrusy pop that made my mouth water. The tortilla was soft and the slaw gave it the perfect crunch. I chewed slowly, taking it all in as the conversation flowed around me—laughs, inside jokes, updates about friends I didn't know. Every so often, one of them tossed a question my way like how late I usually worked, how many hours of sleep I get, whether I'd ever fainted during surgery, and if I'd ever been hit on by a patient. I answered between bites, one eyebrow raised at some of the questions, but more relaxed than I'd expected to be. Their curiosity seemed light and easy rather than intrusive.

I polished off the last of the tacos, then grabbed a Tandy-cake and sat back in the chair to enjoy it. The conversation carried on—stories, teasing, bits of gossip that mostly flew over my head—but no one seemed to mind if I stayed quiet. Then Eve turned and glanced over her shoulder with a smile before looking at us again.

"Max just got home," she said, and a moment later, a guy with dark hair and a friendly face appeared next to her on the screen.

"Hey, ladies," he said with a quick wave. "And gentleman."

"Max, this is Andrew." Eve leaned into him, grinning. "I'll explain about him later."

"Nice to meet you, man," Max said.

"You too," I replied, nodding, kind of curious about what Eve was going to tell him.

"I'm gonna sign off," Eve said. "I love you guys."

A chorus of I love yous and goodbyes followed, then the screen went dark.

After Eve signed off, the energy in the room started to settle. It was still cozy, but softer now, like everyone was easing into the end of the night. Keera, Anjannette, and Sophie started gathering empty glasses, plates, and crumpled napkins from the coffee table, stacking them with practiced ease. I moved to stand, figuring I'd help, but Keera waved me off.

"Sit. You're on Shannon duty," she said with a smirk.

Anjannette nodded as she grabbed the blender jar.

"Yeah, you're doing your part by being here."

I eased back into the seat, glancing over at Shannon. She was tucked under a blanket, looking more relaxed than I'd seen her look in days. I'm not sure if it was the change of scenery, the margaritas, or being surrounded by her people, but she looked content.

"You look nice in your scrubs," Shannon said. "Like a real doctor."

"It's good to know that after all those years of schooling, my clothes make me look the part."

Before she could respond, the ladies returned from the kitchen and started gathering their things.

"I'll talk to you tomorrow," Keera said as she leaned down to give Shannon a hug.

Anjannette kissed her on the cheek and whispered something that made her laugh.

Sophie wrapped her in a hug, giving her a gentle squeeze before pulling back with a smile.

"You staying?" Keera asked, casual but not.

"Yeah. For a bit."

"Good," Anjannette said.

They filed out the door, leaving Shannon and me alone.

She shifted toward me and pulled the blanket tighter around her waist. Her face looked softer in the quiet, tired in a way she hadn't let show earlier.

"I'm glad you decided to come," she said.

"Me too."

She looked at me for a long moment, like she was trying to figure out what to say next.

"I was kind of hoping you would."

"That's the feeling I got from your last text."

"I didn't mean to guilt you."

"You didn't." I shook my head. "I wanted to. And honestly I'm glad I did. I had a good time. You've got good people."

She nodded, her expression soft.

"I didn't always, even though I thought I did. It's different now. I'm so fortunate to have them in my life."

"For what it's worth," I said, "they're lucky to have you too."

Her eyes met mine, surprised, maybe even a little unsure.

"You think?"

"I know."

She glanced at me, and for a second, she looked nervous. Like she wanted to say something but wasn't sure she should.

"You're one of the good ones," she said finally.

My chest tightened. I didn't know what to do with something that meant so much without dropping it.

"Thank you."

She reached for my hand and gave it a gentle squeeze.

"You're welcome," she said, her voice barely above a whisper.

I turned my hand in hers, letting our fingers slide together and lock in place. Hers were warm and fit perfectly against mine, like they'd been there before and found their way back.

As I leaned in toward Shannon, the space between us narrowed with every heartbeat—right up until the front door swung open. I pulled back just as John and Lily stepped inside, their voices spilling into the room.

"Hey, Andrew!" John called out, grinning then turned his attention to Shannon. "How was taco night?"

"It was great," she said. "The tacos and margaritas are all gone, but Sophie made Tandycakes and the leftovers are in the kitchen."

"I'm stuffed," Lily said, then gave John a warning glare. "I'll have one tomorrow so don't eat them all."

"I'd never do that," he said, feigning offense.

"You would and you have," his wife reminded him.

They exchanged a few more words, light and easy, and when there was a break in the conversation, I stood.

"I'm going to head out," I said. "Thanks for the tacos."

"You're welcome," Shannon said. "And thanks for coming."

"Anytime." I gave her a small smile, the kind that said there was more between us than just thanks. "Good night."

Her eyes caught mine, warm and a little hesitant.

"Good night, Andrew."

I said goodbye to John and Lily then stepped out into the cool night air, the door clicking softly behind me. Once in my car, I let the quiet settle around me, replaying the evening—the laughter, the gentle touches, the almost-kiss that hung in the space between us.

What I'm feeling isn't a simple crush anymore. I'm really falling for Shannon.

Not the idea of her, not some memory from high school. Her.

And by some miracle, it seems like she might be falling for me too.

CHAPTER 8

Shannon

THE REHAB CLINIC SMELLED LIKE DISINFECTANT, SWEAT, AND something vaguely minty. Not quite hospital-sterile, but definitely not cozy either. Somewhere between "We're here to help" and "Welcome to the pain cave." But honestly, after being stuck at home for weeks, I was happy to be anywhere but my parents' house, even if it meant trading my familiar walls for a room full of rubber bands and weird exercise balls.

I settled into the chair next to Janet, my physical therapist, who was reviewing my chart.

"Okay, Shannon, you're three weeks post-surgery now." she said, looking up with a reassuring smile. "How's the pain been?"

"Better than the first week, but it still throbs if I'm not careful with elevation."

"Have you been using any meds to manage it?"

"Ibuprofen. I stopped taking my prescription meds a couple weeks ago."

She looked up and nodded.

"Ibuprofen can help with both pain and inflammation, especially this early on. Just make sure you're not overdoing it and stick to the recommended dose. If it stops helping, let your doctor know."

"Okay."

"Have you had any issues with the boot feeling too tight?"

"No, it's fine."

The CAM boot felt bulky and weirdly comforting at the same time—solid, protective, but also a little suffocating. At my post-op appointment last week, they'd finally unwrapped the thick gauze and removed the splint, snipped out the staples lining my incision like tiny silver zip ties, and strapped me into this boot. It was progress, I reminded myself, even if I still wasn't allowed to walk on it.

"The swelling is still your biggest enemy right now." She gestured toward my ankle. "Since you're still non-weight bearing and will be for a few more weeks, we're going to focus on what we can do to keep the rest of your body strong."

I bit back a sigh. I'd been secretly hoping we could finally start doing something with the ankle itself so it could heal faster. But I also knew what the doctor had told me—no weight, no strain, no messing around. The boot could come off for showers and sleeping, and sometimes to flex my toes, but that was it.

"Can I do anything for my ankle?" I asked anyway, because hope dies hard.

"Not yet. Your ankle still needs to stay immobilized while the bones continue to heal. But we can start ankle pumps—flexing and pointing your toes inside the boot to keep your circulation going." She demonstrated the motion with her own foot. "Try that for me."

I followed along, moving my toes and foot enough to feel the stretch in my calf. It was more intense than the toe curls I'd been doing, so it felt like progress.

"Good. Ten reps, a few times a day. It helps prevent blood clots and keeps your muscles awake."

Then she had me lie back on the treatment table and began working on my hip and knee on the affected side.

"We need to keep these joints mobile and your muscles strong. You'll be using crutches for quite a while, so your arms, core, and good leg need to be in the best shape possible," Janet said as I lifted my leg an inch off the table. "The frustrating part is that most of your real recovery happens later. Right now, our goal is to keep the rest of you from falling apart while your ankle does its thing."

I let out a breath.

"You're sure there's no way to speed up recovery?"

Janet chuckled as she shook her head.

"I wish, but nope. It'll be another three to five weeks before your surgeon clears you for weight-bearing. Once that happens, our real work begins—range of motion exercises, strength training, balance work. But for now, patience is your best friend."

I finished the last of my hip exercises and Janet helped me sit up.

"I know it's frustrating, but think of this phase as laying the groundwork. The stronger we keep everything else, the easier your actual ankle rehab will be when the time comes."

She handed me a sheet of exercises to do at home...more

hip and knee work, core strengthening, and those ankle pumps.

"Keep doing these daily, and I'll see you next week. We'll gradually add more as you get stronger."

"I will."

She grabbed my crutches from where they leaned against the wall and handed them to me. After three weeks, I was getting better at maneuvering with them, but it still felt awkward and exhausting. Every trip to the bathroom felt like a major expedition. I thought I was in good shape, but my arms and shoulders begged to differ.

I made my way slowly to the waiting room, the rubber tips of my crutches squeaking against the laminate flooring. Mom looked up from her phone as I approached and immediately stood to gather her purse.

"All done?" she asked, her voice carrying the careful cheerfulness she'd been using since the accident.

"Yep. Ready to go home."

She walked beside me as I made my way to the exit, close enough to help if I needed it but not hovering. Since my surgery, we'd found a balance between her protective instincts and my need to do things myself.

"How was it today?" she asked as we settled into the car.

"Okay." I shrugged. "Frustrating. I know the doctor said I wouldn't be able to put weight on my ankle for at least six weeks, but I was kind of hoping I'd be his first medical miracle."

"Sweetheart, you've always been exceptional, but even you can't out-stubborn your ankle bones."

I smirked.

"You say that like it's a challenge."

She glanced over, raising an eyebrow.

"It's not." We pulled out of the parking lot. "Rushing

things would just set you back and your recovery will take longer."

"That's what Andrew said."

Mom glanced over at me with a small smile.

"He's always been very smart."

Mom hadn't said a word about Andrew hanging around so much, but I have no doubt she knows something has shifted between us. It's probably written all over my face. Besides, she's got a sixth sense when it comes to me and Simon, so there's no way she hasn't picked up on this thing going on between Andrew and me.

We pulled into the driveway, and as I opened my door and waited for Mom to hand me my crutches from the back seat, I noticed Andrew pulling in behind us.

"Andrew definitely has impeccable timing," Mom said with a grin.

Andrew stepped out of his car, his eyes immediately finding me. After greeting him, Mom headed inside leaving Andrew to match my glacial pace as I carefully navigated the uneven sidewalk on crutches.

He closed the door behind us as we stepped into the house, then took the crutches as I settled onto the couch.

"How did PT go?" he asked as he settled into the chair across from me.

"I wiggled my toes and did some leg lifts. Very exciting stuff," I said.

"Not bad for three weeks out."

"That's what everyone keeps telling me."

I heard Mom moving around in the kitchen, no doubt starting dinner.

"Everyone is right," he said. "Your ankle has a lot of healing to do. The bone has to knit back together around those plates and screws."

"I know it in my head, but I feel so useless." I motioned toward my boot. "I can't work, can't drive, and even showering feels like a whole production."

"Shannon, three weeks ago, your ankle was in pieces. Now it's held together with hardware while your body rebuilds the bone. It's not nothing, it's incredible."

I looked at him, struck again by how naturally he'd taken on this caretaker role.

"How do you always know exactly what to say?"

"Medical school and a lot of practice talking patients through recovery." He smiled. "Plus, I care about you. A lot."

The energy between us warmed, like it had been doing more and more lately when we got too close. There was something different in the way he looked at me now and it made my heart race despite the frustration with my situation.

"Andrew," I started, but didn't know how to finish.

"Yeah?" he said.

Before I could respond, Mom appeared from the kitchen.

"Andrew, would you like to stay for dinner?" Mom asked.

He met my gaze, raised an eyebrow, and when I nodded, he looked back at her.

"I'd love to. Thank you."

As Mom headed back to the kitchen, Andrew leaned forward, resting his elbows on his knees.

"I know this is hard," he said quietly. "But you're not useless. You're healing. And I'm going to be right here while you do it."

"Promise?" I asked, the word coming out smaller than I intended.

"Promise."

He reached over and took my hand, and for the first time all day, the frustration with my slow progress faded into the background. Maybe being stuck in one place wasn't the worst thing, especially if it meant figuring out whatever this was between us.

"So," I said, squeezing his hand. "Tell me about your day. And please let it involve something more exciting than toe wiggling."

He laughed, and the sound filled something in my chest I hadn't realized was empty.

"Well, I did replace Mrs. Henderson's knee this morning. Does that count?"

"It does, and it's much better than toe wiggling," I said, settling back against the pillows.

For the first time since leaving physical therapy, I felt content to be exactly where I was.

ANDREW

THE SCOOTER RATTLED IN ITS BOX IN THE BACK OF MY Outback every time I hit a bump. The noise alone made me second-guess the whole idea.

She might think it's dumb. She might love it. Honestly, I had no idea. I knew she'd been going crazy being cooped up and frustrated using crutches, and this seemed like it could help. Still, I couldn't shake the feeling I was crossing some invisible line.

So here I was, pulling into the driveway just after seven, my nerves kicking up like I was showing up with flowers and asking her to prom.

I parked, popped the hatch, and hopped out. The box

wasn't all that heavy—maybe twenty-five or thirty pounds—but it was awkward as hell to carry. Handles would've been nice. I shifted my grip, got it balanced against my chest, and hauled it up the front steps like I was delivering something fragile and hoping not to drop it.

At the door, I leaned the box against the jamb, knocked twice like I always did, and let myself in. I wrapped my arms around the box again as I stepped inside, careful not to clip the doorframe.

"Hey," she said, from the living room. "What's that?"

I lifted it slightly as I walked toward her.

"Hopefully your new favorite thing."

She raised an eyebrow.

"Is that a scooter?"

"Sure is," I said as I set the box on the floor. "A knee scooter to be precise."

Her eyes widened.

"You got me a scooter?"

"I thought maybe it'd make things easier. Especially if you want to go somewhere not crutch-friendly. Like Phoebe's studio."

She looked at me, brows knit together.

"Phoebe's studio?"

"Last week you mentioned she needed a makeup artist, but there was no way you could do it on crutches. I figured with the scooter, maybe you could."

Her expression softened, but she didn't say anything right away. I wasn't sure if that was a good sign or if I'd completely overstepped.

She leaned on one crutch and stared at it like I'd handed her a spaceship.

"Andrew..."

"You don't have to use it," I added quickly. "I figured it might help. If it doesn't, I can return it."

She smiled, slow and soft, like I'd surprised her in a good way.

"You're kind of unbelievable."

"Not the first time I've heard that."

She sat on the couch.

"I want to try it."

"Then let's get it put together."

I knelt beside the box and pulled my keys from my pocket. Using the edge of one, I carefully sliced through the tape and peeled back the flaps. After unpacking all the pieces, I pulled out the instruction sheet. It promised the scooter could be put together with the enclosed Allen wrench, like the man who sold it to me had said.

"Where did you get this?" she asked.

I slid the steering column into the front frame of the base until it clicked. The clamp screwed in easily, and I gave it a little shake to make sure it was locked tight.

"Andrew Brown's," I said as I fed the handlebars into the column, then aligned them to what seemed to be a good height for Shannon and twisted the adjustment knob snug.

"And you just stopped in there to buy this for me."

"Pretty much."

The knee platform slid onto the rear bar easily, and I adjusted the height so her injured leg would rest on it at a ninety degree angle. I tightened the bolts by hand first, then with the Allen wrench for good measure. I gave it a firm shake to be sure it was steady.

"Do you want the basket attached?" I asked, holding up the item in question.

"Obviously," she said. "Where else am I going to put my snacks?"

I clipped it onto the front of the handlebars and gave the whole thing a once-over. Everything looked straight and solid. I squeezed the brake levers and both responded.

"Mission accomplished. Your new ride awaits."

She leaned forward, eyes bright.

"Can I try it?"

"Yeah." I offered her a hand. "Let's get you on it."

She hesitated.

"What if I wipe out in front of you and never live it down?"

"Then I catch you, and you get bonus points for dramatic flair."

She shook her head, laughing.

"Okay. Here goes."

She gripped the handlebars, rested her left leg on the platform, and gave a gentle push. And she was off and rolling.

"This is *amazing*, she said as she headed toward the kitchen. "It's *so* much easier than crutches."

"I'm glad you like it."

She rolled back to me, rested her arms lightly on the handlebars.

"I really might be able to help Phoebe with this."

Before I could say anything else, she wrapped her arms around my neck and pulled me in for a hug. I caught her, automatically sliding my hands to her waist to steady her. The scooter shifted slightly beneath her, but I held firm. Her body fit against mine like she belonged there, warm and close, her cheek brushing mine as she leaned in.

"Thank you," she said against my chest.

When she pulled back, we were still close, her arms around my shoulders, my hands on her waist. She looked up at me, eyes searching mine, lips slightly parted like maybe she was about to say something. But she didn't speak, and she didn't move away.

I leaned in, just enough to give her a second to pull away if she wanted to. Thankfully she he didn't, so I closed the distance and kissed her. Slow at first, careful, because I didn't want to rush it. But once I felt her melt against me, I kissed her like I meant it, like I'd been holding back for way too long, and now that I'd started, I wasn't about to stop.

The scooter shifted beneath her again, and she gave a breathless laugh against my mouth.

"Okay, we need an emergency brake on this thing."

I chuckled and wrapped my arms around her waist, holding her tight against me. I dipped my head and kissed her again, soft and slow, as I tuned into the way she breathed and responded. But I couldn't hold back for long. I nibbled gently on her bottom lip, and when she parted, I slid my tongue inside, deepening the kiss.

Her arms wrapped around my neck, and she melted into me. She matched my tongue, stroke for stroke, and everything else faded as the taste, smell, and feel of her consumed my senses.

But eventually, we had to pull back, both of us gasping for air, hearts racing.

"Damn," she whispered, her voice shaky like she wasn't quite sure what to say.

I pulled back to look her in the eyes, my own breath catching.

"Yeah, that was..."

Before I could find a word to describe my thoughts and feelings, the front door opened. We froze like kids caught making out behind the bleachers. As I heard the door close, I shifted her back onto the scooter.

"Shan?" Lily's voice rang out. "We're home!"

Shannon spun her scooter in their direction as John and Lily walked into the living room.

"Look what Andrew brought me." Shannon gestured to the scooter like it was a show prize. "Isn't it great?"

"Looks like you could do laps in that thing," John said.

"I was zooming around between the foyer and kitchen before you came home."

Lily's eyes flicked between Shannon and me before she glanced down at the scooter and gave a small, approving nod.

"I bet it's a lot easier than crutches."

"It's so much easier."

Lily gave me a warm smile.

"That was really thoughtful of you."

I nodded, trying not to fidget under her gaze.

"I'm glad it helps."

"You staying for dinner?" John asked.

"Thank you, but no," I said. "I just wanted to drop this off."

We chatted for a few more minutes before I headed toward the front door with Shannon rolling beside me. She glanced back toward the living room, then leaned in close.

"The kiss?" she whispered. "We're definitely not done with that."

I smiled.

"Didn't think we were."

"I'm serious. You can't kiss me like that and leave."

I ran a hand through my hair.

"I wish I could stay, but I promised my mom I'd stop by on the way home."

Her eyes widened a little.

"Wait—is everything okay?"

"Yeah, she's good," I said quickly. "I'm just checking in."

Shannon's shoulders relaxed.

"Okay. That's really good to hear."

"I'll see you tomorrow," I said, raising my voice on the last word, turning the sentence into a question.

"You better," she said, smiling. "I've got a list of scooter tricks I want to try."

I laughed as I pulled the door open.

"Promise you won't break anything before I get back."

I made my way to the car, smiling like an idiot and already thinking about tomorrow.

CHAPTER 9

Shannon

DAD PULLED UP IN FRONT OF THE OLD BRICK BUILDING THAT housed Phoebe's studio. It used to be some kind of warehouse, and with its huge arched windows and vintage vibe, it's the perfect place for something artsy and magical, like Phoebe Lee Boudoir.

I remembered this place from when I was a kid, back when the windows were boarded up and the bricks looked like they might give up and crumble to the ground. Now the windows sparkle, the brick has been cleaned and patched, and there are cute little boxwood shrubs in tall planters flanking the door like they're standing guard. The sign over the door has a soft, swoopy script that makes it look like it should be hanging outside a storybook cottage instead of on a building in downtown Scranton.

"Here we are," Dad said, shifting into park. "You ready for this?"

"The test run with Keera went great," I said, unbuckling my seatbelt. "So I'm feeling pretty optimistic."

"Hang tight," he said, already halfway out of the Range Rover before I could respond.

Dad popped the rear door open and easily pulled out the knee scooter as I grabbed my crutches from the back seat. I opened the passenger door as he wheeled the scooter over, handlebars pointed right at me like an open invitation.

"Your chariot awaits," he said with a grin.

I pushed the door open wider and, bracing myself on the crutches, carefully eased out of the seat. Dad steadied the scooter as I carefully rested my knee on the padded platform.

"This thing is a game changer. I don't know how I survived without it the past few weeks."

"Andrew's a good guy for thinking of it."

"Yeah, he is."

The warmth that spreads through my chest at the mention of Andrew's name is becoming familiar, though I try not to let it show on my face. But in case it did, I turned and reached into the SUV to grab my makeup bag and purse.

"He's been hanging out at the house a lot lately," he continued. "I haven't seen him this much since before Simon moved out."

I didn't comment, just shifted the strap of my bag higher on my shoulder and adjusted my grip on the handlebars. Then I started rolling toward the door, pretending to focus on steering instead of the heat creeping up my neck. Dad kept pace, acting like his little comment hadn't been completely intentional.

"Do all his patients get this much follow-up attention?"

I tossed him a half-warning, half-exasperated side-eye.

"Dad."

He chuckled, completely unfazed by my tone.

"Just making conversation."

"Uh-huh."

Leaning in, he kissed the top of my head.

"Text me when you're done."

"Will do." I pushed off, gliding toward the studio entrance. "Thanks for the ride."

With a wave, he walked back to the SUV, and I watched him get behind the wheel and drive away.

I'm pretty sure my parents have caught on to the shift between Andrew and me. Mom's been dropping little comments here and there, and now Dad's chiming in? I can only imagine what they'd say if they knew we kissed two days ago.

The imprint of Andrew's kiss lingered, like it had settled into my skin and decided to stay awhile. And the way he looked at me afterward with a mix of surprise and certainty has been playing on a loop in my head. We haven't seen each other since because his work schedule has been nuts, but the tone of our texts has definitely changed. They feel more personal now...or something.

I opened the door to the studio and rolled inside.

"Shannon!" Phoebe's voice pulled me from my thoughts. "Thank you so much for filling in again, especially with your ankle."

"I'm happy to be here," I said. "It might take me a little longer to get around with this thing, but I practiced on Keera yesterday and got the job done. I'm just a little slower than usual."

"Take all the time you need. Jen's my only client today." Phoebe glanced at her watch. "She should be here in about ten minutes. She's getting the full bridal package and wants photos with both a natural look and something more dramatic."

"Sounds good."

Jen arrived right on schedule. She's a petite brunette with kind eyes and the frazzled energy of someone deep in wedding planning mode. After introductions and a brief consultation, we got started with the natural look first.

I positioned myself at the makeup station, grateful the scooter put me at the right height to work comfortably. As I applied primer then foundation, I found myself settling into the familiar rhythm of the work. This is something I could do, something I'm good at, regardless of whether I'm standing on one foot or two.

"So how long have you been doing makeup?" Jen asked.

"Professionally? About ten years. But I've been playing with it since I was a kid." I blended concealer under her eyes with practiced strokes.

"I'm terrible at makeup. I've watched so many tutorials, but anytime I try something new, it ends up a total disaster. So I stick to the basics and hope for the best."

"There's nothing wrong with the basics," I said. "You've got great features, so it's really about playing them up a little."

Once I finished her makeup, I grabbed the curling iron and moved on to her shoulder-length hair, wrapping each section into soft, loose curls that framed her face perfectly. A quick mist of hairspray locked everything in place, and she was ready to go.

I turned the chair so Jen faced the mirror and moved back to let her look.

She glanced at herself in the mirror, a surprised smile tugging at her lips.

"This looks amazing."

"*You* look amazing," I said, then shrugged and added, "And I simply highlighted what's already there."

"You're too kind."

"I speak the truth."

I held up my right hand as if taking a vow.

Jen gave her reflection one last smile before Phoebe stepped in and walked her to the dressing room to change for her boudoir session. I headed back to Phoebe's office, giving them some privacy until it was time for the bold look.

I settled onto the couch and stretched my leg out, resting it on the cushions. Three weeks ago, I never would have imagined I'd be here, preparing to do someone's makeup while balancing on a knee scooter.

When Dr. Chen said I couldn't put any weight on my ankle for at least six weeks, I figured I'd be stuck at home, chained to my crutches. Using those things for more than five minutes is a total pain in the ass, so I'd pictured a lot of slow, frustrating days. But thanks to Andrew, I'm here now, doing my thing like it's no big deal.

Without overthinking it, I pulled out my phone, brought up his name, and started typing.

> Working at Phoebe's today. This scooter is a total game changer. Thanks again 🤍

> Glad it's helping.

> Yeah, it's making a huge difference. It's so much easier than the crutches.

> Good. I hated seeing you struggle.

Okay, now my heart's doing that stupid little flip again. He really does say the sweetest things.

> Will you be home later?

I will.

> Want some company?

Depends…are you bringing food or just your charming personality?

> Definitely bringing the personality. 😊 Plus maybe some Vince the Pizza Prince. How's that sound?

Delicious.

> Great. I'll text when I'm on the way.

Sounds good.

Glancing down at my phone, I scrolled back through our texts, a small smile tugging at my lips. But before I could bask in it too much, Phoebe popped her head in.

"Jen's ready for her bold look."

I tucked my phone away and scooted back out to the makeup station. The natural look had been pretty, but now it was time for some drama. I started with her eyes, creating a smokey effect with deep browns and blacks, blending until the colors seamlessly transitioned from light to dark. I added more mascara to complement the intensity of the eyes, swiped a deeper blush on her cheeks, and finished with a bold red lip that made Jen's whole face come alive.

Then I moved onto her hair. I spritzed all over with texturizing spray, then teased it at the roots and scrunched the rest to break up the curls enough to make them a little messy in a just-fucked kind of way.

I gave her a quick once-over, making sure every curl and swipe of makeup was exactly where it should be, then turned the chair so Jen could take a look.

"Oh my God," she breathed, staring at herself in the mirror. "I look like...like someone else, but still me. That doesn't even make sense."

"It makes perfect sense," I said.

Jen continued staring at her reflection, turning her head this way and that. Then her expression shifted, becoming almost shy.

"Can I ask you something?"

"Sure."

"The makeup artist I hired for my wedding cancelled on me. Six weeks before the wedding." She let out a breathy, almost-laugh—more stress than amusement. "I've got six bridesmaids and myself to get ready. Would you even consider it? I know it's short notice, and I have no clue what you charge, but..."

"I—" I paused, realizing I was about to say no when part of me wanted to consider it. "I've never done wedding makeup before."

Jen gestured to her face, brows raised.

"Okay, but is it any different from what you just did? Because this looks amazing."

I never really considered doing bridal makeup before, but the idea has its appeal. Plus, Jen's really sweet, and it would feel good to help her out of a bind.

"I'll do it," I said.

"You're a lifesaver!" She grabbed my hand, squeezing it like we'd sealed a secret pact. "Thank you so much. Let me know what your fee is when you have time to figure it out." Her eyes rounded. "Do you want a deposit?"

"No deposit," I said. "And you can pay me whatever the other person was charging."

Probably not the smartest way to conduct business, but these are special circumstances.

We exchanged contact information, and she promised to text me the location details after her session.

Phoebe came over as we were finishing up.

"Need a hand?"

"No thanks, I've got it."

I slipped the last of my supplies into my tote.

"You were amazing today." She gave me a quick hug. "Thank you so much."

"You're welcome." I shifted my bag over my shoulder. "Text me the other dates you need me. I had an easier time than I thought I would, so consider me available."

"Will do. Thanks again, Shannon."

They walked toward the photo area, chatting quietly as Jen got ready for the second half of her shoot. I scooted out the door into the fresh air, pulled out my phone, and texted Dad to come pick me up, feeling like a fifteen-year-old.

Standing there waiting, an unexpected buzz of excitement crept in. I'd spent so much time focused on what I'd lost this past year, I almost forgot how exciting it can be to think about what's next. Wedding makeup isn't something I've ever really considered before, but now? Yeah, I could see it.

Dad pulled up a few minutes later and helped me into the passenger seat then loaded the scooter into the back.

"You look happy," he said as he settled behind the wheel.

"I am, actually. Not only did my makeup-on-a-scooter session go well, I was offered another job."

"That's awesome." He fired up the engine, shooting me a curious look. "What kind of job are we talking about?"

"Wedding makeup."

"Well, look at you."

"Yeah." I grinned. "Look at me."

We eased away from the curb and I leaned my head against the seat watching the world pass by outside the window. I've been home for a little over a month now, still healing emotionally— and now physically too— and unsure how long I'll be here. But with each passing day, the more it feels like maybe I'm exactly where I'm supposed to be.

ANDREW

AS I STEPPED ONTO THE PORCH, I SHIFTED THE STACK OF PIZZA in my arms, nudging the top box into place with my chin. Maybe four trays was overkill, but I've been craving Vince the Pizza Prince for a solid week. Honestly, I'll probably take down a whole tray myself, no problem.

I bumped the side of the house with my elbow, aiming for my usual knock-and-enter routine, except before my knuckles touched the door, it swung open.

"It's about time," Simon said, stepping back with a grin. "I was starting to think you got lost."

I followed him inside and we headed straight for the kitchen.

"Vince's was packed so I had to wait," I said as I set the pizza on the counter.

Keera came in from the hallway as I turned around.

"He's been pacing like a dad in a maternity ward waiting for delivery."

"I just know what matters in life," Simon said, already lifting the lid on the box like it was a national treasure. "And this is sacred."

Shannon rolled in right behind Keera, smooth and steady on her scooter.

"You're looking good on that thing."

She gave a little spin as she parked beside the table.

"Thanks. I've officially graduated from bumping into walls to graceful scooter choreography."

Simon grabbed paper plates and napkins while Keera pulled four bottles of beer from the fridge. They set everything down in the middle of the table and took their seats. I held the scooter steady as Shannon maneuvered into a chair, careful with her leg. Once she was settled, I sat beside her, the smell of pizza making my stomach growl.

"We have three red and one white, because someone's bougie," I said, shooting Shannon a look.

"Excuse you," she said, grabbing a slice of white. "White pizza is elite."

"White pizza is nothing more than a glorified grilled cheese," Simon muttered as he loaded two slices of red onto his plate.

Shannon wrinkled her nose and narrowed her eyes at Simon, then pointed to the tray he'd just pulled from.

"Dibs on the one with the bubble and the burnt cheese."

Simon rolled his eyes.

"Big surprise. You're eating your pizza *and* stealing ours. Classic Shannon."

I swallowed the last bite of my first slice and cleared my throat.

"Children, behave. There's enough pizza here for everyone. Let's keep it civil or I'll have to go get your parents."

"They're not home," Shannon said, then stuck her tongue out at me.

I chuckled then grabbed another slice.

We fell into a familiar rhythm—eating, trading jokes, and talking over each other like we always do. I couldn't count how many times I've sat at this table eating Vince's pizza with Simon, Shannon, and Archer.

Even when we got older and Shannon had plans with her friends, she'd still eat a slice or two with us before heading out, like it was a non-negotiable tradition. And now Keera's here, fitting in like she's always been part of it. Someone tossed a napkin across the table, Simon cracked a joke with his mouth full, and for a second, it felt like nothing had changed. Except something has drastically changed between Shannon and me.

Sitting across from Simon, it hit me that I haven't really let myself think about what he might say if this thing between Shannon and me turns into something more. Will it mess with our friendship? Make things weird?

And her parents—how will they feel about it? About me dating their daughter?

I don't have those answers yet, but sooner or later, I'll have to find out.

"So tell me more about today," Keera said to Shannon, pulling me out of the what-if reel playing on a loop in my head.

"It went really well. I couldn't move around as fast as usual, but once I got the scooter into the right spot, I was able to work without any issues."

"Awesome," Keera said. "Does she have more dates for you?"

"Yeah, she sent me what she has on the calendar. I'll have to make sure someone is around to drive me."

"I'm sure that between all of us you'll be able to get there," Simon said.

"Oh, and her client Jen asked if I'd do her wedding makeup next month. So, I guess I'm accidentally booking gigs now."

"You'd kill it doing weddings," Keera said. "You've got the skills and the calm energy brides need when they're freaking out. And you could totally expand into proms, homecoming, senior portraits. People would book you solid."

"It's something to think about," Shannon said, her tone thoughtful. "I'm not rushing into anything, but I'm open to possibilities."

Simon leaned back in his chair and crumpled his napkin into a loose ball.

"That's dangerously close to growth," he said.

Shannon shot him a look.

"Smartass."

I smirked and knocked back the rest of my beer in one long swallow before setting the bottle on the table. Shannon's pretending to play it cool, but I can see right through it. There's a spark in her eyes I haven't seen since she moved back, and damn if it didn't light something in me too.

"You've always been good at this," I said. "Doesn't matter if it's a *Vogue* cover or someone's wedding day. You make people feel like the best version of themselves. That's kind of a superpower."

Her eyes met mine, soft and unreadable, and for a second, she looked like she might say something. But instead, she just smiled.

Simon cleared his throat.

"Did you see Archer's text about Halo night next Saturday?"

"Yeah, I forgot to answer," I said, pulling out my phone to shoot off a quick reply.

> I'm interested. Will give a definite answer next week.

A second later, Simon's phone buzzed on the table. He chuckled as he picked it up.

"There we go." He sighed, a nostalgic grin tugging at his mouth. "Remember when Saturday nights automatically meant Xbox in the basement with ridiculous amounts of junk food?"

"Yeah, sometimes being a responsible grownup sucks."

"*Glory days, well they'll pass you by...*" Shannon sang.

"Now who's the smartass?" Simon shot back, then turned to me with a grin. "Speaking of glory days...want to relive our youth? The old Xbox 360 is still set up downstairs, along with the Halo 3 disc. Split-screen co-op. It'll be like old times."

I looked over at Shannon, a quiet check-in without saying a word. After all, technically I'm here to hang out with her.

She flashed a sassy smile and saluted me with her beer.

"Go kick his ass, Master Chief."

"I intend to," I said as I stood.

Simon snorted.

"Please. You're more like Sergeant Gets-Dropped-First."

Keera nearly spit out her beer laughing and Shannon shook her head, a big smile on her face.

I rolled my eyes and pushed back from the table.

"Keep talking. You're just fueling the beatdown."

He was already heading for the basement door, shooting me a smug grin over his shoulder. I followed, the familiar creak of the stairs under our feet bringing back so many memories. Some things, like trash talk, Halo, and pizza nights in this house still feel the same, and bring back a familiar sense of comfort

The basement hasn't changed since middle school. It has the same worn couch, old posters, and that familiar early-2000s vibe. Simon fired up the Xbox, and when the Halo 3 theme started playing, we stood there for a moment, caught in a weird mix of nostalgia and "what the hell, we're actually doing this?"

"Damn," I muttered. "This takes me back."

"To the days of dial-up internet and three straight weekends of no sunlight," Simon said, chuckling.

We loaded into campaign co-op, and suddenly, it was 2007 all over again. Plasma grenades, Warthog flips, trash talk, and shared triumphs. It's easy to forget about everything else—work, relationships, expectations—when we're deep in the Covenant fight.

And then, just as we cleared a level, Simon paused the game.

"You got something you want to tell me?" he asked, casually.

"About what?"

"Shannon."

I stayed focused on the screen for a second, before turning to face him.

"What about her?"

"You've been over almost every night since the surgery."

His raised brow asked the question he didn't say out loud.

"There's nothing going on," I said.

Simon waited and as the silence stretched on, I felt the need to fill it.

"Okay, technically nothing's happening, but that doesn't

mean I don't want it to," I said, then paused to choose my next words carefully. "And I think Shannon feels the same way."

"So...are you wondering if I'm cool with it?" he asked.

"Yeah. I guess so."

He set his controller down.

"Honestly, I'd be thrilled. Shannon deserves someone solid. And you're one of the best people I know."

A little of the tension eased from my chest.

"What about your parents?" I asked. "Think they'd be okay with it?"

Simon laughed.

"They'd probably throw a party. My mom already thinks you walk on water."

"I'm glad." I shrugged, half-smiling. "I mean, I'd probably go for it anyway, but..."

"It's nice not to worry about it," he finished for me.

Exactly.

We finished the game, and while I didn't exactly kick Simon's ass, I did come out on top.

After shutting off the Xbox, we dragged ourselves upstairs, still tossing jabs about who actually earned the crown. But as soon as we hit the top step, the laughter from the living room stopped so suddenly it didn't feel natural.

Shannon and Keera were definitely talking about one of us, and I'm betting it was me.

Keera stood, flashing a smile that was anything but subtle.

"We should probably get going," she said to Simon, glancing between Shannon and me like she was wrapping up an episode of a reality show.

"Thanks for dinner," he said, holding out his fist for a

bump. I didn't leave him hanging. Then we all said our goodbyes and they headed out.

Once the door closed behind Simon and Keera, the energy in the room changed to something quieter, but more electric. Shannon rolled across the room and parked her scooter. She eased herself onto the couch and instead of swinging her leg up on the cushions like she normally would, she rested it gently on the coffee table. I took the hint and sat next to her.

"How was the rest of your day?" I asked.

"It was good," she said, then added, "And tonight was a lot of fun."

"Yeah it was."

She glanced at the back of my forearm as I dragged my fingers through my hair.

"Did you always have that tattoo?"

I smirked.

"I mean, I wasn't born with it."

She rolled her eyes.

"You're hilarious."

"I got it about two years ago."

"Can I see?"

I lifted my arm and angled it toward her. She leaned in, studying the thin, dark script.

"What language is it?"

"Elvish," I said.

"Of course it is." She traced the ink with her fingertip, sending a ripple up my spine. "What does it say?"

"No apologies."

She looked up.

"Why that?"

I paused, weighing whether to say too much or just enough. Then I figured I might as well be straight with her.

"It's a reminder not to apologize for who I am or what I want."

"That's pretty deep."

I shifted sideways to face her better.

"One day I decided I'm not going to keep changing to fit someone else's mold. I'm me. Take it or leave it."

She locked eyes with me, her gaze steady and sure, like she wasn't just saying words but meaning every one.

"I'll take it," she said quietly, but there was no doubt in her voice.

I caught my breath for a second, as the weight of her words hit me.

"You sure?"

She nodded, then smirked.

"But this is kind of weird, right?"

"Yeah." I chuckled. "Maybe. But it also feels right."

"It does."

I leaned in, and she met me halfway without hesitation. Our lips brushed, soft and searching, more question than answer at first. Then she exhaled against my mouth, and I kissed her harder, sinking into it like I couldn't get close enough. Our mouths moved against each other in a slow, deliberate rhythm, full of heat and something that felt like a new beginning.

Everything else slipped away until there was only her, only this. Her fingers slid up the back of my neck, holding on like she didn't want this moment to end. I pulled her closer, and the tone of the kiss changed. Slow and searching gave way to something hotter and deeper.

Her fingers curled into my hair, tugging enough to send my pulse racing. My hand slid to the small of her back as I gently eased her down against the arm of the couch. We melted together, giving in to the heat that's been simmering for weeks.

By the time we finally came up for air, my heart was pounding, and I was dangerously close to bursting out of my jeans. I pressed my forehead against hers, trying to catch my breath and pull it together

We stayed still for a moment, lying there together. And in the calm, I settled into the quiet certainty I want something real with Shannon.

When we finally moved, I helped her sit then settled next to her. After a beat, I looked over at her.

"Would you want to go out on a real date?"

"I'd love to," she said, without hesitation. "But can we wait until I'm walking on two feet again? I don't want to scoot into a restaurant for our first date."

"Sure. I'll wait. As long as I can keep coming over." I grinned. "You know, for practice dates."

"It's a deal."

In a single moment, everything that had been unspoken between us was suddenly understood.

CHAPTER 10

Shannon

I stepped back from the mirror and smoothed my palms down the front of my charcoal-gray pants. The soft, buttery fabric draped like a sigh and wouldn't hold a single wrinkle, even after sitting. They cinched at the waist in a way that made my legs look longer than they really were, and the wide leg cut helped camouflage the bulky orthopedic boot strapped to my right foot. Because yeah, standing on two feet comes at a price.

It's been three days since I got the all-clear to put weight on my ankle again. It doesn't hurt, exactly, it's more awkward than anything. Like my body's not entirely sold on the idea yet.

The clunky boot weighed my left foot down like a cinder block. On the right, I'd managed to balance it out by wearing a low-heeled black ankle bootie featuring a sleek toe. It wasn't an exact match, but subtle enough so no one would immediately notice anything was off.

"Shannon?" My mom's voice came from the doorway, followed by a gentle knock. "Can I come in?"

"Sure."

"Oh honey, you look beautiful," she said as I turned to face her.

"Thanks."

"You should wear your hair like that more often."

I'd gone for loose, tousled waves, with a side part so it framed my face. It looked casual but polished, exactly the vibe I was going for.

"It takes me forever to curl, so I only do it like this for special occasions."

"Is this one?" At my raised brow she added, "A special occasion?"

"Well, it's the first date I've had in a long time, so I guess it's something, right?"

"And it's with Andrew. Pretty significant, right?"

She's not wrong. Andrew and I have been circling each other for weeks—sneaking kisses, finding reasons to touch, getting lost in conversations. It's pretty obvious what's going on.

But this is different. It's us officially acknowledging what everyone already knows. And I can't downplay the fact that this is different from any other date I've ever been on.

"Are you nervous?" she asked.

I shrugged and nodded at the same time, not sure how to explain the jumble of nerves and excitement twisting in my stomach.

"What if it's weird? Or what if this doesn't go well and things are awkward between us?"

She reached over and squeezed my hand.

"Trust me when I say nothing is going to feel weird

about tonight except maybe how natural it all feels," she said. "You two are good together."

Before I could respond, Dad's laugh mixing with Andrew's voice drifted up from downstairs.

Mom glanced at her watch.

"Right on time, as always," she said. "I'll let you finish getting ready."

She left my room, and I grabbed my cropped blazer and shrugged into it. I turned and checked my reflection one more time, smoothing the lapel and adjusting my necklace. My heart hammered against my ribs as I grabbed a small crossbody bag and headed downstairs.

I took the stairs one at a time, my hand gripping the railing while I led with my good foot and eased the boot down after it. Not exactly graceful. Each step was slow and deliberate, a quiet reminder I wasn't back to normal yet. Whatever *normal* even meant now.

Frustration buzzed low in my chest. I hated how careful I had to be. How much I had to think about something as simple as walking. But then when I was halfway down, Andrew looked up and the expression on his face chased every trace of annoyance right out of me. His eyes warmed, then widened a little, and the slow smile that spread across his face made me forget how clumsy I felt.

He looked good wearing navy dress pants and a matching sports coat over a crisp white shirt, no tie. It was classic Andrew—clean, put together, and just a little undone, like he'd tugged at his collar or run a hand through his hair on the drive over. The way the light caught in his messy waves made something flutter in my stomach.

"Hi," I said when I finally made it to the bottom, my voice quieter than I meant it to be.

"Hi yourself," he said, his voice low and a little rough.

His eyes swept over me again, and he let out a slow breath. "You look…" He trailed off, shaking his head with a helpless kind of smile. "Incredible."

Dad cleared his throat, and I realized he and Mom were watching our exchange with barely concealed amusement.

"You two have fun tonight," Dad said, but his tone was warm rather than teasing. "Drive safely."

"I always do," Andrew replied, but his eyes never left mine.

Twenty years ago, I would've rolled my eyes at those three words, but now, they sounded hot as hell.

We made our way to the front door, my parents following behind like proud chaperones. The whole situation felt very high school, except we're two adults who'd been circling each other for weeks.

Andrew held my elbow gently as we navigated the front steps, and I felt the warmth of his hand through my blazer. Once we were settled in his car, I let out a breath I didn't realize I'd been holding.

"That was strange," I said, buckling my seatbelt.

"You're telling me." Andrew chuckled as he started the engine. "As I was walking up to the front door, I actually reconsidered my usual knock-and-enter policy. But in the end, I figured after twenty-plus years, it would be weirder to ring the doorbell and wait on the porch like some stranger."

"If you rang the doorbell, my parents would've been so confused," I said, laughing. "Though I think they enjoyed the first-date vibes. Mom looked like she was trying not to take pictures."

"Your mom's been trying not to take pictures of us for weeks," Andrew pointed out, and I realized he was right.

Ever since we started being more demonstrative around

each other, she's been hovering with barely contained excitement.

The drive to Bar Pazzo was short but comfortable, filled with easy conversation about everything and nothing. Andrew parallel parked into a tight spot right out front, then he got out and came around to help me. I laughed as I climbed out, boot first.

"This thing makes everything feel so dramatic," I said, glancing down at it.

"You're pulling it off," he said. "Honestly, I forgot it was there for a second."

"Until I clomped out of the car."

He grinned and offered me his arm.

"Even your clomp is cute."

Inside, Bar Pazzo was warm and cozy. Brick walls, soft lighting, a peek into the open kitchen where flames licked the backs of pizzas. It was busy, but not loud. The kind of place where conversations felt private, like the table had its own little pocket of time.

The hostess led us to an intimate table in the back, away from the bustle of the front entrance. I was grateful for the privacy as Andrew helped me settle into my chair, his hand briefly touching my shoulder, sending warmth spreading through my chest.

"I love this place," I said, looking around at the exposed brick walls and industrial chic décor. "It's very NYC meets rustic Italy."

"I thought you'd like it," Andrew said, settling across from me. "Plus, I figured if we were doing this officially, we should go somewhere special."

The weight of his words settled between us as we opened our menus. I stared at him for a second, my heart doing a ridiculous flutter thing. He really is sweet. Not in some over-the-top, rom-com grand gesture kind of way, but in the way he pays attention. The way he remembers things I didn't even realize I said out loud. And the way he shows up—not only physically but fully—like he's all in, even when we're sitting across from each other with menus and big, unspoken feelings hanging in the air.

He didn't pick this place because it was trendy or impressive. He picked it because it meant something. Because he thought I'd feel comfortable here and he wanted this night to be more than just dinner.

I glanced down at the menu, barely seeing the words, then looked back up at him. He was reading like he hadn't knocked the wind out of me with a single sentence. As if he didn't know I was sitting here falling a little harder for him by the minute.

My foot—well, my boot—nudged his under the table.

"This place *does* feel special," I said softly.

He looked up and smiled, and there it was again—that quiet, unassuming sweetness that made me want to lean over the table and kiss him stupid.

ANDREW

THE WAITRESS ARRIVED WITH SHANNON'S WHISKEY SOUR AND my pale ale and set them down in front of us. I was still staring down at the menu, caught between the pasta brunatta and the spring chicken, both sounding pretty damn good. I weighed the flavors in my head.

"Are you ready to order?" she asked.

Shannon's voice pulled me out of my indecision.

"I'm ready."

I looked up at her, catching a mischievous glint in her eyes, but had no idea what put it there.

"I'll have the pink peppercorn-crusted salmon," she said, folding her menu and sliding it toward the edge of the table.

My brain scrambled to make a call before the moment stretched too long. Pasta brunatta sounded solid and comforting.

I glanced at the waitress and cleared my throat.

"I'll go with the pasta brunatta." I looked at Shannon and asked, "Want to get the honey whipped ricotta to share?"

Her grin widened.

"Definitely."

I turned back to the waitress.

"And the ricotta, please."

She smiled and jotted it down, then paused.

"Is there anything else I can get for you?"

"No, that's it for now," I said.

"Great," she said. "The ricotta will be out shortly."

As the waitress walked away, I noticed Shannon still watching me, an amused smirk tugging at the corner of her mouth.

"What?"

"You still raise your left eyebrow when you're trying to make a decision."

"Still?"

"You've done it as long as I can remember."

I shook my head, grinning despite myself, genuinely surprised she'd picked up on something I didn't even realize I do.

"You've been tracking my eyebrow movements?"

She shrugged, still wearing that smug little smile.

"You spent a lot of time at my house, so I had plenty of opportunities to observe."

I laughed, but beneath it, something in my chest softened. She noticed *me*. Who knew?

By the time our drinks arrived, we had already slid into the familiar rhythm we always seem to find. There weren't any awkward pauses that plagued most of my first dates. No fake small talk. We didn't have to ask about jobs, hometowns, or siblings. We already knew all of it.

And yet, somehow, even after all these years, there were still new things to discover about her. Little details that almost caught me off guard.

I've been watching her for years, in an I-have-a-crush way, not a creepy one. The way you do when someone's quietly taking up more space in your mind than they should. And I thought I knew every little thing about her— the way her lashes caught the light, how she absentmindedly twirled a loose strand of hair when she was lost in thought.

But tonight, it was different. The way she tapped the table in thought. The curve of her smile when she was about to say something mischievous. Every little nuance made her feel more vivid, more tangible. I wanted to reach across the table, to rest my hand over hers and remind myself this wasn't all in my head.

The waitress approached, balancing what looked like a rectangular cutting board piled high with triangles of pita and a small ceramic bowl nestled beside them.

"Your honey whipped ricotta," she said as she set it down in the center of the table.

"Thanks so much," Shannon said with a warm smile.

"Thank you," I echoed, and the waitress gave a quick

nod before heading off, disappearing into the steady rhythm of the dining room.

We sat there for a beat, looking at the board between us like it might be too pretty to mess up. Then Shannon reached for a piece of pita, and I followed suit. She scooped a generous smear of the ricotta onto hers, and I did the same, making sure to snag some pignoli nuts and dried fruit.

"Oh my God," Shannon groaned, her eyes fluttering shut.

A half-groan, half-laugh slipped out as soon as I took the first bite.

"That's insane. Like, stupid good."

"Right? It's creamy and salty and sweet and just—ugh." She looked at the bowl like it had personally changed her life. "I'd eat this every day and be happy."

She laughed, and I was happy to see her reach for a third pita.

I know she hasn't been feeling great about the extra weight she's put on because of her thyroid issues. She mentioned it once in the self-deprecating tone she uses when she doesn't want me to argue. But I'm not lying when I tell her she looks amazing. She does. Always has. Watching her enjoy herself without second-guessing every bite feels like a win, even if she doesn't realize it.

"I'd come back here for this alone," she said. "Forget the rest of the menu."

"Same," I said, reaching for another piece.

"Be honest," she said, licking a smear of ricotta from her thumb, "Is being a doctor everything you thought it'd be? Do you love it?"

I paused for a few seconds before answering.

"I love the actual practice—working with patients, surgeries, problem-solving. But the paperwork is a nightmare. So yeah, I love it, but if I never had to write a single note or fill out another form again, I'd be perfectly happy." I picked up a napkin and wiped my hands. "What about you? Do you still love being an esthetician?"

"I love doing makeup. Filling in at the boudoir studio has reminded me how much. Playing with looks and helping people feel amazing are the parts I live for." She sighed, then added, "But, like you with your paperwork, the rest can be draining. Working for an agency means juggling the politics. There's favoritism, people who get booked more because of who they know or what they do, not just talent. It's frustrating sometimes, trying to get gigs when connections matter as much as skill."

I nodded, watching her carefully.

"Sounds like you're out of all that agency drama now, though. Are you thinking about going back?"

As I waited for her answer, I realized I didn't know how I'd handle it if she did. For years, Shannon has been this impossible crush, like a star I could admire from afar but never touch. But since she's been back, things have been different.

I don't know where this is headed. Hell, I don't even know if it has a destination. All I can do is hope. Because if she goes back to her old life, I don't know what I'll do. It'd be like I was handed my dream then had it ripped away. And I'm not sure my heart could take that.

"Honestly? I don't know what I'm doing," she said quietly. "I'm not sure if I want to eventually dive back into all the chaos or keep carving out something different. I guess I'll figure it out as I go."

"It's good you're taking the time to figure out what you

want," I said, then added, "Whatever you choose, I'm here to support you."

That earned me a shy smile but before she could respond, the waitress returned carrying our entrees. The smell hit first—rich, savory, and absolutely mouthwatering. She set the plates down carefully in front of us.

She placed Shannon's dish in front of her, a pink peppercorn-crusted salmon nestled over lemon-feta orzo, surrounded by bright peas, asparagus, and roasted cucumber. Then she set down mine, a personal pan of bucatini topped with classic bolognese, the edges caramelized to a deep, almost-burnt finish.

Conversation fell away as we ate, not in an awkward way, just comfortable. Every now and then we'd glance at each other or make a small comment about the food, but mostly, we let the silence settle in around us. It felt easy. Natural.

I watched as Shannon carefully cut another bite of salmon, the pink center flaking perfectly against her fork. Her orzo was half gone, the bright green peas and asparagus pushed to one side like she was saving them.

Then, as she reached for her drink, she spoke.

"I'm moving back to my apartment this week," she said, her voice casual, but something else threaded through the words.

"Yeah? That's big."

She nodded.

"It's time. I can walk now—well, boot walk. It's not glamorous, but it's two feet."

"How's your mom feel about it?"

"I think she'd be happy if I stayed longer, but if I'm there, she'll stay stuck in full-on mom mode forever," Shannon said, swirling the ice in her glass. "Ever since I moved in, it's like she's put her own life on pause, like she used to when

Simon and I were kids. She won't make a single plan without checking if someone's going to be home with me, and she shouldn't have to."

"My mom's the same. I don't think she's had a single cup of tea while it was still hot in decades."

She laughed, and the sound filled something in me I hadn't even realized was empty.

The rest of dinner passed in the same easy, light rhythm. We talked about old movies, weird food combos, and the time Simon tried to make grilled cheese with a hotel iron. One ridiculous story led to another, the kind of conversation that didn't need a point, just a flow.

Eventually, I asked for the check, and a few minutes later, we stepped out into the chilly night. I opened the passenger door for her and watched as she carefully climbed in, lifting her boot like it weighed more than the rest of her body.

The drive back was quiet. She leaned her head against the seat, watching the streetlights flicker past the window, and I kept sneaking glances at her like I was afraid she'd disappear.

When we pulled into her parents' driveway, I put the car in park but didn't shut it off. Neither of us moved.

She looked over at me.

"So, this was great."

"Yeah, it was."

She turned in her seat a little, the seatbelt pulling across her chest at the same time I turned toward her. And there it was again, the magnetic pull that's been growing between us. I didn't want to resist it anymore.

I leaned in and at first, she didn't move, just watched me, her eyes warm and sure. And then she tilted her chin slightly, and that was all the permission I needed.

Our lips met, unraveling something deep inside me. Slow, warm, and deliberate. Her mouth is soft and sweet, tasting faintly of whiskey and chocolate. She let out a tiny sound, barely more than a sigh, and I swear it echoed through every nerve ending in my body.

"I've been wanting to kiss you all night," I murmured.

She let out a laugh and her breath brushed my lips.

"Yeah? Could've fooled me."

I smiled, letting my thumb trace the line of her jaw.

"I was trying to be a gentleman."

"You're always a gentleman."

"If you knew what I was thinking right now, you wouldn't say that."

Her eyebrows lifted slightly, but she didn't pull back. She stayed close, curious, and completely unbothered. Then she tilted her head, a playful spark lighting her eyes.

"Oh? And what exactly are you thinking?"

I brushed a stray strand of hair behind her ear.

"I'll tell you another time. Your parents are probably watching us through the window right now."

Her gaze shifted toward the house then met mine again, with a mix of amusement and something softer.

"Okay, another time. But don't think I'll forget."

I stepped out of the car and walked around the front to open her door and help her out. She leaned against me slightly as we slowly made our way to the front porch.

Once there, she turned to face me.

"Thanks for dinner," she said.

"Thanks for saying yes."

She smiled again, and it was more open, like we'd crossed some invisible threshold and there was no going back.

I kissed her again, then stepped back.

"Goodnight, Shannon."

"Goodnight, Andrew."

She opened the door and disappeared inside.

I walked back to my car, slid into the driver's seat, and sat there for a second, my mind racing with everything that just happened.

As I backed out of the driveway, I caught a light turn on in Shannon's bedroom window. For a second, I let myself imagine what it would feel like to be allowed to follow her up those stairs. But that would come, I realized with a surprising sense of certainty.

Tonight has been the beginning, not just of our romantic relationship, but of something deeper. We've officially crossed a line we'd been approaching for weeks, and there's no going back now.

CHAPTER 11

Shannon

THE FAMILIAR CHAOS OF TACO NIGHT WAS IN FULL SWING IN MY parents' kitchen, and I couldn't help but smile as I watched Keera and Anjannette unpack an insane amount of food. Across the room, Sophie was on margarita duty and I watched with wide eyes as she tilted the tequila bottle and dumped at least half of it in.

"That seems excessive," I said, chuckling.

She wiggled her eyebrows and kept pouring.

"Ladies, I present to you the finest tacos Scranton has to offer," Anjannette announced dramatically, sweeping her arm toward the spread on the kitchen island like she was unveiling a five-star feast instead of takeout from Italo's. "Plus margaritas that may or may not be legal to consume."

Sophie set the pitcher in the middle of the table and Keera eyed it warily.

"What exactly did you put in those?" she asked.

"Love," Sophie said with a grin. "And possibly an entire bottle of tequila." She poured us each of us a glass. "It's your last night in the family nest," she said. "We need to send you off in style."

"Or with a hangover," Keera added in a stage whisper.

I accepted my margarita and took a cautious sip. It's strong enough to make my eyes water, but in the best possible way.

Sophie raised her glass in a toast.

"To fresh starts," she said. "And to Shannon moving back to her apartment."

"Cheers," Anjannette said, clinking her glass against mine. "But let the record show I'm going to miss raiding your parents' pantry."

"They do have an alarming number of snack options," I said, laughing. "My mom shops like a blizzard is coming."

Keera raised her glass.

"Here's hoping your pantry is even half as well-stocked."

After their toasts, we loaded our plates with tacos. I reached for the guacamole then I noticed how quiet it got. All three of them were looking right at me, plates full, waiting. I blinked, caught off guard.

"What?" I asked, shifting in my seat.

"We're waiting," Sophie said with a raised eyebrow.

"For the good stuff," Anjannette added.

Keera nodded.

"Spill."

I'm actually surprised it took them so long to ask for details.

"Our date was perfect." I settled back in my chair. "Honestly, completely perfect."

"Details, woman," Keera demanded. "Did he kiss you? How was the kiss? Are you in love? When's the wedding?"

"Let her breathe," Anjannette said.

I told them everything—about getting ready and feeling like a teenager, about my parents' barely contained excitement, about Bar Pazzo and the atmosphere and how natural everything felt. I described Andrew's outfit, the way he looked at me, the easy conversation that flowed between familiarity and discovery.

"And then?" Sophie prompted when I paused to take a bite of my taco.

"And then he drove me home, and we sat in the car talking, and..." I paused for dramatic effect. "We made out like horny teenagers in his car before he walked me to the door."

"How was the kiss?" Anjannette demanded.

"Anjannette!" Sophie scolded, half-laughing.

"What? It's important information! The kiss sets the tone for everything that follows."

"Incredible," I said, my mouth curving into a smile. "It wasn't our first kiss, but it felt different. Like we were stepping into something new together." They waited quietly as I gathered my thoughts. "At first, it was soft and slow, then it deepened. When I rested my hand on his chest, I could feel his heart pounding like crazy." I shook my head with a smile. "Seriously, it was incredible."

"Look at her face!" Sophie said with delight. "She's glowing."

"You know what's weird?" I said, swirling the last bit of margarita in my glass. "All my life, I dated these guys who were...well, kind of crappy if I'm being totally honest. Looking back, I realized they never really fit or made things easy. But with Andrew everything clicks." I shook my head. "I realize it's early days here, but it feels right."

"Sometimes the best things are right in front of us and

we're too busy looking elsewhere to notice," Keera said. "And remember, I'm speaking from experience."

"How long did you and Simon work together and you never thought of him as a romantic prospect?" Sophie asked.

"Almost a decade."

"What made you finally see him differently?" Sophie asked.

"I don't even know what changed, or why," Keera said, then let out a quiet laugh. "But honestly, even if I'd dated Simon back then, it wouldn't have worked. I was a hot mess and had to fix myself first. I wouldn't have been ready for what we have now if I hadn't." Raising her glass, she said, "Cheers to Dr. Green for fixing me."

We all raised our glasses, and as I emptied mine, the tequila settled in—the warm, slow burn that promised either a really good night or an incredibly embarrassing one.

"Not to shame you," Sophie said. "But didn't we have a conversation at your apartment when you first moved back about you being on a dick-free diet?"

"I do remember that," Anjannette said with glee.

"Actually, I think my exact quote was I planned to live a dick-free lifestyle," I said. "I believe Keera's the one who said dick-free diet."

"Regardless." Keera waved her hand as if erasing my words. "We told you those were famous last words. Didn't we?"

"You did, but in my defense, I wasn't looking for a relationship. Especially not with Andrew. It just happened." I shrugged.

"That explains why the dick-free lifestyle is over," Sophie said.

I groaned, dropping my head onto the table with a thunk.

"The lifestyle is technically still in place," I said. "We haven't had sex."

"But it's compromised," Keera said, smirking.

"Violated," Anjannette added.

"Wrecked," Sophie corrected, dramatically wiping a fake tear. "God, I love love."

I lifted my head and tried to glare, but I was smiling too hard.

"You're all the worst."

"Maybe," Anjannette said. "But we're also right."

"With the way Andrew looks at you, I'd say your virtue is hanging on by a thread made of wet spaghetti," Keera said with a grin.

I laughed, but my brain immediately flashed back to what Andrew said the other night, when I called him a gentleman.

"If you knew what I was thinking right now, you wouldn't say that."

Remembering the simmering intensity in his eyes when he said those words made my stomach flip. Andrew's always been super focused and intense. And honestly, the thought of all his energy being aimed at me is pretty damn exciting.

The ladies kept chatting about their love lives—and mine—getting more graphic as the margaritas settled in.

I sat back in my chair, absently toying with the salt-rimmed edge of my empty glass, and let the moment settle around me. For once, I'm not pushing, planning, or mapping out the next ten steps. I'm not stressing about timelines or trying to wrangle my future into a checklist.

I've spent so much of my life treating my dreams like

tasks, something I had to control. But lately, I've just been letting things happen. And surprisingly, it's been working.

Really, the only crappy thing that's happened since I moved back to Scranton is breaking my ankle. But even that had an unexpected upside—it made me slow down and in the stillness, I started seeing Andrew differently. And I like what I see. Even more, I like how I feel when I'm with him.

He's there steady, solid, with a quiet intensity and a certain smile that only ever seems to show up when he's looking at me.

We aren't racing toward anything. We're progressing. And I like the way it feels.

ANDREW

I PULLED UP IN FRONT OF MY PARENTS' HOUSE AND SHIFTED into park. Through the large front window, I caught glimpses of my family already gathered and probably wondering where we were. We're right on time, but they're always early.

Shannon exhaled slowly, like she was bracing herself before plunging into icy water.

"You okay?" I asked.

"Yeah." She gave a half-smile. "But meeting the family is always a little nerve-wracking."

"You already know my family," I said, raising an eyebrow. "And they know you."

"Yes," she said, drawing the word out, "but they know me as Simon's sister, not your..."

She trailed off, eyes dropping to her lap like the next

word might bite. My chest tightened a little, the air between us humming with unspoken questions.

Then, barely louder than a whisper she added, "Girlfriend."

My heart did a full somersault, the kind that makes me want to grin like an idiot. She said it like a question, but to me, it sounded like the answer I've been waiting for my whole life

I reached over, cupped her cheek gently, and kissed her.

"Girlfriend," I said, without hesitation or a question mark.

Her smile started small but grew, warm and real.

"Okay. Girlfriend it is."

I shut off the engine, and the silence settled around us.

"You ready?" I asked.

"As I'll ever be."

I got out and rounded the car just as she opened her door. I offered my hand, and she took it without hesitation. She stood then bent down to adjust the hem of her pants over the boot, making sure it fell right before straightening.

I adjusted my steps to match hers as she walked carefully in the boot, and we made our way along the sidewalk and up the porch steps. I opened the door and stepped aside, letting her go in first.

Mom wiped her hands on a dish towel as she greeted us.

"There you are," she said, kissing my cheek before pulling Shannon into a warm hug. "Honey, it's so good to see you."

"It's good to see you too," Shannon said as Mom released her. "Thank you for having me."

She looked down at Shannon's ankle and frowned.

"You poor thing. How's your ankle feeling?"

"Much better, thanks," Shannon said, glancing down at

her boot. "And as annoying as this thing is, I'm happy to be on two feet again."

"How much longer do you have to wear it?"

"Another three weeks or so." Shannon looked to me for confirmation.

I nodded.

"It all depends on how the bone heals. Dr. Chen will know more at her next appointment."

We followed my mom into the living room, where the familiar hum of family life filled the space. Dad and Bobby were sprawled on the couch, eyes on the game. Maria sat nearby, scrolling through her phone. At the dining room table, Claire and Maddy leaned over an iPad, both of them squinting at whatever they were watching. Harper sat in the recliner, her nose buried in a book as usual, completely absorbed in whatever world she was reading about.

As soon as we entered, all eyes turned in our direction. Karli, sitting cross-legged on the floor, had been absorbed in something on her phone, but the moment she saw us, she looked up with wide eyes.

"Oh my gosh, Uncle Andrew, she's so pretty," she said, her voice full of awe.

The room broke into laughter, and Shannon's cheeks went pink. I couldn't help but grin.

"She is pretty," I said, still looking at her.

Shannon gave me a shy smile, tucking a piece of hair behind her ear like she wasn't used to compliments. Which I know isn't true.

I cleared my throat.

"All right, let me make this official." I gestured toward each person in turn. "You probably remember Bobby and Claire. That's Bobby's wife, Maria. And my nieces, Maddy, Harper, and Karli."

"It's really nice to meet you all," Shannon said.

With the last of the introductions made, my mom nodded toward the dining room.

"We're all here, so let's eat," she said.

"Is there anything I can help with?" Shannon asked.

"No, you take a seat and get off your ankle." Mom walked over to the dining room table and pulled out the chair at the head, the one she usually sits in. "Relax."

"Okay, thank you."

"What do you need me to do?" I asked.

"Just keep Shannon company." She patted my shoulder. "The girls will help bring everything out."

I did as I was told and took the seat next to Shannon. Soon the table was filled with the comforting smells of roast beef, mashed potatoes, and corn. And of course, hard rolls from National Bakery. Mom says it wouldn't be Sunday dinner without them.

The familiar clink of plates and silverware echoed through the room as everyone settled in and filled their plates. Bobby was already digging in, praising the roast with every bite, while Claire passed the rolls around. Shannon offered me a smile as I held the bowl of mashed potatoes for her and she piled some onto her plate. While I did the same, she topped her potatoes and roast beef with a healthy dose of gravy.

She took a bite and her eyes lit up.

"This is delicious," she said, her voice warm with appreciation.

Mom smiled at her.

"I'm so glad you like it."

I buttered a roll for both Shannon and me then dug into my meal. The conversation flowed easily around us, and to my relief, no one was grilling Shannon or tossing out every embarrassing story from my childhood.

Maddy looked up from her half-empty plate and narrowed her eyes at Shannon.

"Can I ask you something?" she said, a little tentative.

Shannon paused mid-bite and smiled.

"Sure."

"I love your makeup. How do you get your eyeshadow so perfect?"

"Thank you! It's all about layering and blending. And practice."

"I try stuff I see on YouTube and TikTok, but I always end up looking like a raccoon," Maddy said.

"Same," Harper said. "Mine always turns into a smudgy mess."

"And I'm no help to them," Maria chimed in, grinning. "I've had the same routine since 2004."

"You all look great," Shannon said. "But I can show you some easy techniques if you want."

"Seriously?" Maddy asked, eyes wide.

"I'd love to."

"Me too?" Harper added.

Shannon turned to her with a grin.

"You too."

Even Claire looked up from her plate.

"I might actually join that lesson."

Maria raised her hand like she was in school.

"Count me in."

They all pulled out their phones like they were gearing up for a military operation, thumbs flying as they compared schedules and locked in plans for Thursday night. Shannon was laughing, holding her own, and I sat back for a second and watched in awe. This woman who used to feel like someone from a separate part of my life now slotted perfectly into the middle of it.

"The plan," Maria declared, tapping her screen with dramatic finality, "is wine, snacks, makeup, and girl talk. Thursday at six-thirty."

Shannon turned to me, her voice low but playful.

"Are you around Thursday night to play chauffeur again?"

"I'm at the clinic until six, but I'm free after that," I said, not bothering to hide the smile tugging at my mouth. "You want me to wear a uniform?"

"If it wouldn't be too much trouble," she said. "But scrubs will do."

"Deal."

After dinner, dessert came and went, and somehow Shannon was still holding her own. She didn't try too hard, just leaned in when it made sense, asked the kind of questions that showed she was paying attention, and smiled like she was truly enjoying herself.

The shift was subtle, but I felt it. Shannon wasn't simply visiting. She was being folded in. My sisters and nieces weren't merely tolerating her, they were letting her in.

Eventually the evening wound down and everyone got up to leave. As we said our goodbyes, my family hugged Shannon like they meant it. Mom told her to come by anytime, and Dad called her "kiddo" without a second thought.

Outside, Shannon leaned into me slightly as we walked to the car.

"So, how do you think it went?" I asked once we were settled.

She smiled, her eyes reflecting the soft glow of the dashboard lights.

"It wasn't a job interview."

"'It's nerve-wracking meeting the family,'" I said, quoting her from earlier.

She smirked, clearly enjoying the playful banter.

"Touché. But seriously, I had a great time," she said. "And to answer your question, I think it went well."

We drove in companionable silence, the hum of the tires filling the space.

I pulled into her driveway and cut the engine. As I shifted into park, Shannon turned to face me.

"Being there with you tonight felt good. Real. Like maybe we're not just figuring this out, we're already in it," she said.

"In a good way, right?"

She smiled, her gaze meeting mine with a spark.

"Definitely."

I unbuckled and leaned over the console to kiss her.

It was meant to be a quick goodnight kiss. A way to seal what we just said and celebrate the night. But the second my lips met hers, it turned into one of those slow, deep, can't-get-close-enough kisses.

I would've kept going, but some small, responsible part of my brain reminded me we're in my car, parked in her parents' driveway. There'll be plenty of time for this—and hopefully a whole lot more—once her ankle's healed a bit more. I've waited this long for her, what's a few more weeks?

Reluctantly, I ended the kiss and pulled back to rest my forehead against hers, breathing her in. Her hand slid to the back of my neck, keeping me close like she wasn't ready to let go either.

We stayed like that for a minute, neither of us moving. Then she leaned back slightly, smiling.

"What?" I asked.

"You kiss like someone who means it."

"I do mean it."

"Good. Because I do too."

She kissed me once more, deliberate and sure, and I swear I felt it in my ribs.

I've waited a long time for her to feel the same way.

Now that she does? I'm not going anywhere.

CHAPTER 12

Shannon

"Do you even remember how to drive?"

My dad grinned as he opened the passenger side door of the Range Rover for me.

"Very funny," I said. "I've borrowed this very vehicle multiple times since I've been home and returned it without a single scratch, thank you very much."

He chuckled as he closed my door, then walked around the front of the car and slid into the driver's seat.

"Here we go," he said. "And please don't blame me when you fall in love with something above your budget."

"Dad, I lived in Manhattan for more than ten years. My tolerance for overpriced things is high." I picked up my phone and opened photos of the cars I'd saved. "But to be safe, I've narrowed it down to three cars I want to check out, so I don't get sidetracked by big shiny things."

We headed to the first dealership and looked at a black Audi Q3. It was sexy and sleek and smelled like ambition. I sank into the buttery leather and gripped the wheel like it belonged to me. Everything about the car whispered city-girl-gone-corporate. And for a minute, I almost convinced myself I needed it. But it's the most expensive of the three so instead of making a snap decision, I waited to see the others.

Next up was a dark blue Toyota RAV4. It was shiny enough to turn heads and rocking tan leather seats that gave off retired-professor-who-still-reads-the-New Yorker energy. The mileage is ridiculously low for the year, like it only left the garage for Sunday brunch and scenic drives. But the previous owner had clearly been a smoker. Even with the dealership's best effort to scrub it down, the stale smoke smell still clung to the interior beneath the layer of citrus cleaning products. Not exactly the vibe I'm going for.

Then we hit the Honda dealership and looked at a white CR-V. It's simple, clean, and practical...three words that wouldn't have caught my attention before. But now they're what made me put it on my list.

I slid into the driver's seat and adjusted the mirrors while my dad stood outside, watching me through the windshield like he was waiting to be proven right. But the minute I put it in gear, I knew.

It didn't roar or purr, just moved smoothly and confidently, like it had nothing to prove.

"This is the one," I said after the test drive.

"Wait, really?" He blinked. "Not the Audi?"

"Nope."

Dad looked genuinely impressed.

"Huh. I thought for sure you'd go with the fancy one."

"Guess I'm full of surprises."

He didn't say anything else, just held out his hand for the fob and slid into the driver's seat. I watched as he pulled out of the lot, leaving me standing there with the salesperson, both of us pretending not to feel the awkward lull. Thankfully, he was back a few minutes later, parking with the kind of precision that said he'd already made up his mind.

When he got out, he popped the hood and leaned in, checking the belts, battery, and fluid levels with practiced ease. Then he crouched to inspect the tires, running a hand along the tread and giving one a quick tap like it was speaking to him. He dropped to one knee and glanced underneath, eyes scanning the undercarriage.

He stood and gave me a nod, like this wasn't only a decent choice, it was a smart one.

"It has good bones, a clean engine, and the tires will last you a while." He glanced over at me. "Yeah, this is the one."

We headed inside, and I haggled enough to get a couple thousand knocked off the price. Once the paperwork was signed and they confirmed the car would be ready for pickup the next day, I made Dad snap a few triumphant photos of me next to my new-to-me CR-V.

We climbed back into the Range Rover, both of us feeling pretty pleased with ourselves. Dad because he raised a daughter who made a smart, practical choice, and me because I officially bought my first grown-up car.

"Lunch?" he asked as we pulled out of the dealership.

"Only if it involves hot roast beef with gravy fries."

Twenty minutes later, we were at the Glider Diner, squeezed into a booth each with a hot roast beef platter in front of us, and zero regrets.

"I can't believe I haven't eaten here since I moved back," I said around a gravy-coated fry. "It's so good."

Dad popped a forkful of roast beef into his mouth and let out a satisfied groan.

We ate in companionable silence for a few minutes, the

kind that only comes from mutual appreciation of hot, juicy perfection. After clearing his plate, Dad wiped his hands, leaned back, and took a long drink.

"So," he said, as he set his glass down, "you're a car owner now."

"I am."

"Guess you're sticking around for a little while?"

"Yeah," I said. "I think so."

"Didn't think I'd see the day."

"Me either."

"I also didn't think I'd see the day you and Andrew started dating."

"I'm impressed you waited this long to bring it up."

"I figured I'd let you buy a car first. You know, build trust."

I laughed and took a sip of my soda.

"Do you think it's weird?"

He didn't answer right away. Just reached for a fry, popped it into his mouth, and chewed like he was considering his answer carefully.

"Do you?" he finally asked.

"I feel like I should." I set my glass down. "He basically grew up in our house. I've witnessed all the nerdy stuff he, Simon, and Archer used to get up to. Full-on debates about *Star Wars*, midnight video game marathons ending in loud arguments and empty chip bags, building some weird cardboard spaceship in the garage one summer. He's always been like another sibling."

"That's what's always been. What about now?"

I took in a breath and let it out on a soft sigh.

"Something happened between when I saw him last and now," I said. "He doesn't seem like another sibling anymore. He feels..." I trailed off, searching for the words. "...natural.

Like being with him makes sense in a way I didn't expect. Like I've finally caught up to something that was always there, waiting."

Dad nodded, giving me a knowing smile.

"That's how it's supposed to feel."

"Still, I didn't exactly plan this."

"The best things are rarely planned."

I looked at him, a smile tugging at the corners of my mouth.

"You know, I really did hit the lottery in the parent department."

He gave me a look that was equal parts touched and trying-not-to-get-mushy, then pointed at my plate with a smirk.

"Now finish your food before I do."

ANDREW

GROOVE BREWING WAS PACKED, BUT NOT IN A SHOULDER-TO-shoulder, can't-hear-yourself-think kind of way. The taproom buzzed with conversation and laughter, and the scent of smoked meat from the food vendor out back drifted in every time the door opened.

On the stage, a two-man band played an acoustic cover of Collective Soul's "Shine." Not trying too hard, just vibing. The guy on vocals had a rasp like he lived on cigarettes and old cassette tapes, which somehow made it all better.

"These ribs are amazing," I said, wiping barbecue sauce off my fingers and tossing another napkin onto the growing pile.

Simon nodded and set down his pulled pork sandwich.

"Solid choice. I haven't had barbecue in forever, and this is seriously hitting the spot." He glanced toward the stage. "And the band's great. This feels like a Friday night in college, but with better food and actual chairs."

Across the table, Archer half-heartedly pushed his mac and cheese around with his fork. I glanced at the bowl he'd barely touched and raised an eyebrow.

"I'm still shocked you didn't get barbecue or at least a hot dog."

"I love mac and cheese," he said. "And this is good."

Simon leaned in.

"Yeah, but good-for-a-side isn't the same as dinner-worthy."

Archer sighed.

"It's sharp cheddar with a garlic breadcrumb topping. This isn't boxed. There's nuance."

I narrowed my eyes.

"Wait...is this a Mirabelle thing?"

He shrugged.

"She's vegetarian."

"We know," Simon said, barely hiding a grin. "The second you told us she was vegetarian, Andrew and I should have bet on how long it would take you to be one, too."

"I'm trying it for a little while."

"For a while?" I repeated.

Archer shrugged.

"It's not that deep."

I took a sip of my beer and leaned back.

"It's fine. We'll support your journey, just don't start pretending tofu tastes like anything."

Archer pointed at me with his fork.

"Wait until Shannon has you trying something new"

"When I start wearing eye shadow, you can tease me all you want."

"Good one," Simon said. "Keera and I are getting married in a few months and I haven't started pole dancing, so I think you're safe."

Archer shook his head.

"You're both smartasses."

"We're just busting you," I said, then decided to change the subject. We've picked on Archer enough. "Speaking of the wedding, Shannon said the girls have already started tossing around bachelorette party ideas. We should probably get moving on your bachelor party. Anything specific you want to do?"

He shook his head.

"Something low-key. No strip clubs or party buses, nothing weird."

"It's not exactly low-key, but we could hit Galaxy's Edge at Disney. And if we've got time, we could Drink Around the World in Epcot."

Simon's eyes lit up.

"That actually sounds incredible."

"I love it," Archer said. "Bachelor weekend with no strippers, just stormtroopers."

We looked at our calendars and came up with a few potential dates. Leo Marakis is in the wedding, but most likely won't be able to make it because it's still baseball season. The only other person we have to coordinate with is Keera's brother Kevin.

"Since you mentioned Shannon...did you talk to her today?" Simon asked.

"For a minute. Anjannette and Keera got there when I called her."

"I was over at my parents' house earlier, and my mom and Shannon were having a *discussion*."

He used air quotes on the last word.

Archer looked up from his now-demolished mac and cheese.

"Was it one of those conversations where your mom smiles the whole time but sounds vaguely threatening?" he asked.

"Exactly," Simon said. "Mom told her she should stay home a little longer, until she's *really* healed. Then she went on about how dangerous stairs can be, like Shannon's about to walk up the Empire State Building instead of into her apartment building. Then she brought up the time in sixth grade when Shannon slipped on ice and nearly broke her wrist, like that somehow proves she can't be trusted with basic movement.

"She's worried," I said. "But Shannon's good. She's got a car now and is back on two feet."

"Try telling my mom," Simon muttered. "Actually, maybe you should. Casually mention how people live alone in walking boots every day without parental supervision."

"I'll try working it into the conversation," I said.

"Make sure you're wearing scrubs if you do," Archer said. "It will have more impact that way."

"Plus there are enough people nearby if she needs help with anything. And I'm sure the girls'll be dropping in to hang out."

Simon looked at me, a little too knowingly.

"And I'm sure you will be too."

I smiled into my beer. There's no need to deny it.

"That too."

"You know, my mom would probably feel better if she knew you were staying there with her."

I raised my eyebrows.

"It's a little early for me to move in, don't you think?

Simon held his hands up in a no offense gesture.

"I just said my mom would feel better. No pressure."

Before I could respond, the band started playing "Friday I'm in Love" by The Cure—one of my favorite songs.

Instead of answering, I took a long drink and settled back into my seat, letting the opening chords wash over me.

No pressure, sure. But I'd be lying if I said I didn't like the way that future sounded.

CHAPTER 13

Shannon

STANDING IN FRONT OF MY BATHROOM MIRROR, I CURLED MY carefully sectioned hair, watching as the strands took shape into soft curls. Once they cooled, I gently brushed them out with my fingers so they fell across my shoulders in loose, effortless waves. Not too fussy, but still date-night worthy.

I opted for a more natural than glam look for my makeup—tinted moisturizer instead of foundation, warm bronzy tones on my lids, a hint of pink blush on my cheeks, and a warm rose lip that made me feel like myself but polished.

After searching through my entire closet, I decided on an off-the-shoulder sage green maxi dress. It's fun and flirty, and will go well with the black combat boots I decided to wear. Ideally I'd pair this with a platform sandal or espadrille, but those aren't structured enough to support my ankle.

I swiped on a coat of gloss to refresh my lips and checked myself in the full-length mirror. The dress skimmed over my curves, flowy in all the right ways. I tugged the off-the-shoulder sleeves into place and gave the bodice a quick smooth-down, watching the tiered skirt sway as I shifted. The hem brushed right above my boots, the two looking unexpectedly perfect together, like softness and edge had called a truce.

This was so different from my Manhattan dating uniform of pencil skirts, silk blouses, and designer heels that cost more than most people's rent. Back then, I'd armor myself in sharp lines and expensive labels, trying to match the energy of men who talked about portfolios over artisanal cocktails and measured success in square footage of their Tribeca lofts.

But Andrew's not like those finance bros who treat people like a placeholder. The ones who only wanted a trophy on their arm or someone who could get them into the right parties. He's real and grounded and doesn't need to name drop or flaunt his Rolex Submariner to feel important.

The doorbell rang, pulling me out of the spiral of comparing the life I used to have to the one I'm building now. My heart gave a stupid little flutter as I walked carefully to the door and pulled it open.

Andrew stood there in dark jeans and a dusty blue-green button-down, the kind meant to be worn untucked. It's casual but put together in that quietly confident way of his. And yeah, the color definitely made his eyes pop.

He held a bouquet of white and yellow daisies with a few sprigs of green. Simple and bright. Thoughtful without making a big deal out of it.

"Hi," I said, with a smile.

"Hi," he said back, and leaned in to kiss my cheek. His hand settled gently on my waist, as he stepped back. "You look beautiful."

"Thank you," I said, taking the flowers from him. "These are so pretty."

"You're welcome."

"Come in while I put these in water."

He followed me into the kitchen, and I grabbed a vase from the top shelf of the pantry. After filling it with water, I set it on the counter, then unwrapped the bouquet and added the flowers one by one, arranging them as I went.

Andrew looked around as I worked, taking everything in.

"This place is nice," he said.

"Oh, I forgot you haven't been here before."

"It's very you."

I looked at him, smiling.

"Is that a compliment?"

He ran a hand along the edge of the counter, still looking around.

"Definitely. It's warm, full of personality, and smells good. Like you."

He added those last two words almost as an afterthought, but the sentiment landed all the same.

My stomach flipped in the way it always does when he catches me off guard. Not with some grand gesture or over-the-top compliment, but with quiet honesty that slips past every wall without even trying.

I glanced at him, trying to keep my voice light even as my heart kicked up a notch.

"You know, for someone who claims he doesn't have game, you're actually kind of charming."

He smiled, and I turned back to the flowers, hoping he

couldn't see the way my cheeks flushed or how hard I was working to tamp down the grin tugging at the corners of my mouth.

I fluffed the last few stems, buying myself a second to breathe, then carried the vase into the living room and set it on the coffee table.

"You ready?"

I straightened and turned to him.

"So ready."

THE 16TH WARD BUZZED WITH THE KIND OF ENERGY THAT felt real—easy conversation, clinking glasses, and that low hum of people genuinely enjoying themselves. Exposed brick, matte black fixtures, and warm wood accents gave it a sleek, modern feel without trying too hard. The air smelled like seared steak and something citrusy, with enough spice to make my stomach grumble in anticipation.

I glanced around, then back at Andrew as I opened the menu.

"I've actually never been here before."

"Me neither," he said. "But one of the nurses I work with comes all the time and raves about it."

"Well, she might be onto something. This all sounds amazing," I said as I scanned the menu, already debating between three different entrees.

"I'm glad I made a reservation," he said, looking around at the packed dining room. "It would've been a pretty lousy date if we had to wander around looking for a backup plan."

Our waitress approached with a bright smile.

"Hi, I'm Kelsey, I'll be taking care of you tonight. Can I get you started with something to drink?"

"I'll have a whiskey sour," I said.

"Draft IPA," Andrew added, glancing up just long enough to catch her eye.

"Perfect. I'll be right back with those," she said, then slipped away toward the bar.

"What are you getting?" I asked Andrew.

"I'm thinking steak," he said. "What about you?"

"I was eyeing the red pepper risotto, but the chipotle-glazed salmon comes with gouda grits, and I'm not strong enough to walk away from that."

He raised an eyebrow.

"Should I be concerned about your cheese dependency?"

"It also comes with veggies," I said. "Plus salmon has omega-3s, so technically, it's a heart-healthy choice. I'm basically making responsible life decisions over here."

"Let me see if I can be as poetic about my meal." He set the menu down and tapped it with his index finger. "I'm going with the ribeye. It comes with fingerling potatoes and sautéed broccoli rabe, which feels classic and dependable."

"Like you?"

"I was gonna say it won't put me in a food coma halfway through the date but sure, let's go with that."

I laughed at his dry tone.

"Just be forewarned I'll be stealing a bite," I warned him.

Kelsey reappeared with our drinks.

"Any decisions yet, or do you need a few more minutes?"

"We're good," I said, and we placed our orders.

As she started to walk away, Andrew caught her attention.

"And can we get the bruschetta to start?"

"Absolutely."

Once she was gone, Andrew raised his glass toward mine.

"To good food and better company."

"I'll drink to that," I said and tapped my glass gently against his.

We clinked glasses, and I took a sip—sweet, tart, with just enough whiskey bite to keep it interesting. I hummed in approval.

"Mmm, so good," I said, setting the glass down.

A few minutes later, the server returned with a wooden board piled high with bruschetta and slid it between us.

"Wow," I said, eyeing the toast points topped with burrata, tomato relish, pesto, and balsamic glaze. "They're almost too pretty to eat."

"Almost," Andrew said, already reaching for one.

I picked up a piece too and we took our first bites, sharing a quiet, satisfied moment when food speaks louder than words. It tasted as good as it looked, and we cleared the whole plate in record time.

He wiped his fingers with a napkin and leaned back a little in his seat, eyes on me.

"So," he said, "how's your ankle feeling?"

"Still feels weird. Kind of like it forgot how to be an ankle." I shrugged. "But it doesn't hurt. And I'm loving the bootless freedom."

"You've come a long way."

"Thanks to a very patient doctor-slash-chauffeur."

"I am a doctor, but I'm technically not *your* doctor."

I rolled my eyes.

"You sound like a lawyer."

"I'm setting the record straight." He smirked. "I don't want you to fall for me because I treated your ankle. That's classic transference, you know, when a patient falls for their doctor."

"Trust me, my feelings have nothing to do with your medical expertise." My mouth curved into a slow smile. "Though I'll admit, your bedside manner is top notch."

Conversation moved easily from there, the way it always does with him. We talked about work, weird TikToks, how neither of us really understood cryptocurrency but felt like we should. We laughed and shared bites, and as the meal went on, a quiet, nervous hum settled in my belly. It's because tonight's going to be another step forward in our relationship.

The tension between us has been simmering for weeks. Each kiss lingered a little longer, each touch grew bolder. Only the timing hadn't been right. The boot had been an issue. It was awkward, bulky, and a constant reminder I wasn't quite myself. And on top of that, I was staying at my parents' house, which didn't exactly lend itself to privacy or spontaneity.

Kelsey returned, expertly balancing both plates as she set them down in front of us with a grin. We each opted to not have a second drink when she asked. The water she'd dropped off earlier was enough, and honestly, with how good everything smelled, I didn't want anything distracting me from the food.

"Okay then, enjoy," she said, then walked back toward the kitchen.

My salmon glistened under its chipotle glaze, the gouda grits buttery and rich beside a rainbow of roasted vegetables. Across the table, Andrew's ribeye was seared to perfection, almost too flawless to be real.

"This looks amazing."

"Yeah, it does," he said as he picked up his fork.

For a while, we didn't talk. Every few bites, we traded a look or a small nod, silently agreeing—the food was just that good. He cut me a bite of his steak without asking, and I nudged a forkful of salmon and grits his way. By the time our plates were clean, I felt full in the best way—satisfied, not stuffed. I leaned back with a contented sigh.

We sat there a little longer, not in any rush. The buzz of the restaurant carried on around us—glasses clinking, laughter from the next table, low music humming in the background—but it all felt distant. Like we were in our own little pocket of calm.

Eventually, I spotted the people waiting by the door and figured it was probably time to give up the table.

Andrew paid the bill, then we made our way to the door, weaving past tables and offering another quick thanks to Kelsey on the way out.

Outside, the night air was soft and breezy in that late-spring way. Streetlights glowed above us, casting everything in a warm haze as we walked side by side down the block.

When we reached the car, Andrew unlocked it and opened the passenger door for me.

"Thank you," I said as I slid into the seat.

As he closed the door behind me, something warm and steady settled in my chest. I'd already made up my mind tonight was the night. This thing between us has been building for weeks in every lingering glance and touch. Now, there's nothing in the way. No boot, no doubts...just him, me, and the quiet certainty we're ready.

He smiled, closed the door gently, then circled around to the driver's side. A moment later, he was behind the wheel, one hand on the gearshift, the other resting casually on the console like we had all the time in the world.

"There's a band playing at Voodoo Brewing Co. if you want to grab a drink and listen."

I turned in my seat, met his eyes, and said, "Or we could go back to my place and have a drink."

He froze for a second then blinked. Slowly, his mouth curled into a smile.

"I'd like that."

As he pulled out of the parking spot, he reached over and took my hand. Our fingers laced together like it was the most natural thing in the world. It still caught me off guard sometimes how someone I've known forever could still make something as simple as holding hands feel like magic.

I looked over at him, my heart picking up speed.

Because for the first time in a long time, I wasn't holding back.

And I had no intention of slowing down.

ANDREW

WE DIDN'T SAY MUCH DURING THE DRIVE TO SHANNON'S apartment. The tension between us had been building for weeks, and was humming like a low-grade current under the surface. It wasn't overwhelming, but it was there, steady and sure.

When she said we could skip the live music and head back to her place instead, I tried to play it cool but didn't really succeed. I'm pretty sure I blinked like I'd been hit in the face with a snowball. But the smile that followed came easy.

She unlocked the door to her apartment and entered

ahead of me, her combat boots thudding softly against the hardwood floor.

"Water?" she asked, already heading for the kitchen. "Or would you like something harder?"

"Water is good."

I lingered at the edge of the living room for a beat before crossing over and sitting on the couch, doing my best to play it cool while my pulse had other plans. It wasn't racing from nerves exactly. More like awareness and anticipation.

Shannon came back with two glasses of water, handed one to me, and settled onto the couch beside me, near enough that I could feel her body heat. She set her glass down, then bent to unlace her boots. One came off, then the other, followed by the ankle brace, which she eased off with care and set beside them.

"It feels so good to be out of the boot," she said as she slowly rotated her ankle.

I looked at her for a second. The way her hair fell over her shoulder in soft waves, the faint flush lingering on her cheeks after the walk from the car, the careful way she moved. She looked relaxed, strong, and so damn beautiful it made my chest ache.

"Feels good to be free?" I asked.

"Free and slightly uncoordinated, but yeah." She laughed and wiggled her toes. "I feel like a baby deer learning to walk again. Graceful is not in the cards yet."

"You get points for effort," I said, smiling over the rim of my glass.

"Oh, good, I live for participation trophies."

We both smiled, and for a few heartbeats, sat there in the quiet and comfortable silence. But there was something under it now. A low hum in the air, like the moment was holding still, waiting.

I set my glass down next to hers, hyper-aware of the space between us.

Shannon turned toward me, her head tilted and a few strands of hair slipped forward. Her eyes met mine, steady and curious, like she was reading every unspoken thought that had been swirling in my head for weeks.

My hand drifted to her thigh, slow and deliberate, and the hitch in her breath sent a jolt straight through me.

"I've been thinking about this all night," I said quietly.

"Me too."

And that was all I needed to hear.

I leaned in and kissed her deliberately, taking my time, savoring the moment we'd been circling for weeks. Her lips were soft, warm, and familiar, and the rest of the world faded away.

She pressed into me like she'd been waiting for this as long as I had. And when she kissed me back, it was sure, deliberate, and just the right amount of greedy.

Our mouths found a rhythm, slow at first, then deeper, more searching. I slid my hand to her waist and pulled her closer. She melted against me, every curve settling perfectly into place, as if we were meant to fit this way. Her fingers curled around the back of my neck, her thumb grazing under my jaw, sending a shiver straight through me.

The kiss deepened, like we'd both been craving it longer than we realized. I dragged my thumb over her nipple through the fabric of her dress. She moaned, low in her chest, and the sound hit me hard.

I cupped her breast and gave a gentle squeeze, and she arched into me. The kiss got hotter and hungrier until we were all hands and mouth and heat. I pinched her nipple between my fingers, and she gasped, threading her hands into my hair and tugging in a way that made me moan.

My cock throbbed against my zipper, and I shifted, trying to relieve some of the pressure. Sliding my hands down to cup her ass, I pulled her against me and opened my mouth wider over hers. She tightened her grip on my hair as our tongues tangled together.

The couch suddenly felt way too small for everything I wanted to do to her.

I pulled back to catch my breath, my forehead resting against hers. We were both breathing hard, our eyes locked, like neither of us was quite ready to break the spell.

She gave a breathless laugh.

"We should probably move this to the bedroom."

"Lead the way," I said, as I stood.

I held out my hand, and she slipped hers into it without hesitation. When she stood, we were close enough to feel each other's breath. Neither of us moved right away.

"You good?" I asked, voice low.

Her smile was a little shy, and a lot sure.

"Very."

We walked to her bedroom hand in hand, quiet but buzzing with anticipation. Warm light filled the room, and the bed looked soft and inviting.

My hands found her waist and then her back, pulling her flush against me. Her fingers gripped the fabric of my shirt, and I leaned down so she could tug it up and over my head. She tossed it to the floor, then stepped back, her eyes roaming over me like she was taking her time memorizing every inch. A slow smile tugged at her lips.

"Damn Andrew." Her fingers skimmed lightly down my chest, then traced along my abs like she couldn't help herself. "You've been holding out on me," she said, her voice low and appreciative, her tone a mix of reverence and teasing.

I let out a breath and closed my eyes for half a second, to savor her touch, her voice, and the way she was looking at me. My stomach tensed under her fingertips, the muscles tightening involuntarily like even they wanted to show off for her.

For several heartbeats, I enjoyed the feel of her hands, but if I let her keep going, it'd be over before we even started. I needed to take the reins, slow things down, and shift the focus to her.

I slid my hands to the hem of her dress and pulled it over her head in one clean motion, revealing a lace bra and matching underwear that did a number on my self-control. Through the years, I'd seen her in a bikini more times than I can count, but this is different.

"Christ Shannon…" My voice came out rough. I took a step back so I could look at her. "You're perfect."

Color crept to her cheeks, but she didn't look away. Instead, she sat on the edge of the bed, and reached for my belt. Her hazel eyes locked onto mine, steady and unflinching, little flecks of green and gold sparkling like a challenge. The leather sliding through the metal buckle sounded loud in the quiet room. My breath caught as she made quick work of the button and eased the zipper down, her knuckles grazing the hard ridge of my cock.

Her fingers lingered at the open fly of my jeans as she flashed me a slow, sexy smirk that said she knew exactly what kind of fire she was playing with. And for a second, I was ready to let her burn me.

Thankfully I still had at least one functioning brain cell, and I knew if she touched me the way I was pretty sure she was about to, it was game over. I couldn't let that happen.

So it was time to take charge.

I wrapped my fingers around her wrists, gentle but firm,

and stepped closer, nudging her knees apart. She wrapped her calves around mine as I bent to kiss her. It was slow for half a second, then turned hot and hungry.

Pulling back, I slid my hands under her thighs and shifted her toward the middle of the bed. I took a second to strip off my jeans, then followed her down. Our mouths met again, the kiss deeper this time, like the last few weeks had been nothing but foreplay leading us to this exact moment.

I settled against her only her lace panties and my boxer briefs keeping me from slipping right into heaven. She shifted beneath me with a little gasp, and the feel of her heat pulled a groan from deep in my chest.

Releasing her mouth, I trailed kisses down her neck, along her collarbone, letting my hands roam over curves I'd been dreaming about for too long.

I pressed a kiss to her stomach, then another a little higher, nipping gently at her navel. Her skin was warm beneath my mouth, and I followed the path upward, taking my time. When my mouth found the swell of her breast, I dragged my tongue over one nipple through the fabric of her bra, teasing until it strained beneath the lace. She arched and the sound that escaped her was low and needy.

"You're so damn beautiful," I murmured.

While my mouth worked over her right breast, my hand slid to the left, rolling the stiff peak between my fingertips. She bowed beneath me again, her hips shifting like she couldn't decide if she wanted to pull me closer or push me over the edge.

I shifted to the left breast, our eyes catching as I ran my tongue slowly around her nipple. She held my gaze as I spiraled closer, then sucked her in deep. Her hands fisted in the sheets, and all I could think was how I wanted to wreck her in the best way possible, one breathless sound at a time.

Reaching behind her, I unhooked her bra with one hand, sliding the straps down her shoulders like I'd done it a hundred times. She shimmied out of her panties while I peeled my boxer briefs off, watching the way her eyes tracked my every movement like she couldn't look away.

She was laid out in front of me, completely bare, and I took in the curve of her waist, softness of her belly, and strong lines of her thighs. I touched her slowly, reverently, my fingers tracing the path my eyes had just followed.

Moving my hand lower, I brushed the pads of my fingers along her core and explored, slow and steady, learning every slick, warm inch. I circled her clit with my thumb, featherlight at first, just enough to make her breath catch again. She shifted beneath me, tilting her hips, silently asking for more. Which I was more than happy to give.

I slid a finger into her, groaning when she clenched around me hot, wet, and so goddamn tight I nearly forgot how to breathe.

Adding a second finger, I stroked until she let out another one of those wrecked sounds that made my whole body tighten in response. Her hips lifted into my hand as her thighs eased fully apart, like her body surrendered to the fact that she was desperate for more.

"Yeah," I said, voice low as I watched her face, curling my fingers to make her gasp again. "That's what I was looking for."

She tightened around me, and I swore under my breath because nothing compared to this. The way her body responded like it had been waiting, needing. Every sound she made, every shift of her hips, it lit something primal in me and I couldn't hold back anymore.

I sank down between her thighs, lowered my mouth, and finally got my first real taste.

Holy. Fucking. Hell.

She was wet and warm and perfect, and I groaned against her like I was starving—because I was starving for her. My hands gripped her hips as I licked her slowly, deliberately, dragging my tongue against her, taking my time because she deserved every bit of pleasure I could give her.

"Andrew..." My name came out more as a sigh than a word.

I dipped my head again and moved my tongue slowly, teasing her with long licks and soft bites until I felt her hips lift searching for more. When I circled her clit, her breath hitched and she gripped my hair tight. Since she seemed to like that, I did it again and again and again.

Her thighs trembled, clamping around my head, while her heels dug into the bed like she needed something to anchor herself. I groaned low against her, the sound swallowed by the wet heat of her, and kept going. Long strokes, tight circles, the right pressure.

She squeezed again—this time around my ears—and it damn near broke me. Not from pain, but from how completely she was falling apart for me.

"Jesus, Shannon..." I murmured against her, not expecting her to answer, just needing to say her name, let her know how completely gone I was.

One of her hands fisted in my hair while the other gripped the sheets. Her breath came fast and shallow, and her hips rocked against my mouth like she couldn't get enough.

"Don't stop," she gasped, her voice trembling. "Don't you dare stop."

No way in hell was I stopping. Not with the way she was shaking, the way she moaned, or the way I needed to feel her come apart underneath me.

I pressed my tongue flat and worked her in tight, focused circles, curling two fingers inside her again and dragging them until she cried out, sharp and wild. Her whole body arched off the bed, as she pulsed around my fingers, slick and hot and completely unguarded.

Watching her come undone was the hottest thing I'd ever seen. Better than I'd imagined, and I'd imagined it more times than I care to admit.

I didn't move until I felt her start to soften beneath me, until her hand in my hair loosened and her body gave a little involuntary shiver that told me she'd had every last thought wiped from her brain.

When I finally lifted my head, she blinked down at me like she wasn't entirely sure what planet she was on.

"You okay?"

She blinked again and nodded.

"But I think I died for a second there."

I chuckled and kissed her inner thigh, then her hip, working my way back up. When I reached her mouth, she pulled me into a kiss that was slow and messy, all tongue and breath and emotion.

She sighed, lazy and satisfied, her fingers trailing through my hair like she never wanted to stop touching me. And hell, I hoped she didn't.

I hovered there for a second, taking in her flushed cheeks and parted lips. She blinked up at me, a little dazed and a lot satisfied, then her lips curved into a smile that just about knocked the breath from my lungs.

"Hey," she whispered.

I brushed a piece of hair off her cheek.

"You okay?" I asked again.

She nodded.

"Better than okay."

"You sure? You've got an I-just-saw-heaven look."

Her smile turned sly.

"You're way too cocky to be an angel."

"I prefer confident."

She tugged me down into a kiss, still smiling against my mouth.

"You're ridiculous."

"Maybe." I brushed my thumb along her cheek. "But you're stunning."

Her smile widened as her fingers slid into my hair again, a satisfied little sigh leaving her lips.

"I might be too blissed out to argue with you."

"Then I must be doing something right," I said, kissing her again, slow and sure, like a promise.

"Mmm, you definitely are," she said. "But I think it's your turn now."

Her hand closed around my cock, stealing the air from my lungs. She started slow, savoring every inch—firm enough to make my thighs tense, smooth enough to drag a groan from my throat.

"Shannon..." I groaned her name in warning, but I didn't stop her. Not yet.

She stroked me with a confident rhythm, her thumb brushing over the head, drawing a sharp thrust from my hips. My breath hitched, and I started mentally reciting anatomical trivia to keep from coming right then and there.

The average adult human has 206 bones and 27 of them are in the hand.

The human foot has 26 bones, 33 joints, and over 100 muscles, tendons, and ligaments.

The average human hand can exert a grip strength of 100 pounds.

Shannon was currently proving that last fact, because

the way she gripped my cock was borderline illegal in at least three states. Maybe four. My eyes rolled back for a second as she twisted her wrist in a way that made me forget what a femur was.

"Fuck," I rasped.

She smiled up at me, all flushed cheeks and wicked delight, like she knew *exactly* what she was doing. And she did. Of course she did. But one more stroke and it'd be game over.

I reached down and covered her hand with mine, so she stopped.

Her gaze flicked up to mine, curious and a little smug.

"Too much?"

"Too good," I said. "And I'm not trying to finish this before it even starts."

After pressing a quick kiss to her lips, I eased off the bed, taking a second to breathe and reset. My jeans were crumpled on the floor, and I crouched to dig through the back pocket, fishing out my wallet.

I found a condom, tore open the wrapper, and glanced over my shoulder just in time to catch her watching me with a bedroom-soft expression. Her eyes flicked down and she flashed a teasing grin.

"You carry those around all the time?"

"Not all the time, only when I'm hopeful."

"Was I such a sure thing?"

I smiled as I rolled the condom on and climbed back into bed.

"Not at all." I braced a knee on the mattress and leaned in. "But I was very, very, *very* hopeful."

Then I kissed her deep and slow, the kind of kiss that made it impossible to tell where one of us ended and the other began. Her arms wrapped around my neck, pulling me closer, her bare skin warm against mine. I shifted, letting my hips settle between hers, feeling the heat of her, the invitation in the way her legs parted to cradle me.

I pulled back and rested my forehead against hers.

"You still sure?"

She lifted her hips, a smile tugging at her lips.

"Andrew, please get inside me before I lose my mind."

"Well since you asked so nicely..."

I eased into her, savoring every second, every inch, until I was fully buried inside and the world shrank to her, me, and everything we'd been building toward. I held still for a beat, letting her breathe, letting us settle, my hand skimming over her hip as I kissed the corner of her mouth. When she shifted beneath me with a quiet invitation, I started to move.

And then we found a rhythm—slow at first, like we were learning each other from the inside out. It built, easy and instinctive, our bodies falling into sync without a single word. There was only heat, hunger, and a sharp, consuming need that left no space for anything else.

Shannon clung to me, her fingers digging into my back. I kissed her jaw, her mouth, the corner of her eye. Every time she whispered my name, I gave more. More pressure, more depth, more of me.

She hooked her legs around my waist and pulled me in deeper, and the last thread of restraint I'd been holding onto snapped. My thrusts grew harder, faster, driven by every sound she made and the way her fingers dug into my back like she never wanted to let go.

The air between us was thick with sweat and want, the mattress shifting as I drove into her over and over, chasing the edge we were both getting closer to with every breath, every sound, every thrust.

All I could focus on was the slick slide of our bodies, the heat between us, and the ragged edge of her breathing that told me she was right there with me. Every time I pulled back, I pushed in deeper.

She tightened around me and moaned my name, and that was it. I followed her over the edge with a groan, burying my face in her neck as we came undone together.

For a long while, I didn't move. I stayed there, breathing her in, my heart pounding like I'd run a damn marathon. Eventually, I pulled back enough to see her face, flushed, glowing, and completely wrecked in the best way. She blinked up at me with a satisfied look, lips parted like she was about to speak but couldn't quite find the words.

I kissed her forehead then rolled to my side, bringing her with me. She curled in close without hesitation, her head on my chest and one leg slung over mine like we did this all the time.

We stayed quiet for a while, her fingers trailing lazy circles over my stomach, then she shifted to look up at me.

"You were really quiet for a while."

"Was I?"

"Yeah." She looked up at me, eyes warm and curious. "I figured you were either having a spiritual experience or doing mental math."

"Close. Anatomical trivia."

"What?"

I hesitated, then shrugged.

"Some guys recite baseball stats or football rosters to keep from finishing too fast, for me anatomical trivia works." I grinned. "I was trying not to embarrass myself."

She laughed, the sound muffled against my chest.

"You *were* muttering."

"Not out loud."

"I swear I heard 'ligaments' at one point."

"You're making that up."

"Am I?" she teased, pressing a kiss to my chest.

I tightened my arm around her, grinning like an idiot.

She settled against me, totally relaxed, completely *here*, I knew this was just the beginning.

CHAPTER 14

Shannon

THE SECOND WE WALKED THROUGH THE DOOR, THE SMELL OF garlic and tomatoes wrapped around me like a hug. Andrew said his mom was making spaghetti and meatballs, and I came prepared, wearing a red shirt because I have zero trust in my ability to avoid a stain.

I'd been to dinner at his parents' house twice now, but today felt different, more familiar somehow. Like I wasn't a guest anymore.

Karli lit up the second she saw me.

"Are we still doing makeup today?"

"Absolutely." I held up the tote in my hand. "And I brought some goodies for you."

Maddy and Harper perked up immediately, both of them practically leaning over the kitchen counter to get a look.

"Wait, seriously?" Maddy asked. "Like what kind of goodies?"

"New palettes, lipsticks, brushes, a few sparkly shadows…" I trailed off, and Karli gasped like I'd just announced a world tour.

"*Sparkly* shadows?"

I grinned.

"I'd never show up without glitter."

"Best. Day. Ever," she declared, spinning in a little circle. "I call dibs on anything with glitter."

"After dinner," Andrew's mom said from the stove, not even turning around.

Then she glanced over her shoulder at us and smiled, wiping her hands on a dish towel as she made her way across the kitchen.

"Hi, sweetheart," she said to Andrew, kissing his cheek before pulling me into a quick hug. "Shannon, they've been talking about this makeup session for days, especially Karli."

Andrew leaned in and murmured against my temple, "I think you just became their favorite."

"Jealous?" I asked, grinning up at him.

"Maybe a little."

"Okay," his mom said, clapping her hands. "Spaghetti and meatballs are hot, the bread is warm, and there's salad for anyone who wants to pretend they're healthy."

Karli grabbed a chair and pulled it out like she'd been saving it for me. I sat with a smile, and she slid into the seat beside me, buzzing with excitement. Harper claimed the other side and they both immediately angled their bodies toward me like we were already in the middle of a conversation.

Andrew sat across from me and gave me a look that sent a little jolt straight to my stomach. Maddy dropped into the seat next to him, already leaning over to tell him something, but his eyes stayed on me for a second longer before he finally looked away.

The first time I'd come to dinner, I'd braced myself for awkward silences and small talk. But there weren't any. Now, it felt like sitting down with my own family.

Dinner was loud in the best way. We ate a ton of pasta, meatballs the size of my head, and way too much garlic bread, all while keeping up with a dozen conversations that somehow didn't miss a beat.

As soon as everyone finished eating, Maddy and Harper jumped up and took charge of clearing the table like it was a team sport. The guys disappeared into the living room, already yelling at the TV about some bad call before they even sat down. Claire and Maria wiped down the table, while Karli hovered nearby, practically vibrating with anticipation. I caught her shooting me looks every thirty seconds, like sheer willpower might speed things up.

"Okay, okay," I said. "Let's do this."

We gathered around the table again, only this time it was covered with makeup. They'd brought their own cosmetic bags packed with favorites, half-used palettes, and well-loved lip glosses. I added in what I had on hand, which was a lot.

I handed them each a brush set. They're nothing fancy, but solid quality. The girls stared at the table like I'd dropped treasure in front of them.

"I used to have a ton of stuff sent to me," I explained. "Most of it came from brands doing shoots with photographers I worked with—promo kits, samples, new product drops. Most of this has never even been opened, and if it has, it's barely touched." I shrugged. "I figured there's enough variety here so we can have some fun playing with color."

Karli stared at the table like she couldn't believe it was real.

"This is insane," she said. "It's like Christmas."

"Seriously," Maddy added, her eyes scanning the table. "Thank you for bringing all this."

"Yeah, this is so cool," Harper said.

Claire looked over the spread and let out a soft laugh.

"I wouldn't even know what to do with half this stuff."

"I'll show you," I said. "We're going to start with a super simple daytime look, something you can wear to work or school or brunch. Then I'll show you how to amp it up for a night out."

"I love that you think I go to brunch," Maria said with a chuckle.

"Or a PTA meeting when you want to feel like a badass. It all works."

They laughed, then leaned in, eyes scanning the table like they didn't want to miss anything. Even Claire, who claimed she was "low maintenance" was already swatching eyeshadow on the back of her hand.

"Rule number one: you don't need a million products to do a solid face once you know how to use what you've got."

Following my lead, they flipped open the light-up mirrors I'd also brought and angled them just right.

I walked them through moisturizer and primer first, then foundation, demonstrating on my own face, careful to go slow. I'd done this more times than I can count, but I remembered what it felt like to be new at it. To want something to look good and have no idea why it didn't.

Harper held up her foundation brush, and shifted her eyes from her mirror to me, frowning.

"Am I doing this right? I feel like I'm painting a wall."

"You kind of are," I said, gently correcting her angle.

"But a wall you love and want to hang art on, one you tear down."

"That's pretty deep," Karli said.

"It's a metaphor *and* a life lesson," I said with a smile.

They kept going, asking questions, getting more confident with each step. I showed them how to blend with a damp sponge, warm up their faces with a touch of bronzer instead of going full contour, and how to feather their brows for a natural look instead of drawing them on like cartoon villains.

When we got to eyeshadow, I passed around the neutral palette.

"This one's perfect for a quick look. Light color all over, medium in the crease, shimmer on the lid if you're feeling fancy."

"I'm always feeling fancy," Karli said, dipping into the shimmer.

"You're thirteen," Claire muttered, but her lips twitched.

I stood behind Maddy to show her how to hold the brush.

"Use soft windshield wiper motions. Think 'back and forth, back and forth.' Blend it out so it's seamless."

She bit her lip and tried again, and this time, it looked perfect.

"Okay, I don't hate this," Claire said as she checked herself in the mirror.

"You look amazing," I said.

Andrew's mom had pulled up a chair at the end of the table, watching with a soft smile, her hands wrapped around a mug of tea. She didn't say much, but I could tell she was enjoying every second of the girls all crowded around the table playing with makeup like it was a sleepover.

Behind me, the TV blared as the Waves loaded the bases. Ever since Keera and Simon got together and started hanging out with Anjannette and Leo, our whole circle has become fans of the team. Even Andrew, who isn't usually big on watching sports, paid attention now. Still, every time I glanced over, he wasn't watching the game, he was looking at me. His soft smile when our eyes met said everything.

It hadn't just been sex between us a couple weeks ago—it was a turning point. One that settled deep in my bones. I felt it now, in the way I laughed with his nieces, in how naturally I moved through his family's space. I hadn't realized how badly I'd needed something that felt this easy.

When I got to lips, I gave everyone two options...tinted balm for a natural look and a long-wear matte for glam.

"Okay," I said, as everyone admired their work. "Your final step is setting spray. Think of it as insurance for your face."

Karli grabbed the bottle like it was a sacred artifact.

"So I mist it on?"

"Exactly. Not too close unless you want to feel like you're walking through a car wash," I said, grinning. "Give it a couple spritzes, let it dry, and you're officially locked in."

She did as I said, then gave herself one last dramatic spritz and grinned.

"I feel unstoppable."

"You *look* unstoppable," Harper said, leaning toward the mirror for a closer look. "We actually look like we know what we're doing."

Maddy glanced at her reflection, then back at me.

"This turned out so much better than I thought. You made it easy."

Across the table, Claire angled her mirror and blinked at her reflection.

"I haven't looked this put together in…" she trailed off, then shook her head. "God, I don't even know."

Right?" Maria said. "My eyes look so big and open."

"This was such a treat," Andrew's mom said. "It's been fun to watch them."

"Thank you for letting us turn your dining room into a glam station," I said. "They've all been naturals."

"Well," Claire said, turning off her mirror, "some of us took a little longer to figure out how to blend, but we got there."

We all cracked up at her dry tone, the kind of laughter that settles into your chest and lingers long after. I started tidying up a few things but wasn't in any rush. The energy in the room felt too good to break. Karli was still snapping selfies, Harper was already planning her next look, and even Claire looked like she wasn't ready for it to end.

Maddy looked at her mom,

"This look would be nice for class night."

"It would," Maria agreed.

Maddy beamed, and I couldn't help but smile. This whole thing started as a fun little idea, something light and easy. But watching them now, laughing, glowing, and hyping each other up, I realized it had always been more than makeup. It was a bonding experience. And I soaked it all in.

"If you want," I said to her, "I can do your makeup for prom. Hair too, as long as you're not thinking full bridal glam. I'm decent at curls and basic updos."

Her head snapped toward me.

"Seriously?"

"Totally serious. It'll be fun."

"I was actually thinking I wanted it curled," Maddy said, twirling her fingers to mimic loose waves, "and then, like—"

she motioned around her forehead, pulling invisible strands upward, "the front pulled up kind of soft?"

"I can definitely do that."

"That would be amazing." Maddy came around the table and hugged me. "Thank you."

I smiled and pulled out my phone.

"Alright, give me the date. I'm putting it in my calendar." She rattled it off, and I tapped it in, adding a little lipstick emoji next to it for fun. "You're officially on my glam schedule."

"Ugh, I wish I had prom so you could do mine," Karli said dramatically, slumping into her chair.

"Don't worry," I said, teasing. "By the time it's your turn, I'll be even better. Maybe I'll have a studio by then."

Claire snorted.

"Or a reality show."

"'Shannon Saves Prom,'" Maria added, and the girls all cracked up.

The banter kept going, light and easy, as everyone started picking through the makeup still scattered across the table. Palettes were opened and compared, lipsticks swatched on hands, brushes claimed like prized treasures.

Karli immediately zeroed in on anything sparkly. Harper pulled a nude gloss from the pile and held it up to her face, checking it in her mirror. Claire and Maria went back and forth over a rose-toned palette until Claire rolled her eyes, handed it over, and muttered something about being the bigger person.

I watched them laugh and hype each other up, everything between them so easy. And somehow, being there with them felt exactly right. I'd never been this comfortable around a boyfriend's family before, not even close. Hell, I hadn't even met the families of half the guys I'd dated.

The game ended with a final cheer from the living room, breaking through my thoughts. I heard footsteps on hardwood, then Andrew leaned in the doorway, arms crossed, watching like he didn't want to interrupt.

His gaze found mine, and that familiar smile tugged at the corner of his mouth.

"You taking new clients?"

I tilted my head.

"Depends. Are you looking for a soft glam or something bold?"

He laughed and stepped closer, his hand brushing the back of my chair as he slid into the seat beside me. It was a small touch, but enough to make my heart trip over itself.

"You know you raised the bar for all future dinners here, right?" he said.

"Good," I said, tying my brush roll. "I like being hard to top."

"You always are."

He said it so casually, like he wasn't even trying to be charming, but somehow still was.

And there it was again, the quiet pull in my chest I kept trying not to name.

I'd been falling for him for weeks. Not in some big, dramatic way, but in the small moments. The steady ones that snuck up on me when I wasn't looking.

And now, I wasn't falling anymore, I'd landed.

ANDREW

· · ·

The sun was already high by the time we pulled into the lot at Lackawanna State Park. I glanced over at Shannon in the passenger seat.

"You ready for this?" I asked as I turned off the engine.

"I watched a YouTube video, does that count?"

"Of course it does." I said. "But I'm sure you'll be fine. I'll be right there to help you."

She slid her sunglasses down her nose and looked at me over the top of them.

"Promise not to laugh if I end up paddling in circles."

"No promises." I bit back a smile. "Especially if you make it look cute."

Her eyes narrowed, but the corner of her mouth twitched.

"Careful, Bowen. I might flip your kayak on purpose."

I opened the center console and I dropped my phone inside.

"We won't be out that long, so I wasn't going to bring my big dry bag."

"Then I better leave mine here too. I don't trust myself to not end up in the water."

She set her phone on top of mine and before I shut the lid, I grabbed the waterproof pouch I keep stashed in there. I dropped my key fob inside, sealed it tight, then looped the strap around my neck so it rested flat against my chest.

"Simon and Archer have come kayaking with me several times. If neither of them ended up in the water, you should be fine."

We got out of the car and I looked around. The water glinted beyond the trees, calm and steady, like it had been waiting for us.

I reached for the tie-down straps, my fingers working through the familiar routine as I loosened the first one.

"You need help?" she asked, shielding her eyes to look up at me.

"I'm good," I said, loosening the second strap. "This is where being tall comes in handy."

She laughed.

"So basically, I'd be completely useless."

"Not completely," I said, glancing down at her. "You've got excellent moral support energy."

I slid the first kayak down and leaned it against the side of the car, then walked to the other side to grab the second. Once both kayaks were resting side by side, I popped the hatch of the Outback and grabbed the life jackets. I handed one to Shannon and she slipped it on, then struck a dramatic little pose, one hand on her hip, chin tilted up like she was modeling for the cover of *Vogue*.

"You look beautiful," I stepped close and kissed her. Just a quick one, but enough to feel the smile tug at the corners of her mouth. "Like a very sexy park ranger who's about to ticket me for unsafe paddling practices."

She raised an eyebrow.

"Are you unsafe?"

"Not yet," I said, grinning. "But I might forget how to steer if you keep looking at me like that."

After grabbing the paddles out of the car, I shut the hatch.

"Alright. Now we're ready."

"Let's do it."

She picked up one of the kayaks and set off on the trail toward the lake slowly, careful with her footing. I followed behind her, doing my best to focus on the lake, the trees, the fluffy white clouds in the impossibly blue sky. But instead, my eyes locked on her ass in those little black athletic shorts. The curve of her hips, the sway of her ponytail, and the fluid way her bare legs moved kept my eyes locked on her and nowhere else.

Because nature is beautiful, but Shannon is something else entirely. She's like some kind of siren song specifically designed to destroy my concentration and, if I wasn't careful, my dignity. The last thing I needed was to roll up to the launch half hard.

As we reached the lake, she glanced back at me over her shoulder, eyes bright, cheeks flushed from the walk.

"You good back there?"

I nodded, smiled, and tried to sound normal.

"Yeah. Just taking in the view."

Her eyebrow lifted like she knew exactly what I meant and wasn't mad about it.

We set her kayak in the water first and I steadied it as she climbed in.

"Okay," I said, kneeling beside her. "Keep your knees slightly bent, and try not to lock your hips. It'll feel weird at first, but you want some flexibility so you don't feel every shift in the water."

She nodded, gripping the paddle.

"Got it. Loose hips, firm core. Sounds like half the workout classes I've taken."

"Exactly." I slid my own kayak into the water beside hers and climbed in. "And if you can climb a pole, you can definitely do this."

"I appreciate the confidence."

"Now follow me out a bit," I said, dipping my paddle into the water. "We'll stick to the edge for a while." I pushed off with one easy stroke and turned to look back at her. "Take slow, even strokes. Don't worry about speed, think more gliding, less splashing."

"So graceful, but with core strength?"

"Exactly. Which means you're probably going to show me up in the first five minutes."

She followed, a little wobbly at first, but she caught on fast.

We paddled in tandem, her strokes becoming more confident the farther we got from the shore. I kept an eye on her, making sure she wasn't shifting her weight awkwardly or pressing too hard with her feet. But she looked relaxed, strong, and completely in the moment.

"This is actually fun," she said after a while, a little surprised.

"I told you. It's the perfect balance between being active and floating around."

"You just like that it's quiet and no one can text you out here."

"Also true."

We drifted for a while, laughing, racing in short bursts, occasionally bumping paddles and exchanging mock glares. When she asked how to steer better, I paddled around and demonstrated, guiding her through a turn. Her brow furrowed in concentration, but when she nailed it, she pumped a fist in the air.

"Okay," she said. "Now I'm feeling pretty badass."

"You are a badass."

After about a half hour of paddling around, I glanced over at her.

"We should probably head back."

"Boo! I was starting to hit my stride," she said, sticking out her bottom lip in the sexiest pout I'd ever seen.

I laughed.

"I know, but you've been sedentary for a couple months, and I don't want you waking up tomorrow feeling like you got hit by a truck."

"Alright," she sighed. "But I think you're scared I was about to leave you in my wake."

"Exactly," I said. "Let me preserve my dignity while I still have it."

She gave me a mock-sympathetic pat on the air between us with her paddle.

"You're doing amazing, sweetie."

Shaking my head, I chuckled as we turned back toward the launch, our boats gliding side by side through the sunlit water.

I paddled in a little ahead of her, climbed out, and dragged my kayak up onto the shore. By the time she reached the edge, I was there waiting. I held out my hand to help her up, steadying her as she climbed out. She gripped my shoulder, her body close to mine as she got her footing.

"Thanks," she said, brushing a damp wisp of hair from her face.

I leaned in and kissed her temple.

"I've got you."

We stood there for a moment, water lapping gently at the shore around us. Then she bumped my arm with her elbow, her smile tugging at the corner of her mouth.

"Let's get back to the car before my body figures out it's been exercising and stops working in protest."

She picked up her kayak and I followed her back to the parking lot. I lifted the kayaks onto the roof rack and once they were secure, I turned toward her and smiled.

"Now, it's time for ice cream."

As I pulled out of the parking lot, Shannon reached for her purse, unzipped the front pocket, and pulled out a brush. She yanked the elastic from her ponytail and shook out her hair, then ran the brush through it with steady, practiced strokes.

I caught a glimpse of her pulling everything back into a sleek ponytail, securing it tight. Then she leaned her head against the seat and let out a slow breath.

"I had so much fun. My arms are gonna hate me tomorrow, but it was totally worth it."

"You did great. Minimal circles," I said, throwing her a grin. "No injuries. You didn't even capsize."

"That's a pretty low bar, Andrew."

"And yet, I'm proud of you," I said, bumping my shoulder lightly into hers as the road opened up into wide stretches of farmland.

She smiled then looked around at the scenery.

"I like it out here," she said after a while, eyes on the horizon. "It's peaceful."

"It always kind of resets me. Reminds me of who I am when I'm not in a white coat or writing progress notes."

She turned to look at me, soft and curious.

"And who is that?"

I thought about it for a second.

"Someone who likes quiet mornings, cold pizza for breakfast, and this girl he used to have a crush on who made his whole week by trusting him enough to paddle out onto a lake with him."

Her lips parted slightly, but she didn't say anything.

I turned onto Manning Road and parked under a big maple tree near the fence and turned off the engine. She unbuckled and slowly looked around.

"I remember coming here as a kid," she said.

"Me too."

We stepped out of the car and walked hand in hand toward the walk-up window and joined the short line. Shannon tilted her head, studying the menu board like it held the answers to life's big questions.

"Too many good choices," she murmured. "Why does this feel like a high-stakes decision?"

"Because it is." I smiled. "But honestly, I don't think there's a bad choice."

When it was our turn, she ordered a scoop of peanut butter crunch in a waffle cone. I went with caramel critter.

"Caramel critter, huh?" Shannon asked as we found an empty picnic table in the shade and settled across from each other.

"I like to mix it up," I said. "But when I was a kid, I got strawberry pretty much every time I came here." I licked my cone and smiled. "My family used to hike at the park most Sundays when I was a kid and I hated it. The ice cream afterwards made it bearable though."

"You hated hiking? Didn't you, Simon, and Archer always go?"

"Yeah, I kind of learned to love it as I got older. And now I appreciate those afternoons even if I whined the whole time."

"I can't imagine you whining."

"Trust me, I did. But mostly because Bobby and Claire turned every hike into a sibling hazing ritual," I said. "They're eight and ten years older than me, so growing up, it felt like it was them against me."

"So they picked on you because you were the baby?"

"Yeah, and because I'm the oddball of the family."

"In what way?"

"Bobby and Claire both excelled at sports. I hated organized sports and pretty much anything that made me put down my gaming controller." I chuckled. "Bobby always says my height is wasted on me, and if he was six-four, he'd be playing in the NFL or MLB."

"But Bobby is tall."

"He's six feet on a good day."

"Yeah, that's short," she said, rolling her eyes.

"Apparently it is for pro sports."

She shrugged.

"You know, I always liked having you over when we were younger. You and Archer always fit right in."

I looked down at the table, then back at her.

"Yeah, your parents accepted us for who we were...nerdy kids who wanted to talk about *Star Wars* and argue about video game strategy."

"They are pretty great," she said. "Even when we were teenagers and my friends complained about their parents, I knew mine were different. Simon and I are total opposites, but they never made us feel like we had to be anything but ourselves."

"That's probably why you were always so nice. Even though you were the most beautiful girl in school, you were never a mean girl."

She laughed softly and looked down at her ice cream.

"I don't know about the most beautiful."

"I do."

We ate in silence for a minute, the quiet broken only by the occasional sound of kids running nearby and the distant hum of a car passing on the road. The kind of peace that didn't need filling.

Then she glanced over at me, a small smile tugging at the corner of her mouth.

"So...you mentioned a crush?"

I raised an eyebrow, fighting a grin.

"I did mention that, didn't I?"

She licked her cone, pretending to think it over.

"So was it like a passing thing, or a full-on teenage pining situation?"

I laughed at her teasing tone.

"Somewhere between a passing thing and a full-blown inability to make eye contact with you."

"I had no idea," she said, then her mouth curved into a sexy smirk. "What about now?"

I thought about it as I popped the last of my cone into my mouth and chewed.

What started as a soft, hopeless thing I carried around for years, had grown into something I couldn't file away as a childhood fantasy anymore.

It wasn't just her beauty, her kindness, or the dry, razor-sharp humor that always caught me off guard. It was the way being with her felt easy, steady, and right.

Somewhere along the way, the old crush turned into something real.

I wiped my hands on a napkin and looked over at her.

"Now?" I said, meeting her eyes. "Now it's not a crush." Her brows lifted slightly, but I didn't look away. "It's more. *You're* more."

Shannon's expression softened, like she hadn't expected me to say that, but she welcomed it. She didn't say anything, just smiled, slow and soft and a little dangerous.

And damn if it didn't make me want to tell her right then, surrounded by sticky-fingered kids and the smell of waffle cones, that I was completely in love with her.

But I didn't. Not yet.

Instead, I let the moment stretch out between us and let it be enough.

For now.

CHAPTER 15

Shannon

Despite all the time we'd spent together, I still hadn't set foot in Andrew's place.

With my busted ankle and the giant boot, climbing stairs or being anywhere without a dozen pillows and a footstool wasn't exactly an option. After that, we were always at my place, his parents' house, or somewhere in between.

But now I was here, standing in the hallway of his building with a Tupperware container full of brownies in my hand.

He opened the door before I could knock, looking like a snack—barefoot, wearing low-slung jeans and a soft gray T-shirt clinging to his chest like it had a personal vendetta against my concentration.

"Hey," he said, then leaned down to kiss my cheek.

"Hey." I held up the container. "I brought dessert."

"Is that what I think it is?"

He stepped aside, and I walked into his apartment as he closed the door behind me.

"Depends. Were you thinking about the brownies I used to make that you, Archer, and Simon inhaled like feral raccoons?"

"Exactly those."

"It smells amazing in here," I said.

He took the container from my hands, set it on the counter behind him, then pulled me in by the waist and gave me a proper kiss.

When he pulled back, I was still trying to catch my breath. My brain felt foggy in the best possible way, like he'd short-circuited every thought I'd had the second his lips touched mine.

"I made chicken strips in butter and garlic," he said.

"Wait." I blinked at him, a little dazed. "What?"

He smirked.

"Exactly the reaction I was going for."

"You can't melt my brain with a kiss, then casually bring up chicken and expect me to keep up."

"I'm just glad I can 'melt your brain with a kiss,'" he said, using air quotes around the last six words.

I chuckled and looked around. His apartment was not what I expected. In the best way.

"I like your place."

The loft was open and airy, with high ceilings and huge windows. One wall was exposed brick, the other painted a rich navy that somehow made the space feel warm instead of echoey.

In the center of the room, a dark leather couch faced a wall-mounted TV. Below, a Nintendo 64 sat like a crown jewel of nerd nostalgia. Next to it, a GameCube, a PS5, and Xbox.

I walked over to check out his floor-to-ceiling bookshelf. It was packed tight with sci-fi paperbacks, some vintage *Star Wars* novelizations, and a row of Stephen King titles. One shelf held retro game cartridges perfectly lined up like museum pieces. A Lego Millennium Falcon sat inside a plexiglass display case on top, angled to look like it was mid-launch.

"Wow," I said, turning in a slow circle, taking it all in. "I always knew you were a nerd, but this is next level."

He raised an eyebrow.

"That sounded like a compliment."

"It is. This place is the real deal. People try to fake this kind of vibe on Instagram. Yours is nerdy in the best way. Smart and lived-in with slightly intimidating shelving."

"Well thank you," he said, then gestured toward the table. "Dinner's ready."

I walked over and blinked. He'd actually set the table with cloth napkins and real placemats, like this was date night in a rom-com. Two plates of pasta sat waiting, piled high with chicken strips sautéed in garlic butter. It looked amazing.

Off to the side was a big bowl of salad and next to it a cruet of Good Seasons Italian dressing, which is my favorite.

"You cooked," I said, eyebrows raised.

"I told you I was going to."

"Yeah, but you also folded napkins. This is a whole event."

He smirked.

"Only the best for my favorite girl."

As we ate, we traded stories about our day the way we always did. He'd had surgery in the morning, then rounds and a string of appointments at the office. I told him about the two boudoir clients I'd glammed up—one nervous, the other extremely confident—and how I was still brushing glitter off my arms.

The food was perfect...simple, cozy, and somehow still kind of swoony. And maybe it wasn't fancy, but it hit in a way nothing else ever had.

No one had ever cooked for me before. I'd been taken to Michelin-star restaurants, ordered tasting menus with wine pairings and everything in between. But a guy making me dinner from scratch in his kitchen because he wanted to was a new experience.

My grandmother always said the way to a man's heart was through his stomach. Sitting there, full, warm and a little gooey inside, I had to admit the reverse was definitely true. There was something about being cooked for thoughtfully and intentionally that hit in a way I hadn't expected.

After we cleaned up, we curled up on the couch with a plate of brownies to watch *Guardians of the Galaxy*. The movie has all the nerdy vibes for him and is funny enough to keep me entertained. Plus, the soundtrack is total perfection.

I curled into his side, legs tucked up, head resting on his shoulder. He wrapped an arm around me, his fingers drawing absentminded circles on my hip. We stayed like that for a long time, warm, full, and quiet.

About halfway through Peter Quill's first dance number, I felt his gaze shift to me.

"What?"

"Nothing," he said, brushing my hair back behind my ear. "I just like having you here."

I leaned up and kissed him, soft at first, but then his mouth tilted into mine, and it wasn't so soft anymore. Everything else faded away—the movie, the brownies, the rest of the world. All I could focus on was the heat of his hands and the way he kissed me like he meant it.

Before I could think twice, I climbed into his lap, resting my knees on either side of his thighs. Warm hands slid beneath my shirt, reacquainting himself with something he already knew by heart.

He pulled back a little, his eyes finding mine like he was checking in. I didn't say anything, I didn't need to. Whatever he saw there must've been enough because he dipped his head and brushed his lips along my neck, slow and deliberate. When he reached my collarbone, he lingered for a beat before gently nipping, enough to send a jolt straight through me. I curled my fingers into his shoulders, and he smiled against my skin.

"I like your place," I whispered.

"Yeah?" His lips skimmed up my neck, then he pulled back and looked at me. "You want to see more of it?"

"Absolutely."

His hands slid down to my ass and he stood, lifting me with him like it was nothing.

I let out a breathless screech, then instinctively wrapped my legs around his waist and arms around his neck, holding on as he grinned like he'd been waiting for this moment forever.

His room was clean, calm, and put-together in a quiet, understated way that felt very him. The bed was made, of course, and a lamp cast a soft glow over the well-read paperback on the nightstand. A hoodie was folded neatly over the back of a chair, like he'd tidied up but still lived here.

He started to guide me back toward the bed like he meant to ease me down onto it, but I wanted to be in charge tonight. I moved back, then gave him a gentle push. He caught on fast, and dropped to the edge of the mattress with that crooked little grin I loved, like he was already enjoying where this was going.

I stepped between his knees, rested my hands on his shoulders, and leaned in close enough to feel his breath catch.

"Tonight it's my turn," I said, soft but certain.

The way his eyes darkened in response let me know he was all in.

I reached for the hem of his shirt and tugged it up. He raised his arms without a word, letting me peel it off him. My hands followed the path down his body, tracing over his shoulders, chest, the dip of his abs. It was familiar territory, but one I never got tired of exploring.

Then I dropped to my knees between his legs and looked up at him. He watched me, eyes dark, hands clenched at his sides like he was trying not to touch me.

I popped the button on his jeans, eased the zipper down, and slid my fingers beneath the waistband. He lifted his hips and I slid both his jeans and boxer briefs down in one steady motion.

I rested my hands on his thighs and leaned in. When I looked up, our eyes locked, and I didn't look away as I dipped my head and licked up one side of his cock, then down the other, deliberately slow, savoring the way his breath caught. He let out a low, wrecked sound that went straight through me, and shot a curl of heat straight through my belly. I did it again, just to hear it one more time.

Opening my mouth wide, I took him in, alternately sucking and rolling my tongue around the tip, teasing him like it was something I'd been craving all day. Then I wrapped my hand around his base, taking him in deeper, inch by inch, until the head of his cock brushed the back of my throat. I paused there, letting him feel all of it before starting to move up and down with a little swirl of my tongue at the top before starting all over again. Each stroke was deliberate, my lips and hand working together, teasing and coaxing.

The muscles in his thighs tensed and his groans went straight through me. The sound and the way his body responded only made me want to give him more. His fingers slid into my hair, curling tight as I sucked him over and over again.

"Shannon."

He tightened his grip and tugged.

I pulled back, releasing him with a soft pop then sat back on my heels, my hand still wrapped around him. He looked like he was barely holding it together, which is exactly where I wanted him.

He sucked in a shaky breath, chest rising like he was still catching up. Then his eyes locked on mine, and without saying a word, he tugged my shirt over my head and flung it behind us. Lacing his fingers through mine, he gave a gentle tug, guiding me to my feet. His eyes never left mine as he undressed me slowly, like he was unwrapping something he'd been waiting for and wanted to savor.

Then his hands were on my ass, like when he picked me up and carried me into the bedroom. He gave a quick tug, guiding me down onto him as he shifted back against the pillows. I settled over his thighs, straddling him, my palms pressed to his chest.

He reached into the nightstand, grabbed a condom, and held it out to me.

I took it with a grin, tore it open, and rolled it onto his cock, loving the way his breath hitched as I did.

"Still good?" I asked, even though I already knew.

"Better than good," he said, voice rough.

Holding his gaze, I sank down, inch by inch, until he was fully inside me, stretching me in the best possible way. My breath caught. His jaw clenched. We stayed still, savoring the feeling of how good we fit, how deep he went.

"Fuck," he muttered, eyes dark. "You feel so damn good."

I smiled, already breathless.

"You too."

I started to move, rocking my hips, rolling forward enough to make us both feel it. He didn't guide me, didn't rush, just held me there, his grip firm on my ass as I found my pace. Up and down. Slow then faster, grinding against him when I reached the bottom, chasing the ache that had been building since the second he touched me.

His fingers flexed, digging in a little as I moved harder, riding him with purpose.

"You're gonna kill me," he groaned, his head tipping back against the pillow.

I leaned forward, palms flat on his chest.

"Not planning on it," I said, my breath hitching. "But if this is how you go..."

He laughed, low and rough, then bit his lip as I picked up the pace again, bouncing now, my movements messier, hungrier. The pressure built fast and low, and a tingle started at my spine spread outward, curling into my fingertips, tightening in my thighs. I was so close it almost hurt.

"Come for me, Shannon," he whispered.

His words broke something open in me. I shifted the angle, held him deep, and ground my hips against him, my clit catching just right. I did it again, faster this time, losing myself in the rhythm of each roll of my hips. His hands gripped tighter, anchoring me as I moved, riding the wave building low and hot in my belly.

One more thrust, and everything snapped. I cried out,

clenching around him as my orgasm tore through me, wave after wave hitting harder than I was ready for. I barely had time to come down before I felt him throb inside me, his grip tightening on my ass as he let go with a low, broken moan, his hips jerking up against me.

I dropped forward, breathless and shaky, collapsing against his chest. He wrapped his arms around me, holding me tight like he needed the contact as much as I did.

We stayed like that until our heartbeats returned to normal. I shifted to the side, rolling off him with a quiet sigh. He pressed a kiss to my shoulder before slipping out of bed and disappearing into the bathroom to take care of the condom.

By the time he came back, I was tucked under the covers, warm and content. He climbed in beside me and pulled me in, his chest to my back, arms wrapping around me like I was his favorite part of the night.

"You good?"

"Mmm hmm," I said, smiling into the pillow. "Not gonna lie...I kind of liked being in charge."

He chuckled and kissed my shoulder.

"I noticed."

"We might have to make that a regular thing."

He tightened his arm around me and brushed his lips against the back of my neck.

"Please do."

I closed my eyes already planning the sequel.

Andrew

. . .

I woke up with her in my arms and couldn't help but smile.

Shannon was still asleep, back pressed to my chest, her breathing soft and steady. My arm was draped over her waist, fingers resting lightly on the hem of the T-shirt she'd pulled last night. My T-shirt. I remembered the way it had looked when she first slipped it on, like it belonged to her all along.

The sun hadn't fully made its way across the loft, but the soft morning light was already creeping through the windows, casting a pale gold glow on the sheets, on her skin, on the quiet stillness between us. Everything in me settled.

Last night had been simple. A homemade dinner, her signature brownies, and a movie we half-watched because we couldn't stop kissing on the couch. And now she was here, tangled up in my bed like she belonged there.

I closed my eyes again and breathed her in. She smelled like coconut shampoo and something soft and warm... maybe her lotion or maybe it was just her. I'd spent years sprinting through mornings chugging coffee, rushing to rounds, scanning emails before my brain was even fully awake. But she made me want to savor the moment.

Eventually, I eased my arm out from under her. She made a soft, sleepy noise and shifted slightly, but didn't open her eyes. Yeah, she's still not a morning person.

I slipped out of bed, pulled on a pair of gym shorts, and padded barefoot to the kitchen, stretching my arms overhead. The loft was quiet, still holding onto the peaceful hush of early morning. Traces of the perfume Shannon wore last night still lingered in the air, and I liked it.

Opening the fridge, I scanned the shelves for breakfast options. I found bacon, a couple of eggs, and milk. With a half loaf of bread on the counter, I have everything I need for French toast. And yeah, that happened to be Shannon's favorite. Sometimes, the universe handed you a win without asking.

I started the coffee first. Measured the grounds, filled the reservoir, and hit the start button all on autopilot. The low hum of the machine filled the quiet, anchoring the space in routine.

But the space wasn't just mine this morning. Shannon was still here. Her purse sat on the counter, her shoes rested near the door, and her sleep-warm body was still tangled in my sheets. And I liked that way too much.

While the coffee brewed, I opened my laptop and skimmed through my inbox. There were a few messages from the office and one from the patient portal, but none were urgent. I shut it again and headed back to the kitchen.

I'm not due at the office for a couple more hours, and right now, all I wanted was to make breakfast and soak up a little more time with Shannon before letting the real world in.

I opened the fridge and pulled out the eggs, milk, and bacon, then grabbed the loaf of bread from the counter.

After pouring myself a cup of coffee and taking a quick sip, I dropped the bacon onto a skillet and set it on the stove. I cracked the eggs into a bowl, added milk, cinnamon, and a little vanilla extract, whisking until it smelled like something worth waking up for. I set the first slices of bread into the egg mixture to let them soak.

Behind me, I heard her bare feet padding across the hardwood floor, quiet but unmistakable. I didn't turn around as I listened to the sound of her footsteps.

"Good morning," I said as I finished flipping the bacon.

"Morning," she mumbled, her voice thick with sleep.

I turned around, and there she was with her hair twisted

into a messy bun, eyes still heavy with sleep, wearing nothing but my T-shirt.

She blinked at me like the light had personally offended her.

"You look...wow." I shook my head, smiling. "Yeah, that's all I've got right now."

Her brows lifted, and she rubbed at her face.

"I literally just woke up. I'm a mess."

"I disagree."

That got a sleepy little smile out of her. She crossed the room and wrapped her arms around me from behind, her cheek resting against my bare back as I added a slice of soaked bread onto the hot griddle.

"It smells incredible in here," she said.

"French toast used to be your favorite."

She gave a soft hum, her fingers brushing across my stomach before letting go.

"Still is."

"Good," I said as I turned to face her. "Would you like some coffee?"

"I'd give my right arm for some."

"There's no need for sacrifices." I pointed toward the cupboard above the coffee maker. "Mugs are in there. Help yourself."

She grabbed a mug from the cabinet, and filled it with coffee. Then she grabbed the milk and added a splash before setting it back on the counter.

The steam curled around her face as she took a sip.

"Okay, that's really good," she said. "I had no idea you were so domestic."

"After last night and this morning, you'll have pretty much witnessed the full extent of my culinary skills, unless you count boxed mac and cheese and the occasional late-night ramen masterpiece."

She gave me a look over the rim of her mug.

"Mmm, I don't buy it. You're way too comfortable in the kitchen for a couple things to be your whole repertoire."

I shrugged, fighting a smile.

"Comfortable doesn't mean skilled."

"Sure," she said, taking another sip.

"But it usually means there's a few go-to recipes stashed up your sleeve. You've got secret-risotto-guy energy and surprise stir-fry-on-a-Wednesday-night vibe."

I laughed.

"Now you're making up imaginary meals."

"And you're not denying them."

"You'll have to spend more time here and find out."

"Is that your way of asking me to stay over more?"

"If it worked, then yeah."

She shook her head, smiling into her coffee like I'd caught her off guard in the best way.

A soft sizzle from the skillet reminded me the bacon was teetering on the edge of perfectly crisp and burned beyond saving. So I turned back to the stove, flipped a few strips, and plated up the French toast while she grabbed silverware and napkins like she'd done it a hundred times before.

A few minutes later, we settled at the table, a platter of French toast and bacon between us.

"So," she said as she cut into her toast, "last night was kind of amazing."

"Yeah?"

"It was comfortable and cozy, and fun."

I nodded as I took a bite of bacon, chewing slowly, letting her words settle.

Some of my past relationships had cracked under the pressure of mismatched expectations. I liked going out once in a while, sure, but I also liked quiet nights in, long hikes, bike rides, and things that didn't require a dress code or a reservation.

"That's exactly what I was hoping for," I said, looking over at her.

She smiled and picked up another piece of French toast, placing it on her plate before reaching for the syrup.

We eased into lighter conversation, with no big declarations or heavy topics. Just the kind of back-and-forth that felt natural and easy.

Afterward, we cleaned up together. I loaded the dishwasher while she rinsed and handed things to me. As I wiped down the counter, she leaned against it, still holding the dish towel, like she wasn't quite ready to let the morning end.

"I really loved last night, Andrew," she said, her voice quieter now.

I froze for a second, my eyes on her. The way she said it, like it wasn't only about dinner or the movie or the night. It felt bigger, like she was talking about *us*. About me.

Setting the towel down, I turned and stepped closer, reaching out to tuck a loose strand of hair behind her ear. Her eyes didn't leave mine.

"I love you, Shannon."

For a second, she didn't say anything. She looked at me with those wide, steady eyes like she was taking me in, piece by piece. Then she set the dish towel on the counter beside her and reached for my hand.

"I was hoping you'd say that," she whispered, fingers lacing through mine.

She leaned in and I closed the distance and kissed her, soft and sure, like the truth had settled between us and finally found its place. When we pulled apart, she smiled up at me, warm and a little breathless.

"And so you know," she said, "I love you too."

Her words settled deep, into a place I didn't know had been empty until she filled it.

I pulled her in again, slower this time, my hands wrapping around the small of her back. She rested her forehead against my chest, and for a moment we stood there, wrapped in the kind of quiet that said everything without a single word. The kind you don't get often, and when you do, you hold on.

This wasn't just a good morning, it was the beginning of something I never wanted to end.

CHAPTER 16

Shannon

THE PLAYLIST DRIFTING THROUGH THE BACKYARD WAS CLASSIC Dad—yacht rock, Jimmy Buffett, and the occasional 80s hair band thrown in just to prove he still had edge. Honestly, I found it comforting. Predictable in the best way, like sunscreen, grilled burgers, and the scent of chlorine clinging to your skin after a long swim.

Andrew's arm brushed mine as we sat at the table, both of us digging into plates loaded with cookout classics.

"Your mom still makes the best macaroni salad." He leaned closer. "But please don't tell my mom I said that."

"Your secret's safe with me," I said, then mimicked locking my lips and throwing away the key.

Near the pool, Simon waved a half-eaten hot dog like it was a whiteboard marker, arguing some dramatic point. Archer countered with even bigger gestures, nearly launching his bun into the grass. Keera sat under the umbrella, her eyes hidden behind oversized sunglasses as she very clearly pretended not to know either of them. Near the pool, Anjannette dipped her toes in the water, talking to Mirabelle who was doing the same next to her.

Mom and Dad moved easily among everyone, checking coolers, offering seconds, and slipping in and out of conversations like they were hosting a backyard wedding instead of a casual Sunday cookout.

Afternoons like this had a way of making everything feel lighter. Like the world pressed pause for a few hours so we could breathe. I couldn't even count how many days we'd spent back here growing up. It was the kind of comfort you didn't have to think about, it lived in your bones.

I nudged Andrew with my elbow.

"Remind me why we're supposed to talk about wedding stuff during a cookout?"

"Because you and Anjannette are both Type A and you're afraid we need supervision planning Simon's bachelor party."

"True. Also, she's trying to get our spa weekend locked in. Hershey, remember?"

"The one with chocolate massages?"

"Yep. Facials, scrubs, massages, wine tastings," I said. "And if she has her way, matching satin pajamas."

He tilted his head.

"I could be into that."

"Not for you."

"I meant on you."

I rolled my eyes, but my cheeks warmed anyway.

"You know," he said, glancing at me, "if you all get matching outfits for the spa weekend, it's only fair we show up to Galaxy's Edge in full costume."

"Matching Jedi robes?" I offered, mostly as a joke, but I should have known better.

Before Andrew could answer, Simon called out from across the yard, "Way ahead of you. They're already ordered."

I blinked. "Wait—seriously?"

He finally looked over, smug as hell.

"I have robes for everyone. Coordinated colors. It's going to be a whole thing."

I stared at him, trying to gauge if he was joking, but honestly, with Simon, it could go either way.

"You're the best man," I said to Andrew. "It's your job to rein him in."

"But what if I don't want to?"

I shot him a look over the rim of my drink.

"You might want to rethink that. You're going to Orlando in August."

He winced.

"Fair point. I'd like to survive Galaxy's Edge without heatstroke."

"If you two are done canoodling over there, maybe we can discuss wedding stuff," Anjannette said as she pulled her feet out of the pool and stood.

"Okay, wedding mode activated," I said, with a grin.

"Let me throw these out first," Andrew said, grabbing our empty plates.

"I'll grab us drinks," I offered, heading for the cooler.

That was all it took for the group to mobilize. Everyone took the chance to toss paper plates and empty cups, grab another drink, and stretch a little in the late-afternoon sun. I bent over the cooler and fished out a watermelon High Noon for myself and cold beer for Andrew, who was walking back from the trash can.

Chairs scraped against the patio as everyone pulled up seats and settled in. The ladies sat at the table and the guys filled in around it. Mirabelle slid into a seat next to Archer. Andrew sat beside me, casually resting his arm along the back of my chair, bumping his knee against mine like he couldn't help it.

Simon dropped into a chair across from us, next to Keera, and gave us a look somewhere between amused and mildly unsettled.

"I'm not gonna lie, it's still weird seeing you two like that." he said, pointing his beer in our direction.

Andrew glanced at me, then back at Simon.

"Like what?"

Although he knew exactly *what*.

"All cozy and flirty." Simon said. "And you keep gazing at each other."

"Oh no, not gazing. Call the authorities," Keera said around a chuckle.

He rolled his eyes at his fiancee, then kept going.

"I'm just saying it's an adjustment," he said, directing his word to Andrew. "You've been part of the family forever, but now it's like...*this.*"

Andrew smirked.

"Would it help if I sat farther away?"

"No," Simon said immediately. "Because then you'd *look* at her from across the table, and I'd have to deal with that too."

I laughed.

"So by being together, we've completely thrown you off?"

"Pretty much," Simon said, with a crooked grin. "It's not bad, just different."

Andrew leaned in, his voice warm and close.

"I think that's as close to a blessing as we're getting."

I smiled, but something tugged at me under the surface. Simon and I had never actually talked about Andrew and me. Not really. There'd been jokes, plenty of sibling-level teasing, but nothing spelled out how he actually felt.

Simon pointed between us.

"Exactly. Give me a minute, alright? My best friend dating my sister requires some rewiring."

"But we're worth the effort," I said, keeping it light even as my heart beat a little louder.

"Absolutely."

Anjannette jumped in, clearly ready to get things moving.

"Bachelorette plans are almost finalized," she said. "Spa treatments are booked, dinner reservations are set, and I'm looking for somewhere to have brunch before we leave on Sunday."

"We'll have time for chocolate martinis, right?" I asked, grinning as I took a sip of my drink.

"Obviously," Anjannette said, eyes on her phone where she had a checklist pulled up. "We'll also have matching robes, silk pajamas, and slippers. Not to mention a highly curated playlist."

"Are we doing anything low-key?" Keera asked, raising an eyebrow. "Like sitting in a hot tub and talking shit?"

Anjannette didn't even look up.

"Of course. With snacks."

"Sold," Keera and I said in unison.

"Anna texted and said that whatever we decide is fine with her and Kevin," Anjannette said, speaking about Keera's brother and sister-in-law.

Mom and dad emerged from the house and made their way over.

"Did we miss anything important?" Mom asked as she slid into the seat Dad had pulled over for her.

"No shower stuff yet, just bachelorette plans," Keera

said, then smiled. "Unless you changed your mind and want to join us."

Her voice lifted on the last word, teasing but hopeful.

"No, I'll leave the bachelorette fun to the bridal crew," she said. "I'll expect full details when you get back, though. Preferably with photos and a little harmless scandal."

"Done," Anjannette said, then pointed at Andrew. "Okay, best man. You're up. Give us the rundown."

Andrew chuckled and leaned back in his chair, casually resting one arm along the back of mine.

"I don't have a checklist, but I'll do my best," he said. "We have a direct flight from Avoca to Orlando Friday afternoon. We'll hit Disney Springs for dinner that night, Saturday is Galaxy's Edge. We have a reservation to build custom lightsabers at Savi's Workshop and dinner reservations at Oga's Cantina. Then we're drinking around the world in Epcot on Sunday. The plan is to have a drink and snack in each country, and have dinner at Le Cellier Steakhouse in Canada. Then we fly back Monday morning."

Simon lit up with his every word.

"I still can't believe we're actually building lightsabers."

"Fully customized," Archer added. "I've already decided mine's going to be green. Classic Jedi Knight energy."

"Mine's going to be purple," Simon said. "Samuel L. Jackson style."

"What about you?" Archer asked Andrew.

"I'm not sure yet," he said. "I'll decide when I'm there."

"Let me guess," Archer said, "you're waiting until the last possible second to decide, hoping the crystal speaks to you?"

Andrew shrugged.

"What can I say? I'm letting the Force guide me."

Simon snorted.

"Right into overthinking the hilt design for three hours."

I looked around at them.

"You guys do realize these aren't *real* lightsabers," I said. "Like they don't actually work aside from lighting up."

"That's exactly what someone without a high midi-chlorian count would say," Simon said, then leaned back, looking smug. "But honestly, this is the most on-brand bachelor party I could've asked for—lightsabers, cocktails, *Star Wars* everything. It's perfect."

Andrew looked at Anjannette and smiled.

"How'd I do?'

"Well it looks like the groom is happy, so I'll give you a B+."

"Not an A?"

She shook her head.

"If you'd actually made a checklist, I would have given you the extra points."

"Wow. Harsh, but fair."

Talk shifted from lightsabers and logistics to bridal shower planning.

"We're moving on to shower stuff," Keera announced, waving the guys off like a benevolent queen. "You're officially excused."

They were up and moving before she even finished the sentence, muttering something about Mario Kart as they disappeared inside. I stood and followed, heading to the bathroom while they went downstairs.

When I came back out, Andrew was in the kitchen, grabbing bottles of water from the fridge. He turned, spotted me, and that soft, crooked smile of his hit me like a punch to the chest.

Without a word, he set the bottles down, slid one arm around my waist, pulled me in, and backed me against the counter as his mouth found mine. I kissed him back, my hands gripping the front of his shirt, the counter cool beneath me and his body warm and steady against mine.

Then we heard a throat clear.

We jumped apart like guilty teenagers. My dad stood in the doorway, one brow raised, clearly amused.

"It's a good thing this didn't start fifteen years ago," he said casually. "I'd have had to sleep outside your bedroom door with a baseball bat every weekend."

My entire body flushed. Apparently, no matter how old you are, it's still embarrassing getting caught making out by your dad.

He walked past with a grin, patting my shoulder on the way to the bathroom like he hadn't permanently scarred my dignity. I didn't even look at Andrew, but I could feel the secondhand awkward radiating off him.

Once the door clicked shut behind my dad, Andrew exhaled dramatically.

"Think he'd be open to pretending that never happened?"

"Not a chance," I said with a smirk. "This'll come up at every family party for at least the next five years."

Andrew groaned.

"Awesome."

"Hey," I said, bumping his hip as I handed him the water bottles. "At least he didn't ask you what your intentions are."

He dragged a hand down his face.

"Don't give him ideas."

I chuckled and gave him a quick kiss.

"Go play your video games."

"Gladly." He started backing toward the basement stairs. "But for the record? Even if he does bring it up every chance he gets to bust our asses, it was totally worth it."

I watched him head downstairs then went back outside grinning like an idiot.

ANDREW

Mondays at the walk-in clinic always had a pace of their own—steady, unpredictable, and just this side of chaos. Between weekend warriors who waited too long to get checked out and people who couldn't snag an appointment with their regular doctor, there was never a dull moment.

By ten o'clock, I'd already seen a teenager with a fractured clavicle from a skateboarding fall, a guy who tore his meniscus playing basketball with his kids, and a woman who finally came in to get her "sprained" ankle looked at and it was actually fractured.

Between patients, I reviewed X-rays, dictated notes, and stopped by the nurse's desk to drop off an insurance form I was given to fill out. Sarah stood there, tapping her index finger against her tablet like it had personally offended her.

"Tablet giving you attitude?" I asked, setting the form down in front of her.

"It's not responding right. I tap one thing, and it jumps somewhere else entirely. It's like trying to chart with a Magic 8-Ball. It only shows me whatever it wants to."

I chuckled.

"Have you tried threatening it?"

"I'm about two taps away," she muttered, narrowing her eyes at the screen. "That or smashing it."

"As tempting as that is, I'm sure it would be frowned upon by IT," I said with a smirk.

Sarah let out a sigh and set the tablet down on the counter with a little more force than necessary.

"There are other ones to use, I know. It's annoying when the tech decides to rebel mid-shift. And I'm not letting it win."

I nodded in sympathy.

"Tech tantrums. The real Monday vibe." I glanced at my watch, more out of habit than anything. "My clinic shift's over. I've got about an hour before my first office patient, so I'm heading to the cafeteria to grab something for lunch. Can I get you anything?"

She shook her head.

"No, but thanks. I brought leftover lasagna from last night."

"Well, enjoy," I said. "I'll see you tomorrow."

I tapped my knuckle on the counter and turned to go, but she stopped me.

"Hey, Andrew?"

I glanced back.

"Yeah?"

She looked at me for a second, brow furrowed like she was trying to puzzle something out.

"Something's different about you lately."

"Different how?"

"You've been smiling more and seem happier. I think I even heard you whistling last week." She crossed her arms over her chest and flashed a smug smirk. "You're either in love or joined a cult."

I opened my mouth to deny the whistling, then paused. I couldn't swear under oath that I hadn't been.

She grinned like she knew exactly what I was thinking.

"Whatever's going on looks good on you."

And the truth was, it felt even better.

I let out a quiet laugh and rubbed the back of my neck.

"Is it really obvious?"

She raised her eyebrows like it wasn't even a question.

"You've got a whole content-and-glowy vibe going on." She rested her elbows on the desk and leaned forward. "So...you gonna tell me who she is?"

I couldn't help the smile that tugged at my mouth.

"Her name's Shannon."

"I *knew* it. You've had a stupidly-happy look for weeks now." She tilted her head. "How'd you meet her?"

"We've actually known each other for a long time. She's my best friend's sister."

"That's straight out of a rom-com."

"I guess." I shrugged. "She moved back to town a few months ago, and somehow it turned into more."

"And now you're glowing," Sarah teased, pointing at me like she'd solved a mystery.

"Apparently," I said with a laugh. "Guess it's hard to hide."

She winked.

"Go eat before all the chocolate chip cookies are gone."

"Will do. See you later," I said.

I headed to the cafeteria, still smiling.

The afternoon settled into a familiar groove—post-op check-ins, a few cortisone injections, and the usual questions about when patients could get back to golf, tennis, or, in one guy's case, competitive axe throwing. One consult turned into an impromptu anatomy lesson when a patient's teenage daughter started asking questions about the shoulder joint. She said she wanted to be a surgeon someday. I liked that. Curiosity was underrated.

I'd finished dictating my last patient's notes when my phone vibrated.

You up for dinner tonight with Simon and Keera?

Definitely.

You didn't even ask what restaurant.

Doesn't matter.

The dots started and stopped three times before her response came through.

Pick me up at six?

See you then.

Love you.

Love you, too.

I wasn't lying when I said it doesn't matter where we go. As long as she's there I'm good.

We'd gone kayaking again, taken a bike ride, and spent more than a few nights with takeout and a movie on the couch. We weren't casually hanging out anymore—we'd fallen into a real relationship routine. It felt good, settled, like we were building something one small moment at a time.

After seeing my last patient, I packed up for the night. My laptop bag slung over one shoulder, keys in hand, I stepped out into the early evening sunlight and headed for the parking lot.

That's when I caught myself whistling. Actually

whistling some random, upbeat melody I hadn't even realized was coming out of my mouth. I laughed quietly and
shook my head, the sound echoing in the space between
rows of cars.

I'm not sure I've ever randomly whistled before. But I
guess it shows just how happy I am.

Things with Shannon made me feel like I'd stumbled
into the version of my life that was always meant to exist.
The one with weeknight dinners with friends, her stealing
half my fries, making me laugh without even trying. The
one where falling asleep next to her felt like home, and
waking up the same way felt even better.

I unlocked the car, tossed my bag into the passenger
seat, and slid in behind the wheel, still humming.

Yeah, I was happy, and I wasn't trying to hide it. Not even
a little.

CHAPTER 17

Shannon

Tuesdays at Italo's were basically a sacred ritual sealed in tequila and guac. We always spend the night eating tacos, sipping margaritas, and talking about everything and nothing until we're too stuffed to move.

With Anjannette in Myrtle Beach for Leo's home stretch, it was just Keera, Sophie, and me tonight, but we still ordered enough food for a small army.

Sophie was telling us about one of her beginner pole students, eyes wide, hands flailing for emphasis.

"So she tried to spin on the static pole, but forgot to grip, and—" Sophie made a whirling motion and mimed falling flat. "Boom. Straight onto her mat. And she laid there like a fainting goat."

Keera nearly choked on her guac-covered chip.

"Please tell me there's video."

"Oh, absolutely. She posted it on Instagram."

We all lost it, laughing so hard I had to grab my napkin to wipe my eyes. Nights like this, with friends, tacos, and complete emotional safety were my favorite.

When the laughter died down, I reached for a chip and said, "God, I miss pole class. I can't wait to get back."

Sophie's smile dimmed a little.

"Any idea when you'll be able to come back?"

"Not for another three to six months," I said. "I'm praying it's closer to three."

"That sucks," Keera said with a frown.

"It does," I agreed. "I mean, the boot's off, and I'm mobile, which is amazing. But I miss how strong I felt on the pole, you know?"

Sophie reached across the table and squeezed my hand.

"It's frustrating, I know, but you want your ankle to heal right. Don't rush it. Pole will still be there when you're ready."

I smiled and took a sip of my margarita, trying to keep the mood light. I didn't want this to turn into a pity party. Especially not when I just started feeling like myself again.

Somewhere between our second taco and Sophie arguing that guacamole should be considered its own food group, I remembered something.

"Oh Keera! I found some pictures of Simon on an old flash drive."

Her brows lifted hopefully.

"Embarrassing pictures?"

"Not full-on blackmail material, but definitely peak awkward phase. Braces. Too-big graphic tees. That one haircut he swore looked cool but absolutely did not.

"Send them." Keera clapped her hands. "All of them."

"I'll do it now so I don't forget again." I opened the folder

I'd put them in and selected the ones I thought she'd like most and texted them to her. "I can make you a copy of the flash drive so you have all the others, too."

Keera flipped through the photos, alternating between bursts of laughter and soft awws. Then she angled her phone toward Sophie.

"Wait, is that Andrew and Archer?" Sophie asked.

Keera turned the screen toward me, and I nodded.

"Yep, in their matching *Star Wars* pajamas holding plastic lightsabers. They took it very seriously."

Sophie took a sip of her margarita, set the glass down, and grinned.

"You know what we should do?" she said. "Make a slideshow for the shower. Like a full-on, embarrassing-but-cute montage."

Keera narrowed her eyes suspiciously.

"Of Simon?"

"Of both of you," Sophie smirked. "I have a feeling Granny Vi and your mom have some real gems of you tucked away in scrapbooks somewhere."

Keera groaned and dropped her head into her hands.

"They absolutely do. There's one of me in a pink cowboy hat and plastic heels that haunts me to this day."

Sophie wiggled her eyebrows.

"Exactly the energy I'm looking for."

Keera lifted her head and pointed at her.

"If I agree to this, I get veto power."

"Done."

While they were still laughing over the photos, I scrolled through the folder to see if there were any other gems worth sharing. Nothing jumped out. I was about to set my phone down when a new email notification caught my eye. I tapped it open without thinking, more out of habit than anything else.

The subject line caught my eye...*Opportunity at Sable West – Training & Education Manager, L.A.*

It could've been spam. I get messages all the time with supposed job offers that promise a lot of money for minimal work. But something in my gut told me this was legit. With a deep breath and slightly shaky fingers, I tapped it open.

Hi Shannon,

I hope you're doing well. I'mSableWest's Talent Acquisition Manager, and you were recommended to us by Oliver Ryan, who spoke highly of your talent and passion for makeup artistry.

We're currently growing our Training & Education team in our Los Angeles office, and I believe your experience and creative energy would make you a fantastic addition. This role plays a key part in bringing our products to life in the field.

As Training & Education Manager, you would:

- Design and deliver hands-on training for our retail artists and staff, in both classroom and in-store settings
- Lead product workshops and seasonal masterclasses to deepen team expertise
- Create engaging training materials—slides, videos, technique guides—aligned with SableWest brand standards
- Collaborate across departments (Retail, Marketing, Product) to launch new collections through our training programs

Would you be open to a quick 15-minute chat to discuss this opportunity? I'd be happy to share more about SableWest's vision, our brand mission, and how we support our creative educators.

I'm excited about the possibility of working together.

Warm regards,

Tiffany Palmer

Talent Acquisition Manager

Sable West Cosmetics

tiffany.palmer@sablewest.com | (323) 555-1234

www.sablewest.com

The breath whooshed right out of me, and I sat back, blinking like maybe I'd misread it. But nope. There it was, clear as day, sitting in my inbox like it hadn't tilted my whole world sideways.

"What's wrong?" Keera asked.

"Nothing," I said quickly, setting my phone down but not flipping it over.

"Your whole vibe changed," Sophie said with narrowed eyes.

She wasn't lying. I could feel it in my shoulders, in the way my brain had suddenly veered off the road of tacos and margaritas and dropped straight into the land of what ifs.

If I told them, it would make the email more real. But if I didn't tell, I'd be sitting here pretending I wasn't freaking out inside. And I didn't want to do that, either. And honestly, if anyone could help me make sense of it all, it was them.

I exhaled slowly and looked up.

"Okay, fine. I got an email from Sable West about a job."

Both of their heads snapped toward me at the same time, like I'd just said Pedro Pascal slid into my DMs.

"Wait, like *the* Sable West?" Keera blinked. "Your holy grail brand?"

I nodded, pressing my palms flat against the table to ground myself.

"Yeah. I don't have all the details yet, but they said I was recommended by a photographer I used to work with."

"Shan, that's huge," Sophie said.

"I know." My throat felt tight. "It's an amazing opportunity."

"Then why do you look like someone ran over your favorite lipstick?" Keera asked.

I glanced down at my phone, like it was ticking and about to detonate my entire life.

"The job is in Los Angeles."

Keera's brows shot up so fast I was surprised they didn't fly off her face.

"The one in California?" she asked, like maybe there was another one I'd forgotten about.

"Shan, that's huge," Sophie said.

"I know."

"But it's in L.A.," Keera said gently.

"I know that, too."

The mood at the table shifted. It wasn't exactly dark, but definitely heavier. The kind of weight that came with knowing things might change.

Sophie flashed a forced smile.

"Jamie and I did long distance for about a year," she said, obviously trying to be supportive. "It wasn't easy, but we made it work."

"Jamie was in New York," Keera pointed out. "Not three thousand miles away."

"We're getting ahead of ourselves here," I said, trying to

keep my voice steady. "It was only a recruiting email, not an actual offer. I haven't even responded yet."

"Are you going to?" Keera asked.

"Yeah. I mean, I should at least see what they're offering."

"You'd be crazy not to," Sophie agreed.

"I'll read it again when I get home and message them back."

I tried to keep smiling, to focus on the lingering scent of cilantro and lime, the sound of laughter from another table, the hum of music overhead. But my mind kept spinning between L.A., a dream job, and Andrew. Add in my friends and family and I was basically a human Tilt-A-Whirl.

The image of Andrew leaning over my kitchen counter, coffee mug in one hand and half-eaten brownie in the other, flashed into my brain. We'd fallen into such a good rhythm. Waking up together, cooking dinner, binge-watching TV, and arguing over plot twists. He felt like home.

"But this? An opportunity at Sable West, my favorite brand since middle school. The chance to work with them wasn't just big, it was scream-into-a-pillow huge."

I looked up to find both Sophie and Keera watching me with matching expressions of concern, support, and the smallest flicker of fear.

I forced a smile.

"I'll keep you posted."

"We'll be here for you," Keera said.

"Whatever happens," Sophie added.

Keera watched me for a second, then asked, "Are you gonna tell Andrew?"

A knot twisted low in my stomach. I took a sip of my margarita, mostly to stall.

"I will," I said. "I have to...I want to wait until I know more."

Sophie raised a brow.

"How much more?"

"They want to set up a fifteen-minute call to talk about the role and see if I'm even interested. I'll take it from there."

Keera nodded slowly, her expression softening.

"Sounds like a good plan."

Neither of them pushed, and I loved them for it.

We gathered our things and stepped out into the warm night air. The scent of citrus and grilled tortillas still clung to my clothes, and would probably make my car smell like taco night for days. But right now, even that felt comforting.

For most of my life, all I wanted was to leave Scranton. I used to lie awake in high school dreaming of somewhere bigger, louder, glossier. I thought success meant skyscrapers and coastlines I didn't grow up with. And I'd achieved that dream. I lived in Manhattan for ten years.

But now the idea of leaving twisted something low in my gut. Not just because of Andrew—though he was a huge part of it—but because of everything. My friends. My family. This town suddenly didn't feel like a detour, but a destination.

"You okay?" Keera asked as we reached our cars.

"Yeah, it's a lot to think about."

And it was.

The kind of *a lot* that didn't come with instructions. That settled in your chest like a weight and stretched the edges of your world in opposite directions.

Eighteen months ago, I would've been over the moon to get an interview request from Sable West. I would've prayed for it. Manifested it. But things are different now. Or maybe I am.

Because for the first time in forever, I wasn't trying to get away from anything.

I was building something with Andrew, my friends, and this version of myself I actually liked. And if I chased one dream, I might have to let go of the one I never saw coming.

ANDREW

I HAD AN EARLY SURGERY IN THE MORNING, WHICH MADE FOR A long day, even by my standards. As I left the office, all I could think about was dinner, a couch, and Shannon.

We'd been trading off shows lately, binging series we thought the other might appreciate. *Fringe* had been my pick. She enjoyed the weird science and alternate timelines and we finished watching the series last week. Now it was her turn and we're starting *Outlander*. She says it has time travel, historical drama, and some pretty explicit sex scenes, so I'm intrigued.

I went to knock, but the door was already swinging open before I could lower my hand.

"Hey," she said, a soft smile tugging at her lips, warm enough to melt every thought out of my head.

I stepped inside and kissed her hello, slow and unhurried, because there was nowhere else I'd rather be. Her hands slid up my chest and looped behind my neck, holding me there for a second longer, like maybe she needed it too. Eventually, we pulled apart, her fingers trailing down my chest as she stepped back with a smile that didn't quite reach her eyes.

"Come on," she said, taking my hand and leading me toward the kitchen. "Let's eat while everything's still hot."

The table was covered in takeout containers and a few paper-wrapped bundles I could only assume were Texas wieners.

"Are they from Green Ridge News?"

"Of course." She smiled as we settled across from each other at the table. "I know they're your favorite."

"I know that's practically hot dog heresy around in this city," I said, unwrapping one of the bundles. "Everyone swears by Coney Island, but I think Green Ridge News has them beat."

She handed me a napkin, grinning.

"You've always been loyal to the underdog."

"Damn right," I said. "And these taste like weekend gaming tournaments and midnight *Star Wars* marathons at your house."

"So basically, the food equivalent of a core memory."

"Exactly." I looked across the table at her, my chest going soft in a now-familiar way. "And you remembered."

"Of course I did," she said, then nodded toward the rest of the spread. "There are also fries—gravy for me and cheese for you—and a tray of pizza."

"There's a lot of food here for two people."

She shrugged.

"I know you like cold pizza for breakfast."

I leaned across the table and gave her another kiss.

"You know me too well."

As I settled back in my seat, I caught something. A beat of distance behind her smile. Like she was trying too hard to keep things light. I shook it off, figuring I was imagining things.

"So how was your day?"

"Long," I said. "But this morning's surgery went well, and all the post-op patients I saw today are healing well, so all in all, it was good. How about yours?"

"Pretty uneventful." She shifted in her seat, reaching for her drink. "I washed clothes, cleaned the apartment. Nothing major."

She smiled when she said it, but something in her tone tugged at the back of my brain. Her words were too careful, too composed. And for someone claiming the day had been boring, she sure wasn't making much eye contact.

I didn't say anything, but the feeling stuck with me, quiet and persistent, like a song playing under the noise. It followed me through dinner, through throwing away empty containers and rinsing plates. By the time we settled on the couch, it was still there, pressing at the edges. I couldn't pretend not to notice anymore.

"Is everything okay?"

She angled toward me, her gaze meeting mine. Her expression was tight, like she was working through what to say, or whether to say it at all.

"There's something I need to tell you."

Everything in me stilled. Like my body knew something big was coming and wanted a head start bracing for it. I didn't say anything, just sat there and waited.

"I got a job offer," she said finally. "Well, not an offer exactly. A recruiter from Sable West emailed me yesterday and I had a call with them today. They're hiring a training and education manager, and a photographer I used to work with recommended me for the job." A breath hitched in her chest, and she looked down at her fingers twisting in her lap like they had the words she couldn't quite say. Then her eyes came back to mine. "They want me to fly out to L.A. for a formal interview and see the office, meet the team."

I blinked.

Sable West.

The name hit like a punch.

Los Angeles.

That hit even harder.

"Wow." I swallowed. "That's big."

"I know."

"So, when are you going out there?"

"In the next couple weeks."

I kept it together on the outside, but inside, it felt like the floor gave out beneath me.

"It's a good opportunity?" I asked.

She nodded.

"But like I said, nothing has been decided," she said.

I gave her a small smile, even though my chest still felt tight.

"Well, if they've got any sense at all, they'll offer you the job. You're incredible."

"If they do, we can figure things out. Sophie and Jamie did the long-distance thing for almost a year. She said it was hard, but they made it work."

I nodded slowly, but the comparison didn't land right. Not because I didn't believe in us, but because I knew the logistics.

"Jamie was in New York, though. That's a two-hour drive, not a cross-country flight."

The silence that followed wasn't angry or cold, just full. Packed with everything we weren't saying, and all the things I wasn't ready to hear.

"Would you ever consider moving to L.A.?"

"I don't think so."

"Not right away obviously. We'd have to date a little longer before making a decision so big."

I shook my head.

"No."

Her brows knit.

"Just...no?"

"I like it here," I said. "I like being close to my family. I've never had the itch to leave like you did."

"But you lived in Arizona for residency."

"Yeah," I said. "And those were the longest five years of my life. Especially when my mom got diagnosed with breast cancer halfway through. I wanted to defer a year and come home, but she wouldn't let me. She said I needed to finish what I started."

Shannon reached for my hand, lacing her fingers through mine. Her thumb brushed across my knuckles, gentle and steady as I continued.

"I hated being so far away from her. From everyone. I missed birthdays and family dinners and stupid things like helping Dad fix the snowblower. I don't want to do that again."

She didn't say anything right away, just held my hand a little tighter. Her eyes were glossy, like she was blinking back everything she didn't want me to see. Or maybe didn't want to feel.

"I don't want to mess this up," she whispered. "You and me."

"Shannon, I love you." I slid my free hand to her cheek, brushing my thumb along her jaw. "I love you so much it scares the hell out of me sometimes, but I'd be miserable out there. I'm not an L.A. kind of guy."

She closed her eyes for a beat, then leaned into my hand.

"I know," she murmured.

"But all that being said, *when* you get offered the job, we'll figure it out." I leaned in and rested my forehead against hers. "Because losing you is the one thing I know I could never handle."

That earned me a soft kiss. Then she reached for the remote and hit play on *Outlander*, and the haunting theme music kicked in.

The show didn't waste any time dropping viewers into the past. Claire was in World War II-era England, then bam, 18th-century Scotland. I half focused, catching the gist of the setup while Shannon curled against my side like it was any other night. But it didn't feel like any other night. Not with what she'd just told me.

Her head rested on my shoulder, her fingers gently tracing patterns on my thigh. I kept my arm around her, holding her close, hoping it grounded both of us.

I wanted to believe we'd figure it out. That the job might not pan out. Or the distance wouldn't matter if it did. And love really could be enough.

But part of me knew better.

I couldn't imagine not having her in my life, but I also couldn't picture myself in Los Angeles, sweating in traffic and missing Sunday dinners while pretending video calls made up for being gone.

Maybe I'm being too negative. After all, Anjannette and Leo made it work. But he was also home for months at a time during the offseason, and even in-season, he was often playing within driving distance. And when there was a home stretch in Myrtle Beach, she'd go down for a week or more, and they'd have real time together. Built-in breaks. Proximity. A plan.

Shannon and I wouldn't have any of those things.

But if we're really determined to be together, we'll do it, right?

I mean, Claire Fraser had crossed through ancient

stones and traveled two hundred years into the past to be with her true love. Surely I could manage flying across the country.

I kissed the top of Shannon's head and pulled her closer, letting the sounds of the show fill the space between us. We were okay for now. But the future was coming, and when it got here, we'd either make it work or learn how much love could bend before it broke.

CHAPTER 18

Shannon

Tall buildings gleamed outside my hotel window. Glass giants framed a skyline floating above gridlocked streets—L.A. alive in daylight. I'd landed last evening and checked into the Conrad, too distracted to take in much more than the glow of the streetlights and the blur of palm trees as my rideshare wound through the city.

Now, bathed in morning sun and coffee-fueled nerves, it all felt more real.

This trip wasn't a vacation, brand event, or even a training gig—it was a three-day pitch. Their chance to see if I was the right fit. My chance to figure out if I could really picture myself living here.

The weight of it all pressed in as I walked back to the bathroom.

Tiffany's text came through as I was giving myself a final once-over in the mirror.

Car will arrive in 10 min.

I looked back at my reflection, happy nothing was wrinkled, stained, or out of place. It's been a while since I had to look this professional and I'm a little out of practice. But I think what I put together for today works.

I'd gone with a structured blazer over a white silk blouse with a subtle abstract print and tailored charcoal trousers that hit right at the ankle.

I'd treated myself to a Brazilian blowout before flying out yesterday, so my hair cascaded over my shoulders smooth and sleek. And it should behave for the rest of the trip too.

For my makeup, I'd gone for a full look complete with dewy skin, soft contour, a subtle rose-gold shimmer on my lids, and a crisp winged liner sharp enough to cut glass. My lip color is a warm nude with just enough sheen to look effortless. Every product was from Sable West's latest collection, of course. If I was going to sell it, I had to wear it like I meant it.

A smile tugged at my lips. If I don't get this job, it's not because I don't look good.

I slipped into my six-inch black Louboutins. I'd debated on wearing them, but they always made me feel like a badass. I'm sure I'll be nursing a sore ankle later, but the confidence boost will be worth it.

Purse in hand, I took one last breath, and headed down to the lobby.

As I stepped outside to wait, the heat wrapped around me, warmer than I thought it would be based on the temperature, but not unbearable.

A sleek black SUV pulled up and it wasn't hard to guess it was mine. Tiffany had mentioned in the itinerary she had emailed a few days ago that I'd be picked up by a black Escalade.

As I stepped forward, the driver climbed out and circled to the sidewalk.

"Ms. Parker?" he asked, reaching for the door handle.

"That's me," I said, tucking my hair behind my ear.

He opened the door, and I slid into the back seat and was greeted by a rush of cold air and Tiffany Palmer's bright, polished smile.

"Good morning!" she chirped, looking every bit the West Coast professional in tailored trousers and oversized sunglasses pushed up into her glossy waves. "Did you sleep okay?"

"Like a rock," I lied, offering a smile as I buckled in.

The truth was I'd tossed and turned for hours, my brain cycling through all the what-ifs this trip carried with it. But as we pulled out into the street, Tiffany launched into a rundown of the day ahead, and I shoved my doubts and nerves aside as the city passed by in a blur of possibility.

"When we get to the office, I'll introduce you to the team, show you around a little bit, and then you'll meet with a few department heads. Nothing formal, just the usual 'let's see if we click' kind of chat." she added, which I'm guessing was code for still bring your A-game.

Entering Sable West's lobby felt like stepping inside a giant camera lens. Everything looked sharp, reflective, and poised. I wondered if it was too late to pretend I was sick. Although I wouldn't be totally pretending. My stomach was in knots and my coffee from earlier was threatening to reappear.

But instead of focusing on that, I straightened my spine, squared my shoulders, and followed Tiffany toward the elevators like I belonged here. Even if I wasn't totally sure I did.

The next two days passed in a blur of polished conference rooms, curated conversations, and smiles that felt a bit too tight. I met with department heads, toured training spaces, sat in on a product launch brainstorm, and even got walked through their onboarding platform like I was already halfway to being hired.

They took me to lunch each day, and we ate outdoors on fabulous patios where the umbrellas were chic and the salads cost more than most people's weekly groceries. But I couldn't deny it, the energy around the team was electric. Everything about the job...the innovation, the momentum, and the way they talked about beauty like it was both art and science...lit something up in me.

At night, they whisked me off to flashy rooftop spots with skyline views, artisanal cocktails, and the whole curated L.A. experience. They kept calling me words I used to chase like impressive and visionary,

And I *was* flattered. At least, part of me was. Another part wanted to lie down in a dark room and just breathe.

The weird thing was, two years ago, I would've eaten it up, every bite of it. Every name-drop and neon-lit elevator ride. Back then, this would've been the dream. Now I had some doubts. Maybe I'd been out of the corporate game too long. Or maybe it wasn't only the game that had changed.

Now, with one dinner left before my flight home tomorrow morning, I should have been getting dressed, but instead, I decided to carve out a pocket of quiet in my hotel room.

Propped up on the bed in the hotel robe, I balanced my phone in one hand and waved at Andrew through FaceTime with the other. His face filled the screen, familiar and steady.

Seeing him made something in my chest unclench, like I'd been holding my breath without realizing it.

"Look at you, living that luxury hotel robe life," he said, his smile tugging at the corners of his mouth.

I let out a quiet laugh and smoothed a hand over the lapel.

"For the next half hour or so, yeah. I've got one more dinner with the team, and then it's lights out before my flight tomorrow morning."

"So how's it going?"

We talked the night I got here, but just texted the last couple days, so I didn't fill him in on too many details yet.

"It's been a whirlwind. Incredible in a lot of ways," I said. "They've really rolled out the red carpet and everyone has been super nice."

I gave him a quick summary of what I'd been doing out here, and he asked all the right questions, but there was an underlying melancholy beneath them. Which I totally understood, because even with how excited I was about the opportunity, there was a heaviness I couldn't quite shake either.

"But I'll fill you in on more when I get home tomorrow."

"Can't wait," he said with a genuine smile. "I'll be at the airport when you land."

"Fair warning...I'll probably be puffy-eyed and running on airport coffee and two hours of sleep."

"You'll still be the best thing I've seen all week."

And with those words, the sparkle of L.A. lost a bit of its shine, while the thought of home—of him—glowed brighter than anything the skyline had to offer.

ANDREW

AFTER DISCONNECTING THE CALL, I STEPPED OUT OF MY bedroom and into the soft glow of the living room, rubbing the back of my neck like that would do anything to unknot the tension. Simon was exactly where I'd left him, half-sprawled across my couch, one socked foot on the coffee table like he paid rent, scrolling on his phone.

He didn't look up right away, which was probably his version of giving me space. Or pretending he hadn't been listening through the wall like a nosy neighbor in a sitcom.

I dropped into the armchair across from him and leaned my head back, staring at the ceiling like it might have answers.

"You don't have to stay, you know."

Simon snorted without looking up.

"Yeah, and you didn't have to spend twenty minutes pacing in your room like you were about to be voted off *Survivor*, but here we are."

"Fair."

"So, what'd she say?" he asked. "Did they make her an offer?"

I rubbed my hands over my face.

"She didn't say."

"Did you ask?"

"No." I dropped my hands into my lap. "She gave me a recap of everything, but she didn't say if they offered her the job outright. Just that she'd fill me in on more details when she gets back."

Simon tossed his cell onto the cushion beside him.

"What do you think she'll do if they do offer it?"

"You tell me," I said. "You've got the whole twin connection. Don't you usually have a read on this kind of thing?"

His mouth curved into a half-smile.

"Two years ago, I would've said yeah. I'd have told you exactly what she was gonna do and probably what shoes she'd wear while doing it."

I raised an eyebrow.

"And now?"

"Now," he said, dragging out the word on a sigh, "I don't know. She's different since moving back...calmer, more grounded. And since she got with you, she's been happier than I've ever seen her. But..."

"But..." I prompted when he didn't continue.

"She's always had a clear vision of what she wanted to do with her life and she always wanted to live in a big city," he said. "And Sable West is possibly offering her both of those things." He paused, his brow furrowed like he was trying to do the math in his head and the numbers weren't lining up. "So yeah, she's happy here. Calmer, more settled, and happier than I've ever seen her, especially with you. But I don't know if that means she's ready to let go of everything else she's worked for. So I honestly don't know."

He's not wrong. I'd love to believe Shannon's dreams had changed, and she'd realized all the big shiny things she thought she wanted weren't actually the things that would make her happiest. But I didn't know if I was being hopeful or selfish.

We could debate it all night, but ultimately, Shannon is the only one who can tell us what she's going to do. And she'll be home tomorrow.

Simon let out a quiet breath and gave a slow nod, as if he could read my mind and knew there was nothing left to say. He stood, stretching his arms over his head with a yawn.

"Alright. I've lingered long enough," he said. "My emotional support shift is over."

I cracked a tired smile.

"You're not exactly a regular around here. You sure you don't want to stick around and watch me stare at the ceiling for the next five hours?"

"Tempting," he said dryly. "But I think I'll leave you to spiral in peace."

I stood and followed him to the door, dragging my hand through my hair on the way.

"Thanks for hanging out with me the past few nights. You didn't have to."

"You'd do the same for me."

He shrugged like it was nothing, even though we both knew it wasn't.

"Good night," I said as he walked out the door.

Before I closed it, he turned around.

"Seriously though. No matter what happens, you two will figure it out. She loves you. That part's not in question."

"Yeah. I know."

"I'll talk to you tomorrow."

"Drive safe."

He waved over his shoulder as he headed down the stairs. I waited until the door clicked shut behind him before closing mine.

I flipped off the lights and headed to my bedroom. After taking a quick shower, brushing my teeth, and pulling on a pair of boxer briefs, I climbed into bed.

But sleep didn't come easy.

My mind wouldn't shut up long enough to drift off. Every time I got close, a new question snuck in through the cracks. What if she takes it? What if she doesn't? What if she regrets staying? What if we try and it all falls apart?

I turned over for what felt like the tenth time, punching my pillow into a new shape, but it didn't help at all. The room was too quiet, too dark, too full of her. I swear my sheets still smelled like her hair, which is impossible because they've been washed since she slept here last.

Her charger was still plugged in beside the bed. There was a half-empty bottle of her moisturizer on the bathroom counter I'd started using on my hands without even thinking.

It would really suck if she left.

I'd support her, of course. When I told her to go for her dream job, I wasn't just saying what she wanted to hear, I meant every word. But that wouldn't make it suck any less.

Because she'd be in California, and I'd be here, trying to fill in the space she left behind with FaceTime calls, long-distance visits, and hope.

And maybe that could be enough.

But I didn't want *enough*. I wanted it all.

Eventually, I flipped onto my back and stared at the ceiling again.

"One day at a time," I muttered, like saying it out loud would make it easier.

But the truth was, I'd already taken a lifetime's worth of steps toward her. I just had no idea if she'd be there to meet me at the end of the path.

And if she wasn't?

Well...I'd still be there waiting.

CHAPTER 19

Shannon

T HE SECOND I SPOTTED ANDREW, EVERY TIGHT, ANXIOUS thread in my chest loosened.

He was holding a coffee in one hand, the other shoved into his pocket like he'd been trying to look casual, but had checked the arrivals board three times already. His eyes scanned the crowd until they found me, and when they did, his smile melted my heart. It wasn't over-the-top or showy. It was the soft, real smile he saved for me, the one that always made me feel like the most important person in the room.

I didn't even try to play it cool. My carry-on slid from my hand and hit the floor with a thud, and I closed the space between us in seconds, wrapping my arms around his neck like I needed him to hold me together. Which, maybe I did.

His arms came around me immediately, warm and firm, pulling me in like we were magnetic. He kissed the side of my head, then held me there like he wasn't in a rush to let go.

"There you are," he murmured.

"I missed you," I said, my voice muffled against his chest.

"Missed you too."

The airport noise faded into the background, a blur of rolling luggage and overhead announcements. He was solid and warm and familiar in all the right ways, and suddenly I didn't feel so overwhelmed by everything. Being in his arms was the first time all week I felt like I could take a full breath and I didn't want to let go. So I held on a little longer, breathing him in, absorbing his warmth, steadiness, and the quiet way he made everything feel calm. And even with people weaving around us in the middle of the arrivals area at the Avoca Airport, he didn't rush me. He pulled me closer and held on like we had all the time in the world.

Eventually, I eased back, not because I wanted to, but because I realized the sooner we get out of here, the sooner we'll be alone in my apartment. He brushed his thumb across my cheek like he was checking I was real, then took the bag from my hand and laced our fingers together as we walked to the parking lot.

We slid into his car and he started the engine. "Creep" by Radiohead blasted through the speakers, and he quickly turned the volume down.

I raised an eyebrow, smirking.

"Having a little solo jam session?"

"I was driving down the highway with the windows down."

"Nice."

He nodded and pulled out of the lot, his mouth curled into a half-smile.

Neither of us said much after that, we just shared the occasional glance. At some point, he rested his hand on my thigh and I covered it with mine, tracing small circles with my thumb.

My heart was still doing gymnastics from the weight of the trip and the feel of him next to me again. But the silence wasn't awkward, it felt like an exhale. Like we were both trying to come down from a week spent orbiting the what-ifs.

We made it into my apartment, and Andrew carried my bag inside and set it gently on the living room floor.

"You hungry?" he asked.

I shook my head, already stepping in close, my hands finding his waist.

"No," I murmured. "I just want to be with you. Feel you."

I rose onto my toes and kissed him like I'd been waiting all week for this moment—because I had. And Andrew kissed me back like he'd been starving for it too, like the feel of my mouth was the only thing that could take the edge off.

His hands slid up my sides, then down again, tracing the curve of my hips before slipping beneath the hem of my shirt. I leaned into him, my fingers gripping the back of his neck, pulling him closer until there wasn't an inch between us.

As his mouth opened over mine, the kiss turned hot and hungry. He backed me against the wall, his mouth still on mine, his body pressed full against me. The hard length of his cock throbbed against my stomach, thick and insistent. I shifted, rubbing against him with a slow grind that drew a groan from deep in his chest, like it was pulled straight from his soul.

He broke the kiss, breathing hard, his forehead dropping to mine. His hands were still on my hips, holding me there like he needed the contact as much as I did.

"Jesus, Shannon," he murmured, his voice rough. "You're gonna kill me."

My stomach clenched, heat curling low and heavy. If I was wrecking him, it was only fair, because he was turning me inside out.

Without saying a word, I laced my fingers through his and we walked together toward the bedroom.

My shirt was the first to go, then his, and we kept moving like we couldn't get undressed fast enough. I let out a soft laugh when I fumbled with my bra clasp, and he stepped in to help, his fingers brushing along my skin like he couldn't help himself.

When he looked at me, fully bare in the soft light filtering in through the hallway, his gaze was reverent.

"God, I missed you."

My throat tightened.

"I missed you, too."

We fell onto the bed in a tangle of limbs and heat, all urgency and want. He was above me, beside me, somehow everywhere at once. His hands moved with purpose, rediscovering every curve like he was memorizing me all over again. He kissed the hollow of my throat, the slope of my shoulder, the delicate skin inside my wrist, each one tender and deliberate.

And when he finally sank into me, we both let out shaky breaths that sounded like relief. For a moment, we stayed still, pressed together, wrapped in the kind of quiet that said everything without a single word.

Then he started to move, slow and deliberate. My body responded instantly, tightening around him, demanding more. Every thrust was deep and steady, sending heat curling low and sharp, stealing whatever breath I had left. I held onto him, my fingers digging into his back, completely lost in the connection.

I wrapped my legs around his waist, pulling him in deeper and holding tight. Our breath mingled and each thrust was more urgent than the last. My nails dug into his shoulders as pleasure coiled low and sharp, then surged through me in waves. I came hard, and a beat later, he followed with a broken sound against my neck.

After, we lay tangled together, the sheet draped over us, our legs still intertwined. He kissed the top of my head and pulled me closer. I melted into him, resting my cheek on his chest. His hand moved in absentminded circles across my back while I listened to the steady thump of his heartbeat. Neither of us said anything, we stayed there, quiet and warm, letting our bodies settle.

Then his stomach growled loud enough to break the silence, and we both burst out laughing. I shifted up onto my elbow to look at him.

"Guess you're hungry."

He gave me a crooked smile.

"Yeah, I only had a protein bar for lunch."

"That's not lunch, it's barely a snack."

He shrugged.

"My morning was insane, and if I took time to eat, I'd still be catching up."

His stomach growled again, even louder this time, and I shot him a look.

"We're ordering food before you waste away." I slid off the bed and picked up my T-shirt. "Thai sound good?" I asked as I pulled it over my head.

"Always."

"My phone's in my purse," I said as I slid on a pair of boy shorts. "I'll go order."

I grabbed my purse, fished out my phone, and dropped

onto the couch. As I opened the delivery app, I added our usual meals plus two orders of dumplings, since Andrew had stolen half of mine last time.

I glanced over my shoulder, taking in the shirtless, jeans-zipped-but-not-buttoned, messy-haired look he was casually rocking. I wasn't sure when the nerdy Andrew I grew up with turned into *this*, but I wasn't mad about it.

"Did you order dumplings?" he asked, leaning against the back of the couch.

"Yep."

He raised an eyebrow.

"Am I allowed to have any?"

"Depends."

"On what?"

"How nice you are to me while we wait."

He flashed a grin, the one that always made it a little harder to breathe. And before I could blink, he climbed over the back of the couch, and I screeched, twisting just in time to keep my phone from flying.

"Andrew!" I laughed, half-scolding, half-delighted as he pulled me underneath him.

"Challenge accepted," he murmured, then kissed me like a man trying to prove a point.

And suddenly, dumplings were the last thing on my mind. All I could focus on was round two.

ANDREW

WE ATE STRAIGHT OUT OF THE TAKEOUT CONTAINERS ON THE couch, our legs tangled together. I'd finished my Drunken

Noodles as well as my dumplings. She'd given me my own order, so I must have been extra nice. She was still picking at her Pad Thai, talking between bites, lit up in a way I wasn't sure she even realized.

And she had a reason to be animated, because everything she described sounded incredible. The meetings. The studio, the energy in the building, and how every person she met all seemed to be on the same page, speaking the same language, and pushing toward the same goal.

"It was a whirlwind." She leaned forward to set her container on the coffee table, then sank back into the couch with a soft sigh. "On the plane ride home, I kept thinking how surreal it all was. Like, did that even happen?"

It absolutely happened. She was still riding the high, and I wanted to be excited for her, and on one level, I was. She deserved every bit of this opportunity and the chance to do something she was excited about.

But on another level, I was already starting to mourn it. Not her success—*this*. Us. The way things were right now. Because I was confident they were going to offer the job, and once they did, everything would shift. Maybe not overnight or all at once, but still, our whole relationship would be different.

I wouldn't give her an ultimatum, and I sure as hell wouldn't let her go without at least trying. But pretending our relationship would be the same felt naive.

"Any idea when they're making a decision?" I asked.

"Last night after dinner, Tiffany told me they'd let me know either way within the next few days."

"At least they don't plan on dragging it out," I said.

She nodded, then leaned into me with a soft sigh. I wrapped my arm around her shoulders, and the quiet that followed wasn't tense—it was the kind you settle into after too much food, great sex, and a few long days apart.

Her hand found mine and her fingers brushed lazily against my knuckles. Then she tilted her head toward me, smiling.

"So what did you do while I was gone?"

"Not much," I said, settling deeper into the couch. "Work was busy. I had a couple of long days at the office, some post-op follow-ups, and one emergency surgery. I saw Simon once or twice. Nothing exciting."

"Sounds like a quiet week."

"It was."

What I didn't say was I'd stayed away from my parents' house, because my mom would've taken one look at me and known something was off. She'd ask if everything was okay, and I wouldn't have had an answer that didn't sound like I was unraveling.

It had been a quiet week. Too quiet. The kind that made you hyperaware of everything missing. Before Shannon, it would've felt normal. My life was full enough with work, family, the occasional dinner or night out. I wasn't unhappy. If anything, I was content.

But now she was part of my days and nights, part of my routines without even trying to be, and everything had shifted. The quiet didn't feel peaceful anymore. It felt like an empty house after a door slams shut. Like something important had been moved slightly out of reach.

If she took the job and moved, it wouldn't just be an adjustment, it would be a loss. A sharp one. And I didn't know what the hell I was supposed to do about it.

She tilted her head and looked up at me and smiled.

"I missed you."

"I missed you, too."

I kissed her forehead and gave her shoulder a light squeeze.

She settled back against me with a sigh.

"I should probably send thank-you notes to Tiffany and the team."

"You should," I said. "I'll get your laptop if you want to do it now. I have to hit the bathroom anyway."

"That'd be great." She shifted so I could get up. "Thanks."

I grabbed her laptop case from where she'd left it near the door and handed it to her as I walked past. She was already opening it by the time I disappeared down the hall.

When I came back, the look on her face hit me like a punch to the chest.

She was sitting up straight, laptop open, her fingers hovering over the keys like she'd forgotten what she was doing. Her expression was somewhere between stunned and overwhelmed, like she'd been caught off guard by something huge and wasn't sure whether to be excited or terrified.

She didn't need to say anything, I knew.

"They offered me the job," she said, her voice low.

And even though I'd already known, her words made my stomach drop.

I sank down next to her on the couch.

"Told you they would," I said, trying to sound excited and light-hearted, but didn't quite pull it off. "Is it a good offer?"

"It's really good," she said, her eyes still wide as she turned the screen toward me.

I scanned the email, nodded as each word registered. It wasn't good, it was incredible.

A generous salary, benefits package, relocation

allowance, and travel stipend. All the perks that told you they didn't just want someone, they wanted Shannon.

I shifted the laptop back to her and leaned against the cushion, trying to keep my expression steady.

"They're not playing around," I said.

She gave a small, shaky laugh.

"Yeah. It's a lot."

And I nodded, because it was. But it was everything she deserved. And it scared the hell out of me.

She stared at the screen a second longer before closing the laptop and placing it on the coffee table. Then she looked at me, eyes glassy with unshed tears.

"I don't know what to do," she whispered.

"Why?"

She blinked, like she didn't even know how to start.

"Because if I take it, everything will change."

"That's not necessarily a bad thing," I said gently.

"It is when you have to leave your friends, your family, and the love of your life."

If those last four words hadn't knocked the breath out of me, the wobble in her voice when she said them would have.

I reached for her hand, lifted it to my mouth, and kissed her fingertips, one by one, like it might ease the ache growing between us.

"We'll figure it out. I'm not giving up on this because your zip code changes," I said. "I'm not going anywhere unless you tell me to."

She squeezed my hand.

"I could turn this down and stay," she said. "Keep working freelance at the boudoir studio, look for other opportunities."

"That would've made sense if this offer hadn't come

along," I said gently. "But it did, and now the game's changed."

She exhaled, frustrated.

"I don't want things to change."

"That's kind of funny, Shan," I said around a chuckle. "You've wanted adventure your whole life. Something big. Something new. I remember you saying you wanted a life you had to grow into, not one that made you feel smaller."

She looked at me, startled for a second, like she hadn't realized I'd been paying attention.

"I know," she whispered. "But maybe I've changed."

"Maybe you have," I said. "But a part of you is excited about this opportunity."

"It's definitely flattering to be chosen."

"So the thing is, no matter what you decide, things will change," I said. "If you take it, you'll move across the country. But if you don't, you'll be here wondering *what if*. And I don't want that hanging over us the rest of our lives."

"I wish this was easier," she said, her voice barely above a whisper. "I wish I could want one thing without feeling like I'm betraying another."

"I know," I said.

She leaned over and kissed me, soft and aching, like maybe if she held on long enough, she could carry us both through whatever came next.

CHAPTER 20

Shannon

I DIDN'T REMEMBER OWNING THIS MANY BREAKABLE THINGS when I moved in. Had I seriously bought this much glass since getting here?

Anjannette was carefully packing my glasses like they were heirlooms, Keera was elbow-deep in a box she'd labeled "miscellaneous kitchen," and Sophie had taken charge of wrapping dishes with layers of bubble wrap like it was an art form.

My mom was standing at the open hall closet, holding up an unopened bottle of Windex like it was some kind of offering.

"Do you want to keep this?" she asked. "It's not open."

"No, you can take any cleaning supplies. My car will be packed as it is," I said. "I'm not taking any non-Sable West makeup either."

Anjannette chuckled from across the room.

"You don't want to get caught holding contraband, huh?"

"Exactly. It's probably best if I only use Sable West going forward, considering they'll be signing my paychecks."

Keera grinned.

"Good thing it's your favorite anyway."

"Seriously," I said. "It would've been awkward if I had to pretend to love a brand that made my face itch."

"If that was the case, you probably wouldn't have even interviewed for the job," my mom said. "You'd never promote something you don't believe in."

"True," I agreed. "Nothing pisses me off more than the TikTok influencers who promote stuff they either don't use or don't like because they're being paid."

"I can't believe we're packing you up already. It feels like we just welcomed you back," my mom said, then held up her hands in an apologetic gesture. "I'm sorry, I had to say it. Now I done, I promise."

I wrapped my arm around my mom's shoulders and pulled her in for a quick side hug.

"I know," I said, tugging a roll of tape off the table. "But I'll be visiting all the time like I did when I lived in Manhattan."

Keera smirked as she taped up a box.

"Yeah, and Andrew will keep you locked in his bedroom the whole time you're here."

She froze, eyes going wide as they flicked toward my mom.

"No need to censor around me," Mom said with a smirk. "I get it. Back when John was traveling all the time, that's pretty much how we spent our time when he came home."

I scrunched my nose.

"I do not remember that."

"You wouldn't," she said, giving me a sly look. "But I'm sure you do remember how you and your brother always happened to end up at your grandparents' for a couple days right after your dad got home from a trip."

My jaw dropped.

"Oh my God. La-la-la," I said, slapping my hands over my ears, shaking my head. "Nope. Way too much information."

They all thought my reaction was hysterical, and it took several minutes for the laughter to die down.

Eventually, the room settled again, the kind of quiet that made space for everything else—the goodbyes, the packing, the weight of leaving.

I glanced around at my little apartment, at the boxes everywhere, bubble wrap curled across the table, and empty wall hooks where art used to hang. It hadn't been mine for long, and with the whole ankle debacle, I'd only actually lived in it for a fraction of the time I'd been back in Scranton.

Still, it felt like home. I'd decorated it just enough. Filled it with pieces of me...gifts from friends, framed memories, cheap throw pillows that somehow made the place feel warm.

Mom checked her watch and sighed.

"Alright, I need to get going. I have a Zoom in an hour and I need to look at my files first."

I stood to hug her, trying to pretend I hadn't already started missing her even though I wasn't leaving until next week.

"Thanks for helping."

"Of course," she said, hugging me back tightly. "And you're not escaping that easily. We're having dinner later this week."

"Wouldn't miss it."

She kissed my cheek and waved to the girls.

"Don't break anything."

"We'd never," Sophie said with mock innocence as she clinked two plates together.

Once the door shut behind Mom, the energy shifted a little. It was lighter and more chaotic in the way only happens when your closest friends are left alone in your apartment with bubble wrap and opinions.

We worked for a while longer before ordering pizza and wings. When the order arrived, we grabbed drinks and headed to the living room, settling onto the couch and chairs like we had when I first moved in and they brought taco night to me.

"So," Anjannette said, "what's the plan? Have you and Andrew figured things out yet?"

I shook my head and swallowed the bite of pizza I'd just taken.

"There's no set plan yet. Once I'm out there and have a better sense of my schedule, we'll figure it out," I said. "I negotiated some extra vacation time and the option to work remotely sometimes, so whether I fly here, he flies there, or we meet somewhere in between, I'll have a little flexibility."

Anjannette nodded.

"Leo and I made a no-more-than-three-weeks rule during the season. Two is ideal, but three's the max."

"That's smart," I said, though part of me wondered how realistic it would be from two different coasts. Still, seeing each other regularly, even if it wasn't often, was better than not seeing each other at all.

"And don't forget to loop me in on all the wedding stuff," I said, pointing at them with a chicken wing.

"Well, we'll see you in less than a month for the bachelorette," Anjannette said.

"Exactly." I nodded. "I'm not disappearing."

Keera's smile wobbled.

"I'm really happy for you, I am. But I'm so freaking sad you're leaving."

"I know." I swallowed past the lump in my throat. "Me too."

"Taco night won't be the same without you," Sophie said, reaching over to squeeze my hand.

"You better not ghost us," Anjannette added, blinking fast like she wasn't about to cry. "We expect group chats, FaceTimes, memes at all hours, like we get with Eve."

I managed to smile, even as my eyes stung.

"I won't disappear." I held up my hand as though taking a pledge. "Promise."

And I meant it. These women had become my people. The kind of friends who didn't only show up for the fun stuff, they showed up for the messy, painful, ugly-cry moments too. We'd clicked from the beginning, like the universe had known I needed them. Somehow, they'd come to mean more to me than some friends I'd known for decades.

They helped me find my footing again after everything fell apart in Manhattan and reminded me I was still worthy, still strong, and still me. They didn't just help me heal, they helped me learn how to love myself again.

And between them, my family, and Andrew showing up, holding space, and believing in me, I felt like I'd been loved back to life.

And I wasn't giving that up.

ANDREW

. . .

THE PAST TWO WEEKS HAD SUCKED.

I'd swung between wanting to hide out to lick my wounds and wanting to spend every last second with Shannon. There wasn't a moment of balance, just a constant whiplash of too much and not enough.

Tonight, I picked her up after work and we drove to her parents' for a going-away dinner. The car ride was quiet. She reached for my hand and I laced my fingers through hers like it might anchor us both. I didn't say much, mostly because I didn't trust what might come out. In four days she'd be packing up her car and heading West and I couldn't pretend it wasn't breaking my heart.

At the house, everyone put on a happy face. Her dad was at the grill with his usual intensity, flipping burgers like the fate of the world depended on perfectly seared edges. Her mom had her "party playlist" playing to fill the house with good energy. It almost worked, but there was an underlying melancholy beneath the joyful vibe.

I tried to absorb the upbeat mood, to feel festive and normal and happy for her, but I couldn't quite get there. The smile I wore felt like one of those ill-fitting Halloween masks...plastic, too tight, and hard to breathe in.

Right then, her dad called out from the grill, "Burgers are ready!"

After filling my plate, I settled at the table and Shannon slid into the seat beside me. Her dad sat across from us and turned toward her with a look of half love, half concern.

"You're sure you don't want me to drive with you?" he asked, wiping his hands on a dish towel. "We can have a fun road trip then I'll fly home."

Shannon smiled at him, soft and affectionate.

"I'm sure, but thanks." She smiled. "I'll be fine, Dad."

She'd be driving roughly 2,700 miles. Three long days if

she drove like a machine, which is what she planned on doing. She said she'd listen to podcasts, eat too much gas station candy, and stay at kitschy roadside motels along the way. She made it sound like an adventure.

I'd offered to go with her, too. I told her I could take a few days off, keep her company on the drive, and help her settle in. She turned me down gently but firmly.

"Saying goodbye to you in L.A. would be too hard," she'd said. "I don't think I could do it."

I'm not sure how saying goodbye here would be any easier, but I didn't push. Neither did her dad.

Dinner passed in a blur of second helpings, side dishes, and stories we'd all heard before. I laughed when I was supposed to, kept my arm resting on the back of Shannon's chair, and focused on the way her hand occasionally found my knee under the table like she knew I needed her touch.

After we finished eating, Shannon and her pole crew wasted no time stripping down to their swimsuits and diving into the pool. It took all of five minutes for their laid-back splash-around to morph into an all-out, cutthroat game of volleyball, complete with trash talk, dramatic dives, and enough intensity to make it look like the finals of the Olympic trials.

Simon and I stayed at the table, finishing our drinks, and watching the chaos unfold like spectators at a water-bound gladiator match.

"You ever see anyone take pool volleyball so seriously?" he asked, raising an eyebrow as Keera launched herself halfway across the shallow end to spike the ball with a battle cry.

"Only your sister," I said, watching Shannon laugh as Sophie accused her of cheating.

"Yeah, she doesn't half-ass anything," he said. "Not even fun."

He wasn't wrong. Shannon was all in or nothing. And that made everything about her leaving even harder to swallow. Because I knew whatever came next for her in L.A., she'd give it everything. And I'd be here, giving everything I had to missing her.

Simon stood.

"I'm gonna grab another beer," he said. "Want one?"

"No, I'm good."

He walked across the patio and a moment later, Lily showed up beside me, holding two paper plates stacked with what looked like slices of lemon cake.

"You okay?" she asked.

I knew what she meant. Not *okay right now,* but *okay with all of this.* And yeah, I'd been trying to play it cool, but Lily's never been the kind of person you can fool for long.

So I didn't bother pretending.

"I'm trying to be, but it's hard."

She handed me the cake without asking if I wanted it and sat beside me with a tired sigh.

"She's got a big heart, and it's all yours," Lily added gently. "And even though she's packing up and leaving, don't think for a second she's leaving you behind. She loves you too much."

I stared down at the lemon cake in my hands, blinking a few times before I could even speak.

"I know she does," I said eventually, my voice rough.

She smiled, watching Shannon in the pool as she tossed the volleyball over the net and let out a victory yell.

"She's been putting on a brave face, but I know she's scared," Lily said. "Excited yeah, but still scared. Of leaving. Of staying. Of screwing things up with you."

"She's not the only one who's scared," I admitted, my eyes still fixed on Shannon. "I want her to chase this dream, I just don't know what to do with the part of me that doesn't want to let her out of my sight."

Lily leaned over and gave my arm a squeeze.

"Then don't let go. Not where it counts."

We sat there for a while, quiet again. Shannon's laughter echoed across the yard, and something about it felt like a countdown.

Eventually, the game wound down. The volleyball drifted lazily to the edge of the pool while the girls climbed out, breathless and laughing, wrapped in colorful towels and still talking trash about who actually won. Shannon caught my eye from across the yard and shot me a grin, then gave a quick wave before disappearing inside.

I watched the door swing shut behind her and let out a slow breath I didn't realize I'd been holding. The weight in my chest didn't ease, it shifted.

A little while later, she came back out, wearing dry clothes, fresh lip gloss, and her hair braided down her back. She walked over and I stood as she reached me, my hands already itching to hold hers.

"You ready to head out?" she asked, her voice softer now.

"Yeah."

The ride back to my place was quiet like the ride there, but different. Her hand stayed on my knee the whole time, her thumb tracing circles I felt down to my bones.

Back at my place, she kicked off her sandals by the door and padded over to the couch, grabbing the throw blanket and tossing me a look over her shoulder.

"Last episode?" she asked.

I nodded.

"Let's do it."

We curled up on the couch to watch the finale of *Outlander's* first season. Her body fit against mine like it was made to be there, warm and familiar. The opening credits rolled, the haunting theme song drifting through the room.

I rested my chin on top of her head, breathing her in and trying not to think about the limited nights like this we had left.

About halfway through the show, she shifted and looked up at me, her brows pulling in slightly.

"Are you gonna decide I'm not worth the headache of a long-distance relationship?" she asked, barely above a whisper.

I sat up a little and cupped her face in my hands, brushing my thumbs along her cheeks.

"Shannon," I said, holding her gaze, "I've been in love with you most of my life. I used to think it was a ridiculous crush, but it wasn't. It was always you. And now that I finally have you, I'm not letting you go. Not for distance. Not for anything."

Her eyes welled up instantly, tears slipping down her cheeks. She let out a shaky breath and leaned into my touch like she needed it to breathe.

"I love you," she said, her voice cracking as she wrapped her arms around me and pulled me close. "I love you so much."

I held her tight, anchoring us both. Her head rested against my chest, and I felt every tremble and deep breath like it was my own.

We stayed wrapped in each other while the show played on, forgotten in the background. This wasn't how I imagined the night would end, but it was everything I needed.

She was still leaving. That part hurt.

But sometimes loving someone meant letting them go,

not because it was easy, but because their happiness mattered more than your fear.

She was reaching for something big, and wherever the road took her, my heart was going too. Because she wasn't just the girl I'd been in love with forever, she was the one I planned on spending the rest of my life with.

CHAPTER 21

Shannon

I folded another shirt and put it in the suitcase like I could somehow pack away the panic along with it. The room around me looked like chaos. My clothes were in piles, empty hangers littered the floor, and boxes lined the walls.

I sat down on the edge of the bed and stared at my half-empty closet and felt the knot in my stomach pull tighter.

Last night had wrecked me.

Curling up on Andrew's couch, watching *Outlander* with his arms around me, should've been perfect. And in a lot of ways, it was. But the whole time, I could feel a visceral countdown ticking in the back of my mind, loud and relentless, reminding me everything was about to change.

I thought I was ready for this, that I knew what saying goodbye would feel like. But it wasn't just hard, it was gutting. The kind of awful that pressed down on your chest and stole the air right out of your lungs.

What if it felt like this every time we said goodbye? What

if I never got used to it? What if my heart cracked a little more each time we left each other, until I didn't have anything left to give?

I pressed my palms to my eyes and took a shaky breath. My fingers were still trembling when I pulled out my phone.

Anyone available for an emergency taco and margarita lunch?

It took all of two minutes for the responses to start rolling in.

Sophie: I'm in the car and will head there now.

Keera: I'll meet you there.

Anjannette: See you soon.

Within a half hour, we were sitting at Italo's, guac and chips in front of us, frozen margaritas sweating on the table.

"I don't think I want to go," I said.

Keera's chip-laden hand paused halfway to her mouth.

"Like, *at all*?"

I shook my head.

"I mean...I do. I did. It's a dream job, right?" I shook my head. "But it doesn't feel like mine anymore. Not in the way it used to."

Anjannette frowned.

"Because of Andrew?"

"Not only because of Andrew, although he's a huge part of it," I said. "But it's more than that. I don't want to leave you guys. I don't want to miss birthdays and wedding stuff and Taco Tuesdays and random porch hangs. I don't want to be a visitor in my own life."

The table was quiet for a second.

"Okay," Sophie said, setting down her drink. "So don't."

I blinked.

"What?"

Sophie leaned forward, resting her arms on the table, her expression shifting from casual to laser-focused.

"Didn't you already negotiate more vacation time and some remote work?"

"Yeah."

"Then push," she said, like it was obvious. "What's stopping you from asking to be fully remote and travel when needed?"

"Can I do that?"

"Why not?" Keera chimed in. "You won't know unless you ask."

Anjannette shrugged, like it was the simplest thing in the world.

"Worst they can say is no. Best case is you get to have your cake and eat it too."

I sat back in the chair, picked up my margarita, and took a sip, considering what they'd said. It felt wild to even consider asking for that kind of arrangement, but also kind of right. Maybe this didn't have to be all or nothing. And maybe I didn't have to leave everything behind to move forward.

Our waitress returned, balancing our plates with the kind of grace I could never pull off.

"Chorizo tacos?"

"That's me," I said.

She set down the rest of the plates and promised to bring another round of margaritas. I usually limit myself to one when I'm here, but this was turning into a sort of celebration. Possibility hummed low in my chest, like hope cracked open the door.

The table buzzed with renewed energy as everyone dug into their meals, conversation overlapping with the clink of silverware and the occasional moan of appreciation over perfectly seasoned tacos.

I enjoyed every bite of mine—the spicy chorizo, soft tortilla, and bright lime. For the first time in days, I wasn't overwhelmed or panicked. I felt curious and excited.

After popping the last bite of taco into my mouth, I wiped my hands on my napkin, grabbed my phone, and opened my email.

> Subject: Quick Chat About Role Logistics
>
> Hi Tiffany,
>
> I've been giving some thought to the logistics of the role and would love to discuss the possibility of a hybrid or remote setup—particularly with flexibility for travel along the East Coast.
>
> Would you be available for a quick call today to talk it through?
>
> Best,
>
> Shannon Parker

I read the email out loud, half expecting one of them to suggest a rewrite, but when I looked up, all three of them gave me a thumbs-up.

"That's boss energy," Keera said, grinning.

"Professional but still totally you," Sophie added.

Anjannette gave an approving nod.

"Hit send."

So I did.

My heart thudded as the message vanished from my screen, leaving behind a swirl of nerves and cautious relief.

There's no taking it back now, it was officially out in the world.

By the time we paid the bill, I had a reply.

> Subject: Quick Chat About Role Logistics
> Let's hop on Zoom in 90 minutes.
> Warm regards,
> Tiffany Palmer
> Talent Acquisition Manager
> Sable West Cosmetics
> tiffany.palmer@sablewest.com | (323) 555-1234
> www.sablewest.com

I hugged the ladies goodbye, and they wished me luck with the kind of warmth that made it harder to leave and easier to believe I could do this.

A grin tugged at my lips as I stepped out onto the sidewalk.

If I could find a way to make it all work—this job, these people, this version of myself that had clawed her way back to joy—then I owed it to myself to try.

I drove home, kicked off my shoes, and stood in the middle of my bedroom, eyeing the half-packed suitcase that looked like it was waiting for me to make up my mind.

Maybe it was still headed to L.A., maybe not. Either way, this wasn't just about geography, it was about who I am now, what I want, and what I'm willing to fight for.

The future was still a question mark, but something had shifted. I was standing in the middle of my own life, finally asking for what I wanted.

Andrew

I was standing at the end of the hallway dictating notes for my last patient. He was a nine-year-old boy who'd tripped over his own shoelaces trying to race a friend across a gravel driveway and ended up with a fractured wrist. Not the best way to end the summer, but honestly, it could have been worse.

I'd just finished when I caught the end of an announcement. Then I heard the full thing the second time.

Dr. Bowen to reception.

"What the hell?" I mumbled to myself as I pocketed my phone and made my way down the hall.

We didn't use the intercom often at the clinic, so I wondered if there was an emergency out there. Which didn't really make sense since the hospital was next door, but it was the only thing I could think of.

I burst through the door leading to reception and looked at the nurse at the desk.

"What's going on, Jill?"

She nodded toward the sitting area and when I looked in that direction, my heart skipped a beat then pounded.

Standing amid the chairs, flushed and glowing, phone clutched in her hand was Shannon. She looked like she'd either run a sprint, won the lottery, or both.

"Hi," she said, a little breathless, smiling like she couldn't hold it in.

I walked over and put my hands on her shoulders.

"Are you okay?"

"Perfectly okay," she said. "Are you busy?"

"Technically." I looked her up and down. "You're not hurt, are you?"

She shook her head.

"I just got off a Zoom with Tiffany."

"From Sable West?"

Shannon nodded.

"She got back to me. They approved it."

Her words came out fast and jumbled.

"Approved what?" I asked. "Shan, what's going on?"

"The remote option. And they want me to focus on the East Coast. Minimal travel to L.A., and monthly Zooms to stay in the loop. I don't have to move."

She was talking so fast, it was hard to understand, but that last sentence caught my attention.

"You don't have to move?"

"No."

"You're serious?"

She nodded again, barely able to stand still.

"I'm serious."

"You're staying?"

"I'm staying."

Every cell in my body exhaled.

I stepped in, wrapped an arm around her waist, and kissed her right there in the middle of the clinic lobby. Shannon kissed me back immediately, her free hand bracing against my chest.

When we finally broke apart, I realized we'd just put on a bit of a show.

Jill was smiling as she handed paperwork to a patient who was checking out. A teenage boy said "That was intense" to the woman beside him, who looked mildly amused.

Shannon laughed quietly.

"That's one way to make an announcement."

"I regret nothing," I murmured.

Jill raised an eyebrow as I reached for Shannon's hand.

"Try to keep it PG out here, Dr. Bowen," she said with a teasing grin.

"Noted," I said, already leading Shannon through the door.

We passed Sarah, who gave me a knowing smile and a thumbs-up. Shannon gave her a small wave as we kept walking.

I opened my office door and let her in first, then shut it behind us. She walked over and leaned back against the desk, still grinning.

"Sorry for the dramatic entrance."

"Are you kidding?" I walked over and stood in front of her. "You made my day."

"But I got off the call and couldn't wait. I figured worst-case, I'd have to fake an injury to see you."

"How'd you get them to call me out there?"

Shannon shrugged.

"I told the lady at the desk I was your girlfriend and I needed to tell you something important." She let out a quiet chuckle, eyes dancing. "Now that I think about it, she probably thinks I'm pregnant."

I blinked, then laughed.

"Well, that explains the look she gave me on the way out here." I took a step closer, dropping my voice. "For the record, if you were pregnant, I'd still be thrilled."

Shannon's smile softened, eyes flicking up to meet mine.

"Good to know."

"But we'll discuss that another time," I said. "Right now, tell me about how you're staying."

She laughed again and told me the rest—how she'd been freaking out about leaving and asked the girls to meet her for lunch. How Sophie suggested asking about working remotely. How, fueled by tequila courage, she emailed Tiffany to pitch the idea of working remotely, with some travel.

Tiffany ran it by the leadership team, and they agreed. They want her to focus on the East Coast since she has so many contacts in New York. She'll work from home, check in with the L.A. team over Zoom once a week, and fly out to California once a quarter. But mostly she'll be here with me.

"I was so sure they'd say no," she said, her voice softer now. "That it would be all or nothing."

"Instead, they gave you both."

"Yeah," she said, nodding. "I still can't believe it."

I reached for her hand and pulled her closer.

"I would've supported you no matter what."

"I know," she said, smiling up at me. "But I didn't want to choose between my life and my career. And now I don't have to."

"I'm so proud of you for asking.."

"It was terrifying," she admitted. "But also, kind of exhilarating."

I grinned.

"Makes sense."

Her eyes searched mine for a moment.

"You okay with this? Really?"

"I'm better than okay," I said. "You're doing what you love, and you'll still be here. What's not to be okay with?"

She leaned up and kissed me, slower this time. Just long enough to make my brain fog over.

When she pulled back, her fingers played with the collar of my white coat.

"So do you think your schedule's clear enough tonight for a celebration?"

"Absolutely," I said. "What'd you have in mind? Champagne? Dinner? Or making out in public again?"

She raised an eyebrow.

"All of the above?"

I leaned in, my mouth pressed against her ear.

"Okay, but let's try to keep the PDA contained to places without a sign-in sheet."

"Sounds like a plan."

I stepped back to really take in the spark in her eyes, the calm beneath the excitement, and the way she looked more relaxed than I'd seen in weeks. I imagined I looked the same.

We'd spent so long bracing for impact, waiting for the job to pull her away and leave us figuring out how to make the distance work.

But now she's staying, and the relief is almost dizzying.

Shannon glanced at the clock.

"You probably need to get back to work."

"Eventually," I said, still not moving. "You showed up and changed the entire future. That earns you a little extra time."

She smiled, but it wasn't just playful anymore. There was something behind it—relief, maybe gratitude. That same quiet certainty I'd seen in her eyes when she first said *I'm staying.*

"I didn't know if it would work out," she said softly. "I wanted it to. I hoped. But—"

I reached for her hand, threading my fingers through hers.

"You made it work. You asked for what you wanted, and now we get to figure out the rest together."

Her eyes glistened, but she didn't look away.

"This feels right," she said. "Like all the noise finally stopped."

"Yeah. It does."

And it wasn't about perfect timing, or some flawless plan we'd followed to get here. It was about the messy in-between—the waiting, the wondering, the almosts—and still ending up right where we were supposed to.

She squeezed my hand.

"So what now?"

I leaned in, close enough to kiss her temple.

"Now we live every messy, beautiful second together."

And for the first time in weeks, it didn't feel like something was ending.

It felt like everything was finally beginning.

EPILOGUE

The fairy lights strung across the ceiling of the reception tent glowed softly, casting a warm, golden haze over the tables, dance floor, and the sea of people who'd come to celebrate Keera and Simon's big day.

Someone clinked a glass and a cheer went up in response as laughter rang out from the table next to ours. The smell of late-summer roses mixed with a hint of citronella from the candles flickering near the edge of the tent. And right there in the center of everything good in my life was Andrew.

The ceremony had taken place across the field, at the edge of the same dreamy little property we're standing on now— stone path, open-air altar, and trees blazing with gold, amber, and deep rust. A late October wedding might've been a gamble, but the weather had cooperated like it was written in the stars.

Keera's always been a little witchy in the best way, and this whole day had her vibe written all over it. Moody florals, black taper candles, rich, fall tones. It felt romantic and grounded and real. Perfect for her.

And Simon? He'd have married her in a bathroom stall if that's what she wanted. My brother looked so happy all day I half expected him to start levitating.

The ceremony had been sweet and honest and so very them. But the best part of the day, hands down, had been watching it all unfold with Andrew standing across from me in a perfectly tailored charcoal suit. His tie matched my dress, a deep burgundy that felt romantic and was perfect for autumn. And when I'd walked down the aisle, all fitted bodice and floaty skirt, he'd looked at me like I was the only person on the planet.

"Beautiful," he'd mouthed.

And three months after the wildest, most unexpected shift in my life, I felt like I was. Honestly, I never imagined I could be this happy.

Once I knew I was staying in Scranton, moving in with Andrew felt right. I'd already packed up my apartment and given my landlord notice, so we moved my things into his place.

Living together has been both easier and better than I ever expected. His loft has become our home. I added some plants, candles, and a vintage makeup table I found at an estate sale. We converted the second bedroom into my office. It had been filled with Andrew's collectibles, which we moved to shelves he built in the dining room area, so now they're all on display.

And I love my job. I've even gone into Manhattan a few times for training or launch meetings, and surprisingly, I didn't hate it. The heavy, negative energy I felt the last year I lived there is gone. Probably because now I'm not chasing something anymore. I'm grounded, centered, and deliriously happy. I have a great job, amazing friends, an incredible family, and Andrew, who is more than I ever dreamed of.

How had I known him my whole life and never seen him like this?

Probably because I wasn't ready. That's the only explanation I can come up with. Because once I saw him—*really* saw him—there was no un-seeing it.

The DJ's voice rang out over the speakers.

"All right, let's get the wedding party out on the dance floor!"

A cheer went up and Keera gave a mock-curtsy as she pulled Simon up with her. He kissed her hand like the adorable nerd he is, and together they led the way.

I turned and found Andrew already reaching for me, one hand out, palm up.

"Shall we?"

I nodded and let him lead me onto the floor.

Elvis's voice rumbled over the speakers with the first strains of "Can't Help Falling in Love," rich and familiar, sending a soft hush across the tent. I smiled as Andrew pulled me close, one arm sliding around my waist, the other hand finding mine with an easy confidence that always makes me feel steady.

He looked down at me, his smile soft and a little crooked, like he still couldn't believe this was real.

"You look happy," he murmured.

"I am," I said. "So do you."

"I am," he replied, brushing his thumb over the back of my hand. "You look beautiful, too."

"So do you."

He chuckled.

"I don't know if I'd go that far."

"I would," I said. "Those eyes, that jawline..." I hummed in appreciation. "And you're killing it in your charcoal suit."

His eyes crinkled as he smiled, then rested his forehead lightly against mine.

The music swelled, and we moved together slowly, like the rest of the world had fallen away. It felt easy, familiar, like we'd been dancing around each other for years and had finally found the right rhythm.

I used to dream about my future all the time, but it always stopped at a certain point. Get out of Scranton, build a career, make something of myself. I never let myself picture what came next. I didn't even know what I wanted it to look like.

But now it's so clear.

Mornings with Andrew, coffee in mismatched mugs. Date nights. Family dinners. Maybe someday, a little more. All of it right here in Scranton—or wherever we decide to go —as long as we're doing it together.

He pulled back slightly and smiled down at me, and for a second, I forgot the music, the tent, the hundred other people twirling around us.

Because this man is my everything, and he always will be.

ABOUT THE AUTHOR

As a tween, Tina Gallagher and her best friend would create happily ever afters for their favorite soap opera couples. Eventually, the soap operas lost their appeal, but the writing never did.

Before living her dream as a full-time author, she worked a spectrum of jobs ranging from baking and cake decorating to marketing and project management.

In between creating memorable characters, traveling, and taking pole dance lessons, Tina enjoys spending time with her two grown children and Golden Irish named Thea.